MW00459748

SECRETS AND PIES

A CALLIE'S KITCHEN MYSTERY, BOOK 3

Jenny Kales

Copyright © 2017 by Jenny Kales

Cover design by Renee Barratt, The Cover Counts.
www.thecovercounts.com

All rights reserved. No part of this publication may be reproduced, distribut-
ed or transmitted in any form or by any means, including photocopying, re-
cording, or other electronic or mechanical methods, without the prior
written permission of the publisher, except in the case of brief quotations
embodied in critical reviews and certain other noncommercial uses permit-
ted by copyright law.

Note: This is a work of fiction. Names, characters, places, and incidents are a
product of the author's imagination. Locales and public names are sometimes
used for atmospheric purposes. Any resemblance to actual people, living or
dead, or to businesses, companies, events, institutions, or locales is completely coincidental.

Book Layout ©2017 BookDesignTemplates.com

ISBN: 9781549933912

*"A hungry stomach will not allow its owner to forget it,
whatever his cares and sorrows."*

HOMER

*"There are only the pursued, the pursuing,
the busy and the tired."*

F. SCOTT FITZGERALD, *THE GREAT GATSBY*

Contents

One

L ike a good pie crust, life needs a balance of ingredients, or you may be disappointed by the results.

In the case of pie crust, you need the right ratio of fat to flour, and just the right amount of ice water. If you follow this method, then presto: perfect pie crust.

For Callie Costas, a busy single mom and business owner, balancing life was a little bit more complicated. She wasn't sure she had the recipe for balance, or if she ever would. Her penchant for biting off more than she could sometimes chew didn't help matters.

"Easy as pie," Callie grumbled to herself as she walked up the elegant pathway of The Harris House, a 1920s-themed hotel with an onsite restaurant and bar. "What's easy about it? How did I ever let myself get roped into making so many pies?"

Or rather, *pites*. Callie was tasked, along with her father, George, of making dozens of the Greek delicacies. Her mind spun as she considered the hours of baking that awaited her. She was slated to make dozens of *spanakopita*, aka, spinach-feta pie, as well as a hefty number of zucchini *pites* for the upcoming Greek Festival, an annual summer event in Crystal Bay. Hosted by the local Greek Orthodox Church, the event featured traditional Greek music and folk dancing, plus games, rides and a craft market, along with mountains and mountains of food.

The pie-making didn't stop there. As proprietor of Callie's Kitchen, a Mediterranean meets Midwestern bakery and eatery, Callie was also in the midst of summer pie season. Her clients craved the classics: cherry, strawberry and blueberry; Callie couldn't blame them.

1

Still, whoever had coined the phrase "easy as pie" had clearly never had to make oodles of them in a bakery – or for a Greek festival. No wonder she had pies on the brain.

Callie paused a minute to collect herself. A soft summer breeze blew off of the water, ruffling her wavy brown hair. Shifting the pastry boxes she was carrying, she stopped and gazed up at The Harris House, which was featuring a murder mystery dinner on this warm summer evening. Late afternoon sun slanted against gleaming windows with billowy white curtains. Multi-level turrets stood up like peaked witches hats against the blue, nearly cloudless sky.

The murder mystery dinner was a sell-out event. Callie wasn't attending merely as a guest. Her 10-year-old daughter Olivia's grade school teacher, an amateur actress, had hired her to bring treats to the cast party. Callie had readily agreed to drop off the goodies, not always her usual practice. But then again, Holly Tennyson was one of Olivia's favorite teachers.

Even though Callie had been to The Harris House before, the gaudy grandeur of the place never ceased to enthrall her. The four-story Victorian structure was massive, with an elegantly ornate design that also somehow managed to be flamboyant. Elaborate scrollwork and mauve and white paint highlighted each eye-catching architectural detail. The home had been built in the storied Gilded Age, which dated from the late 1800s to about 1900. For many years, the various owners of The Harris House had decided to go with a 1920s decorating theme, which appeared to be a hit with tourists and locals alike.

Visible from the water and decorated with tiny Christmas lights all year round, the mansion was nonetheless a bit Gothic and dare Callie even think it – slightly creepy – even though The Harris House's beauty was impossible to deny. A sense of danger could be the very thing that drew people to it. Sitting in the dimly lit bar, with its red wallpapered walls, black and white photos, old paintings and

Art Deco lamps, you could easily picture bumping into a silent film star or even Al Capone. The original owner of the house, Nathan Harris, had been a successful Chicago businessman and this was his summer home. Rumors of shady dealings had permeated his legend. Whoever had decided to host the murder mystery dinner here had definitely had the right idea in terms of atmosphere.

Carefully navigating the steep staircase that led to a stunning wraparound porch, Callie balanced the pastry boxes in her left hand while opening the front door with her right. She'd never contributed to an event at The Harris House before. While she knew that her food was tasty, she wondered if it was elegant enough for an establishment with such a glamorous aura. Shaking off these needling doubts, Callie swallowed the lump in her throat and sallied forth.

"Hi! I'm here for the murder!" Callie sang to the woman behind the desk and promptly blushed. "I mean, the murder *mystery night*," she reiterated, feeling her cheeks flush until she was sure they'd burn right off her face. Given the events of the recent year, her words wouldn't necessarily be construed as a misstatement. She assumed that most everyone in Crystal Bay was aware of her involvement in not one but two murders, not as a perpetrator of course, but as an innocent bystander.

The petite blonde woman on the other side of the desk was glancing quizzically at her, eyebrows slightly raised.

"Let me start again," Callie offered. "I'm Callie Costas and I'm here to deliver some food for the murder mystery night cast party. I'm also staying for the show."

The woman smiled back at Callie. She had a sleek haircut, pushed back behind her ears, and wore a crisp white blouse and black pencil skirt. Despite her sartorial polish, the woman wore a harried expression and what looked like a permanent crease between her brows. This must be the new owner of The Harris House, Callie decided. The building's previous owner, a friend of Callie's father, had recently retired. Almost immediately, he'd retreated "up North" to be near his son and four grandchildren. Maybe this new owner hadn't heard about Callie's checkered past after all.

"Pleased to meet you." The other woman smiled and nodded at Callie as she extended one slim hand, graciously choosing to ignore Callie's awkwardness. "I'm Lisa Linley, owner of this barn."

Callie shifted her bulky pastry boxes and held out her hand. Lisa, she was pleased to see, had a strong grip. George, her father, had always warned her to be leery of people who shook hands "like a dead fish," as he so colorfully put it.

"Barn?" Callie repeated, charmed by Lisa's humility. "Hardly. The Harris House is simply stunning!" Choosing to omit her feelings about the slightly sinister air to the home, Callie gestured to the sparkling chandeliers, gleaming furniture and the sunlight streaming through the sun porch, a favorite spot of visitors judging from the group leisurely sipping drinks and chatting. Did Lisa have buyer's remorse already?

"Well, it *is* beautiful, but it has been a challenge taking over a place like this." Lisa's gaze swept the elegant lobby. "You'd be surprised at the emotions some of these old, historical homes stir up, especially when they're inherited! Not to mention the upkeep required. I could tell you stories, but you don't want me to bore you with all of that right now."

Lisa joined Callie on the other side of the desk. "Let me help you lighten your load a little bit." She relieved Callie of the topmost box and placed it on the concierge desk next to the counter.

Gratefully, Callie set the remaining pastry boxes on the desk, determined not to have her lovingly baked treats spilled out onto the red flocked carpet of The Harris House. She and Max had been up early twisting the dough for the Greek butter cookies known as *koularakia*, a Callie's Kitchen specialty. She and Max had also baked an extra-large batch of deep, dark chocolate brownies with ganache frosting.

"These are for the cast party," Callie said, nodding at the oversized pastry boxes with her blue-and-white "Callie's Kitchen" logo on them.

Lisa inhaled deeply. "That smells delicious. I keep meaning to go to Callie's Kitchen, but with running this place, I never seem to have the time to go anywhere anymore." Lisa shrugged. It appeared that while visiting The Harris House was a glamorous experience, running it was not.

Callie understood Lisa's feelings. As the owner of Callie's Kitchen, her from-scratch Mediterranean inspired meals and baking business, long days and lots of worry were part of her daily repertoire as well.

Clearly, Lisa needed some cheering up and Callie knew that the offer of free food usually did the trick. "Please drop by Callie's Kitchen anytime and sample something on the house. We've got lots of good Greek dishes and of course, Midwestern classics. You can't go wrong!"

"That sounds wonderful. And I don't mean to seem ungracious about The Harris House. It's a dream to run this place, it's just that it's due for some major renovations and well, you know how that is."

"I do. In fact, I recently did some renovation at my business and it isn't nearly this large or this old. I'm sure you need someone who specializes in historic homes. My ex-husband has recently taken up home renovation, and his specialty is beautiful old homes like this one. I know he's been working on some of the historic lake mansions near the bay. I don't have his card on me right now, but the name of the company he works with is Vintage Reno."

"Sounds like exactly what I need," Lisa said with enthusiasm. "Can I mention your name or is that a no-no?"

Callie laughed. "Don't worry, we're amicable. Can you believe it? He just moved two blocks away from me with his new wife!" Woops.

She didn't mean to share so much with a stranger, but it had just popped out.

"Oh, my! Good for you." Lisa beamed at Callie. "I'm not sure I could be so tolerant."

Tolerant. Callie wasn't sure if she had achieved that status, but for her daughter's sake, she was giving it her best effort.

Not wanting to share any other personal details, Callie decided to change the subject. "I'd love to chat with one of the actors before the show. I hear they get here early to get dressed and set up, so do you mind if I bring the pastries to the dining room? I assume that's where you're having the murder mystery dinner."

"Absolutely. You go right ahead. And it was a pleasure to chat with you. Talk to you later!" She waggled her fingers at Callie and started writing something down on a notepad. Hugh's company name? He'd be pleased, and possibly surprised, that Callie had offered him a referral.

Callie carefully lifted her pastry boxes and walked in the direction of the dining room, a place she'd been to with Sands, her detective boyfriend, though not recently. No, at her age, *boyfriend* didn't sound right. Man friend? That sounded even weirder. Sighing, she decided she'd probably have to call him her "significant other," even though that term wasn't her favorite.

No matter how she referred to him, Callie couldn't think of Sands without smiling. To everyone else, he was "Ian." He'd come to Wisconsin from England years ago to attend the University of Wisconsin as an international student and stayed after getting married to a fellow student. His marriage had ended as well. Callie felt like he understood her in ways a lot of people didn't since they'd been through similar things.

Sands and Callie had been too busy with work to go on the "warm weather vacation" he had offered to her for a Christmas present. Still, despite their busy, often conflicting schedules, they had grown much closer in recent months and stole time together whenever they could. Callie was content with the way things were even though her father, George, her grandmother and even Sweetie, her aunt, who'd returned to Greece, kept inquiring as to the status of their relationship.

Shaking off thoughts of familial meddling for the time being, anyway, Callie entered the dining room and surveyed the space. She didn't see anyone, but she heard the rise and fall of voices coming from the restroom area. The actors must be getting changed into their costumes. Callie didn't envy them wrestling into their vintage 1920s outfits and wigs in that small space. She strode to the front of the room and decided she'd put the cookies and brownies down on a table while she waited for the actors to emerge.

Enchanted by the décor, Callie wandered around the dining room. It was truly a period set piece, with loads of atmosphere. Jacquard wallpaper gave the room a dark and intimate feeling. A slew of sparkling chandeliers dazzled from the ornate ceiling, which was painted ivory and gold. The cloth-covered tables appeared to float in the wide room which offered dazzling views of the bay. Callie wondered if they'd shut the curtains for the murder mystery dinner. With that view as competition, guests might not watch the actors.

Callie strode back to the front of the room to take a seat and wait for Holly Tennyson, Olivia's teacher. As she did, she happened to glance down at the floor. What she saw made her do a double take. Callie felt her throat open in a piercing scream.

A woman with a black flapper wig was sprawled on the plush carpet. A long strand of creamy pearls trailed across the bodice of her drop waist fringed dress. Her mesh-stockinged legs were askew on the ground as if she were running. The woman's eyes were closed and she was a still as the grave.

Not again. I can't believe this is happening again.

Slowly, Callie knelt down to get a closer look. Just then, the flapper opened her eyes and smiled.

Callie shrieked again and backed up straight into one of the tables. Pain reverberated through her shoulders and back as she made contact with heavy wood. To her dismay and embarrassment, she felt the table overturn behind her with a crash of flatware and candelabra.

In disbelief, she looked again at the flapper on the floor.

"Sorry!" the woman squealed through glossy red lips. "I was just practicing my death scene. I guess it's gotten pretty good." Grinning, she rose awkwardly from the floor and brushed herself off.

"It certainly has," Callie agreed, her knees feeling rubbery. Still, she was starting to see the funny side of the situation. Shaking her head at her own foolishness, Callie started towards the table she'd upended and the flapper rushed to help her. Together they turned the table upright and Callie smoothed the tablecloth. They'd have to get new silverware, she thought, still in shock.

"I was just so surprised to see you on the floor like that," Callie stammered to the costumed woman. "You were so...motionless. I thought you were..."

"Dead?" the flapper asked gleefully, a gleam in her eye. When she saw Callie's expression, she changed her tone. "I'm sorry," she repeated. "But this is good news! I was doing a lousy job of lying still. I kept shifting and blinking. Allan Browne, the director, was ready to kill me for real!" The young woman paused and exhaled loudly. The blunt bangs of her glossy wig blew upward.

She extended her hand to Callie. "I'm Tammy Heckstrom. Nice to meet you. And I'm sorry to have scared you."

Callie shook Tammy's hand, which was soft and slightly damp. "I'm Callie Costas, and I brought some treats for the cast party at the request of Holly Tennyson. She's my daughter's grade school teacher."

"Oh, sure, Holly and I go way back. Besides acting together, we're both in grad school."

"Really? How nice. Well, I'm happy to meet you and I'm just as happy you're alive and well." Tammy giggled and Callie dimly remembered grad school as something that Holly had mentioned during one of their chats at school.

"Want me to go find Holly?" Tammy asked. "It's the least I can do after scaring you half to death," Tammy touched Callie's arm. "I have to fix my makeup and run some lines."

Callie decided that she'd experienced enough pre-show drama. "That's OK. I'm going to look for my family and friends. They'll be here tonight, too. And, uh, break a leg!" She turned to leave, anxious to distance herself from the embarrassing situation. She was also considering attempting to nurse her shoulder and back pain with one of The Harris House's signature martinis. That is, until a peppy voice behind her stopped her in her tracks.

"Callie! I thought that was you!"

Taking a deep breath before turning around, Callie found herself staring into the grinning face of Raine, Hugh's new wife, Olivia's new stepmother and Callie's new neighbor.

"Raine," Callie said flatly. "What are you doing here?" she asked, before she could stop herself. She hadn't meant to sound so rude.

But Raine, bless her, didn't appear to notice. Tall and curvy with big blue eyes and long blonde hair, Raine and Callie couldn't be more different physically or personality-wise. Where Callie was dark and more on the petite side, Raine towered over her, her fair skin and rosy cheeks making her look like the Swiss Miss girl.

"Didn't Hugh tell you? I'm doing costumes for the murder mystery dinner!" She beamed at Callie, all dimples and white teeth.

Callie gave Raine a quick once-over. She wore a rumpled black T-shirt and leggings, with a pink tape measure worn around her neck like a skinny scarf. She certainly looked like someone who was working backstage. The question was: why? She didn't need to ask, though, because Raine was burbling away in a friendly manner.

"Well, with moving to Crystal Bay and trying to get a permanent job, I thought it would be a good idea to network. And I always did love the theater. I used to perform at Saint Mary's, my high school, but I wasn't that good." She giggled. "I admit it. But Kathy said that they needed volunteers and I'm a better seamstress than I am an actress. So here I am."

Raine was certainly a sunbeam. Kathy, her realtor aunt, was dating Callie's father, something that Callie still hadn't gotten quite used to yet. Yep, small town life at its finest, Callie thought. Most of the time, small town life was just fine, unless you really didn't want to see someone. Then you saw them everywhere you went.

"Well, it's certainly a surprise to see you here." Callie attempted a smile. "I suppose Hugh will be here, too?"

"No, not this time," said Raine, her voice losing some of its enthusiasm. "He's finishing up some work on a house because a new project just came in."

Well, that was a lucky break, Callie thought. At least it wouldn't be awkward when Sands showed up.

"I don't want to keep you," Callie said, feeling her shoulders start to ache. "I hope everything goes well with the show!"

"Thanks," Raine replied, her blue eyes blinking. "It's nice to finally be back home in Crystal Bay. Maybe..." she stopped.

"Yes?" Callie prompted.

"Well, I'm hoping we can be friends. You know, with living so close to each other and all." Raine batted her big blue eyes at Callie. They appeared totally guileless and sincere. Darn it.

"Uh...sure."

Inwardly, she cringed. She and Raine had plenty of obstacles to a friendship, but it would be best for everyone if they at least got along. She smiled as warmly as she could, while Raine said goodbye and scurried away, mumbling something about loose fringe on a flap-per dress.

Callie made her way to the front of The Harris House in search of the sun room. Lisa was on the phone and didn't look up. Sinking down into one of the cushioned wicker chairs, Callie let out a deep sigh.

It looked like it was going to be a long night.

Two

A glass of wine in hand, Callie was happy to discover that she was able to enjoy the murder mystery dinner. The actors were funny and entertaining. Every one of them seemed to be having a great time playing their over-the-top roles. Even better, Callie didn't jump a mile high during Tammy Heckstrom's dramatic death scene. Due to her slapstick incident before the show, she was prepared for it. The killer was well hidden, but in an interesting twist, it had turned out to be Holly Tennyson's character. When the play ended, Callie stretched and looked around the table.

Sands, who had shown up a few minutes late, was to her right. When he saw her glance at him, he smiled at and put his arm around her shoulders. Callie felt her face relax into a Cheshire cat grin. Blushing, she noticed that her Irish-American maternal grandmother, Viv, was smiling her dimpled smile across the table at her. Viv, who had cared for Callie when she'd lost her mother at a young age, enjoyed Agatha Christie-style anything, and she'd been among the first to sign on for the dinner. Next to Viv was Samantha, Callie's best friend, a criminal attorney. Sam yawned.

"That was cute, but a little corny," she observed. "Still, it's nice to be able to solve a fictional mystery for a change."

"Yes, a fictional mystery suits me just fine," answered Sands. "I quite enjoyed it. What about you, Viv?" Sands winked at Callie.

"Oh, I just loved it," Viv gushed. "The costumes, the intrigue, the humor: all of it was wonderful. Who knew that Olivia's teacher was such a good actress? That gal is really talented."

As if summoned by Viv's praise, Holly Tennyson walked over to their table, a red-lipsticked smile on her pretty face. "Callie! It's great to see you!" She nodded at the rest of the group. "I'm so glad you all could come to the play tonight." She leaned forward with a mischievous grin. "I'll bet you didn't know that I would be the *killer*!" Holly's normally long, light brown hair was covered with a glossy blonde flapper wig set in vintage marcel waves. She was wearing a black fringed gown and vintage jewelry. Her long, chandelier earrings sparkled and danced as she dipped her head pertly at them.

"Hon, you were delightfully evil," Viv said, and they all laughed.

"Thanks," Holly said, tugging off one of her elbow-length gloves. "I wasn't sure if I'd have time for acting this summer, since I've been busy writing a thesis for graduate school but I'm sure glad I did. It's a lot of fun."

"Yes, Tammy Heckstrom, tonight's murder victim, happened to mention that you're in grad school together," Callie replied.

"I thought I'd told you. I'm going for my Master's degree. I'm writing a paper on F. Scott Fitzgerald. So you could say that acting in a 1920s-style play in a 1920s-style hotel/restaurant almost counts as research." Holly grinned at them.

"How fascinating," Viv remarked, clearly wanting to engage Holly in conversation about the topic. Viv was a big reader and a frequent volunteer at the Crystal Bay Public Library. However, Holly seemed pre-occupied by someone standing behind Sands. She smiled shakily at the group.

"Well, well. Holly, what do we have here? More of your devoted *fans*?" said a man's voice.

Callie turned to look at the source of the snarky words. A tall, portly man with a shock of red hair and a full beard was smiling tolerantly at Holly as if she were amusing to him, like a puppy or kitten. He had a booming voice and an impressive belly to match.

"As a matter of fact, yes. We *are* fans of Holly," Callie said firmly, not caring for the man's jeering tone. "We came here specifically to see her perform tonight."

"Is that so? Well, I certainly hope you got your money's worth. Holly plays an excellent villainess, don't you think?"

"Uh, allow me to introduce you all to Allan Browne," Holly said through teeth clenched in a pasted-on smile. She made a queenly gesture at him. "Director of our little theatre troupe."

"*Little!*" Allan Browne's eyebrows drew together over his Roman nose. "Why, we perform all over the state, and we were at a Chicago theater festival just last year." He stammered a bit and Callie winked at Holly who tried to stifle a laugh.

"It's a pleasure, sir." Sands spoke to Allan in his smooth voice. Allan Browne raised his eyebrows, perhaps surprised at Sands' British accent still evident despite his many years in Wisconsin.

"I really should let you all get back to your evening," Holly was saying. "Tell Olivia I said hello." She directed this last remark at Callie, who nodded in assent.

Allan Browne leaned toward the group, an ingratiating grin on his face. "Yes, yes. It's wonderful to have you in the audience tonight. Please tell your friends about us; we plan to have more shows here at The Harris House." A little too late to try for the charming salesman act, Callie thought.

"We certainly will, dear boy." Viv twinkled at the group while Allan Browne grumbled a bit more at Viv's use of the endearment. Allan Browne had to be at least 55 if he was a day.

When they were clearly out of earshot, Sam chimed in. "What a character." She paused. "And that's putting it nicely."

"Well, you know what they say," Sands drawled. "All the world's a stage."

"Yes, and he's playing Holly for a fool," Callie retorted. "He should be thrilled to have her. She's really good!"

"Oh, Callie, honey," Viv admonished. "These creative and artistic types are all so temperamental. In any case, it looks like Holly can take care of herself."

"She certainly does. Still, I'm glad we were able to give her some support tonight," Callie said. She watched as Holly and Allan Browne spoke briefly to the group at another table, but the two soon parted. Callie couldn't blame Holly for wanting to get away.

Sands squeezed Callie's forearm, diverting her attention away from the pair. "I'm glad we showed up, too. It was a fun evening. Next time, let's bring Olivia, shall we?" She nodded and smiled at the warmth in his words and his hazel eyes. Since he'd lost his own daughter in an accident years prior, Callie was happy that he and Olivia had become such good pals.

"I'll be here, too. But I bet I know who Holly wishes was the murder victim, fictional or not," Viv said, draining the last of her chardonnay. Everybody laughed.

***

"Callie, we've got issues," Max, Callie's assistant was saying. It was the day following the murder mystery dinner and Callie was wondering if she should have spent the time baking instead of watching a play with her friends and family. Tourist season in Crystal Bay was in full swing, and Callie's Kitchen was experiencing a resurgence of clientele. This was welcome news to Callie's bank account, but it did mean that she often felt as if she spent her workday on roller skates. Come to think of it, roller skates might not be a bad idea.

"What is it, Max?" Callie said. "Please tell me it's not serious."

"I guess it depends on what you mean by serious. We're running out of food."

"Oh, no! Like what?" Callie pushed damp hair off of her forehead. The sunnier and hotter it grew outside, the more the kitchen felt like an inferno.

"We're running really low on the *loukoumades* and some of the other Greek pastries." Max, his spiky hair drooping slightly, didn't want to seem to meet her eyes.

"Oh," Callie said, puzzled. "I thought you stayed late to bake last night." That was the usual deal. Max's vintage clothing-wearing, social media-expert girlfriend, Piper, was supposed to be helping him. She worked part-time at Callie's Kitchen, and Callie didn't know how she would get along without either of them. She could hear Piper's sing-song voice chatting to customers in the front of the shop.

"I was supposed to," Max said slowly. He folded his arms across his Callie's Kitchen apron, offering Callie a look at his colorfully tattooed forearms. Max was big and muscular, but with a boyishly handsome face that was a magnet to Callie's clientele.

"Well, what happened?" Callie was growing frustrated.

"I'll admit it. I had some things going on at home. I didn't get as much done as I promised. I'm sorry!"

Callie started to admonish him, but he interrupted her. "You're totally justified in being angry at me. I'll stay late tonight and finish up whatever we need to do. What do you say?"

Callie nodded at him. He was such a hard-working employee that this type of thing was completely out of character. "Fine. What about in the meantime, though?"

"I'll get some stuff out of the freezer. It won't be as good, but you never know. People might come in earlier next time to get the good stuff. You know, if they think we'll sell out of everybody's favorites, it could work in our favor."

It was difficult to stay angry at Max. "All right." She went back to mixing the Greek meatballs she was making, one of her favorite dishes. They would be served with a tangy *tzatziki*, the cucumber-yogurt sauce that was a hallmark of Greek warm weather cuisine. She was also making Greek rice pudding that she would serve chilled and sprinkled with cinnamon. Delightful sweet and savory fragrances filled her kitchen workspace, and she inhaled them deeply, finding that the food smells had a calming effect.

As Max rummaged in the freezer, Callie had a thought. "I'm not happy about running out of food, but it's not like you to shirk a responsibility." She turned to face him. "Is everything all right with you?"

Max emerged from the walk-in freezer with a grim look on his face. "You sound like my father."

"What do you mean?"

Max piled his muscled arms with frozen spinach triangles and butter cookie dough before laying the foodstuffs on a large worktable. He rubbed his face tiredly before answering.

"He wants me to come back home and work the farm. He knows that I want to cook but..." Max took a deep breath. "He's getting older."

Max looked at Callie, his expression glum. "I'm the only one left in Wisconsin. You remember my brother got married last year and moved to Seattle. It's only me. There's just one problem: I don't want that life. I want to keep doing what I'm doing. I love to work with food, with the customers." He smiled. "With you. The best boss ever."

Callie laughed. "You don't need to butter me up, Max. I like working with you, too. You know that." She gave him a sympathetic smile. "Family is always an issue, isn't it?"

Callie could certainly identify with Max's dilemma. Her father, George, hailed from Greece and had wanted Callie, as his only child, to work with him at his diner The Olympia. His dream was for her to take it over one day when he retired, though he certainly did not show signs of doing so. However, Callie had stood firm. She loved her father, but she wanted to create her own business, and that's how Callie's Kitchen was born. George had finally accepted the situation and was one of her staunchest supporters, but it hadn't been easy at first.

"It's just that my dad and I have never really seen eye to eye." Max was saying. "I love him, of course, and I don't want to let him down." He paused. "I don't really even get home that much. He must be desperate if he wants me to take over."

"Now, now," Callie replied. "I'm sure you'd do a fine job wherever you landed. It's more a matter of...do you see yourself as a farmer? And if the answer is no, I guess you'll have to have a talk with your dad. Let him know so that he can find another option."

"That's just it, Callie." Max stared glumly at the countertops, covered with food. "I think I *am* the only option."

Callie didn't like the sound of that. Before she could respond, the phone rang. Distractedly, she picked it up.

"Hello?" shouted Hugh, Callie's ex-husband. It sounded like he was speaking to her from on top of a jackhammer.

"Hugh, what's going on? I can't hear you very well," Callie shouted back into the phone. Max, she noticed, was busying himself placing frozen *spanakopita* triangles onto industrial-sized cookie sheets.

"I'm at a job site. Just about to leave, actually, and I've got Olivia with me. She wanted to see the site, so I brought her along. Don't worry. I didn't let her near anything dangerous," he said preemptively, before Callie could interject any motherly concerns about her daughter's safety.

"The problem," he continued, "is that they want me to go get some measurements at a new house that I'll be working on next week. I was wondering if you could meet me there. I'm really crunched for time." Loud sounds of construction drowned out whatever he said next.

Callie felt her frustration rising. Still, the important thing was to retrieve her daughter

"Sure, OK. Just give me the address. It's not too far away, I hope."

Hugh hemmed and hawed. "To tell you the truth, it's not that close to you, or I'd drop Olivia off myself." *Wonderful!*

"All right, where is it?" Callie asked, wiping her hands on a towel.

"150 E. Elm, right off of Lakeshore, but on the far side of the bay."

"Hey," Callie said, brightening. "Isn't that the house that's been closed up for several years? Grandma Viv told me about it." If it was the house she was thinking of, it was a glamorous affair. The previous owners had fallen on hard times, and the home had foreclosed. No one had lived in the house for quite some time, and Callie was happy it would have a chance at its former glory.

"That's the one. Thanks, Callie. I really appreciate it. I won't make a habit out of this. By the way, how's the boyfriend?"

"Don't push your luck, Hugh," Callie said. "See you soon." She hung up.

***

Callie finished putting together her Greek meatball mix and left Max with instructions on how to finish the dish. As soon as she was in her car with the windows down, she realized how delightful it was to be out of her hot kitchen.

Windows down, radio blaring, Callie savored the warm, but not too hot June sunshine. Hugh's new worksite wasn't exactly around the corner from the main part of town, but the fact that she got to enjoy views of the water for most of the ride made it a pleasant trip.

Before she knew it, Callie was pulling up in front of the house on Elm. She got out and drank deeply from a water bottle she had brought with her. Looking around, she didn't see Hugh's car.

Callie decided that she'd call Hugh if he didn't show up in ten minutes. For now, her curiosity was getting the better of her. She decided to take a look around.

The house had seen better days, but it was clear to Callie what a beauty it must have been in its heyday. Like many of the older mansions on Crystal Bay's historic lakefront, this house had clearly been built in "The Gilded Age," and it had all the architectural hallmarks of a home built during that period of economic prosperity. Despite the peeling paint and crumbling columns, the house had an aura of gaudy glamour about it. *Like The Harris House*, Callie thought.

Callie had parked in the circular drive, which was bordered with overgrown and scraggly flowers and grass. A rainbow of colors made up for the messiness of the landscaping. Particularly striking were the perennials that burst forth, beautiful despite being untended. Callie admired the luxurious purple bee balm and paler astilbe, with its showy lavender-hued flowers atop fern-like stems, as they swayed in the mild breeze. Alongside them, coneflowers nodded their shaggy heads.

Shielding her eyes from the sun, Callie strolled up to the spacious front porch and peered into one of the dusty windows. She'd love to take have a look around. Maybe Hugh would let her take a tour, provided the building was structurally sound. Just for fun, Callie tried the doorknob, and to her surprise, it opened. Slowly she stepped inside.

The house had a musty smell, but thankfully, no rodents skittered in front of her as she made her way to the center of a large living room. Vaulted ceilings soared. The sunlight, so bright outdoors, was filtered through the immense windows by a film of dust and dirt that had accumulated over the years. Thinking of the home's many previous inhabitants gave Callie a funny feeling. She didn't believe in ghosts, but she was feeling a little spooked.

Callie peered down at the hardwood floors. She loved hardwood floors, and when they weren't covered with dust and dirt, these must be beautiful.

Wait a minute. Callie looked more closely. She'd created some footprints in the dust when she'd walked in but now she realized that the floor was filled with footprints. Workmen? Hugh said they were just beginning work. In fact, hadn't he said he was the one taking measurements? Who had been here before her?

Gathering her courage, Callie shouted, "Hello?" but nobody answered. Her voice echoed throughout the empty, darkened rooms. Callie started to walk towards the back of the house, where she assumed the kitchen would be. Spooked or not, Callie always wanted to see what other people's kitchens looked like.

As she made her way through the living room, Callie noticed that one of the sets of footsteps had ended and instead, two lines were smeared in the dust. The lines led to the back door, which appeared to open up into an overgrown garden.

Bending down to look more closely, Callie saw a small piece of yellowed paper with torn-looking edges. She picked it up and saw some handwriting scribbled on it, just a few letters. The paper was a brittle as an autumn leaf. Out of habitual neatness, she shoved it in her pocket, thinking she'd dispose of it later.

Callie decided it was time to see if Hugh had arrived with Olivia yet. Rising carefully from her crouching position, she exited through the back door, which opened up into a large backyard that sloped gently towards the water.

The grass looked recently mowed and Callie guessed that the bank that currently owned the home had kept up the lawn, if not the rest of the landscaping. A strong smell of fresh spearmint wafted towards her, and she went in search of it, planning to surreptitiously pick some of the herb.

The spearmint smell grew stronger as Callie approached a large grouping of overgrown perennials and prairie grass that stood up tall and bristly like a jar full of bushy paintbrushes. She bent down to grab a handful of spearmint and fell over onto her backside with an exclamation of horror.

Lying in the center of prairie grass was Holly Tennyson, eyes wide open and lips blue in death.

Three

Her breath coming in terrified gasps, instinct took over and Callie scuttled away, crablike, until she was several feet away from the body. Quickly she righted herself and took some steadying breaths before approaching Holly Tennyson once more.

Callie's stared at the young teacher, her eyes blinking back tears of horror and sadness. She willed herself to remain calm. Gently, she bent down to examine Holly for any signs of life, careful not to touch any part of her. Unfortunately, she had been around enough crime scenes at this point to know the drill.

Holly was definitely deceased. The teacher's once-beautiful eyes were clouded and her face was grey as a stone. She was wearing a yellow cotton T-shirt dress and tennis shoes. There was no blood, but the Callie noticed that Holly had thin, deep red lines burrowed deeply into the skin at her bare neck. Had someone strangled her? If so, there was no weapon apparent anywhere near the poor woman. In the warm weather, Holly wasn't wearing a scarf.

Feeling sick, Callie backed away. Her fingers trembled as she first called Sands and got his voicemail. She stammered out a message, then called 911 and told them to hurry. As if from a great distance, the operator told her to stay on the line.

Callie tried to form coherent responses while she stared, stricken, at Holly's body from a safe distance away. Callie heard herself babbling answers to the basic questions the 911 operator was asking her, but despite the humid air, her entire body froze at the sound of a familiar voice. *Olivia.*

"Mom!" Olivia sang. She sounded close, but not too close. Maybe Callie could catch her before she stumbled onto the crime scene.

"No!" Callie started running, still holding onto the phone. She raced to the gate and burst into the front yard, ignoring the flurry of questions from the 911 operator.

"Get back!" Callie yelled to a confused Olivia, who was standing on the circular drive, contentedly sipping from a plastic Tastee Freeze cup. Callie could hear the 911 operator's voice asking her what was going on. "My daughter's here. Just a minute," she begged the operator, but didn't wait for an answer. Callie gripped the phone and regarded her daughter gravely.

"What is it, Mom? I'm here. Can't we go home?"

"No," Callie repeated in a gentler tone. She ran to her daughter and crushed her in an embrace that sloshed some of Olivia's milkshake onto her shoes.

"You're sure acting weird, Mom," Olivia said, her face muffled against Callie's chest. "I've only been gone two days."

"It's not that, honey." She held firmly to her young daughter's hand. "Something's happened."

Clicking off of a cell phone call, Hugh strode up to the two, a concerned look on his face.

"Hey," greeted her casually. "Is something wrong? What were you doing in the back yard?"

Callie held up a hand and stared into Olivia's face, her voice urgent. "Olivia, go get in Dad's car and lock the door, OK?"

"Why? It's hot in there," Olivia asked in almost a whine. Her face was flushed and she looked hot and tired.

"Just make sure the windows are open. I'll explain in a minute." She looked at Hugh. "Please tell her. It's important."

He shrugged. "Olivia, do what your mother says. I'll be right there." Suddenly, the thin scream of a siren penetrated the air.

Hugh didn't seem to notice the sound, but Callie felt weak with relief.

"What happened?" Hugh's voice was sharp.

"There's a body in the garden. I got here early and found Olivia's teacher, Holly Tennyson. She's dead. In fact, it's worse than that. It looks like she's been murdered." Callie hated the sob she heard in her voice and took a deep breath to steady herself. "I think she's been strangled."

"What?" The single word was like a shot. "Let me go look." He started towards the back yard.

"Don't go!" Callie shouted, more loudly than she had intended. She grabbed his arm to stop him and softened her tone. "Can you please stay with Olivia?" The sirens grew louder. "Help is on the way. Please, just stay with Olivia." She realized she was repeating herself, but she was terrified. She dropped Hugh's arm and hugged herself, suddenly freezing. What if the killer was still nearby?

Hugh's face was grim. He looked at her searchingly. "Are you sure it's Holly?"

"Yes. I'm positive. I don't want Olivia anywhere near the murder scene." She choked back tears. "Holly was her favorite teacher."

Hugh started to say something and thought the better of it. He walked quickly back towards his car as two police cars drove up the scene, followed by an ambulance. Callie craned her neck, but didn't see Sands' familiar black vehicle.

In minutes, the place was a hive of activity. Callie signed off with the frustrated 911 operator and began filling the police in on what she'd found and the identity of the deceased. She led the EMTs who had arrived with the police to poor Holly's body but couldn't look while they examined her for signs of life. She knew that was a futile exercise.

Two officers led her away from the body and continued their questions. Dutifully Callie told them about the many sets of footprints inside of the abandoned house.

"What were you doing in the house if you're not a resident?" asked one of the officers. He was tall and broad and his face revealed absolutely no trace of friendliness.

"I admit it. I was nosy. My ex-husband had me meet him here to pick up our daughter because he works for a firm that is going to be renovating this home. I thought I'd see if I could look inside." She went for the charm factor. "I don't know about you, but I don't normally get a chance to look inside one of these historic mansions."

"There are paid tours for that kind of thing, lady."

Callie hung her head. "I know I shouldn't have gone inside. I'm sorry." One of the officers started to write something down, but the other held up a hand in greeting to someone standing behind Callie.

"I see there's been another incident. Can somebody fill me in?" Sands' sandpapery voice with its strong hint of British accent was suddenly the most welcome sound in the world. Callie turned to look at him and he gazed at her with an expression of concern and, if she were being honest, more than a little bit of irritation. Well, she couldn't say she blamed him. She was irritated with herself. Why did she have a sudden knack for finding dead bodies?

Callie shivered. The warm sun was giving way to dusk and with it, a slight chill. She wished she were in front of a fireplace with a cup of hot chocolate and a *paxemathia*, aka Greek biscotti. Most of all she wished that darling Holly Tennyson was still alive and well.

"This woman found the deceased," the tall officer was saying to Sands, who nodded once and gave Callie a sidelong glance.

"I see. Mind if I question her a bit?"

"Go right ahead. We've got other witnesses to talk to." That would be Hugh and Olivia. Callie's heart ached for her daughter.

"Ian," she said urgently, using his first name, something she rarely did. "The woman I found was Olivia's teacher. I don't think Livvie knows she's dead yet. Is there any way they can avoid telling her right now?"

"I'm sorry," Sands said. He put a hand on her shoulder. "Truly I am. But we've got to interview everyone. She's a minor, so you or your ex-husband will be with her if anyone questions her."

Callie took a shuddery breath, but she knew he was right. If they were going to get to the bottom of this, then difficult questions would need to be asked.

"What in the bloody hell were you doing at an abandoned house anyway?" Looking around to see if the other officers were watching, Sands grabbed her hand and gave it a warm squeeze. "You're not catering a séance, are you? This place looks downright haunted."

Callie never had thought so before, but taking another look and considering what she had found there, she saw the house in a whole new light. "I was here to meet Hugh." Sands raised an eyebrow at her unintended innuendo. "Don't be silly," she huffed. "Hugh asked me to meet him here for our scheduled drop-off of Olivia. I was doing him a favor."

"I see. Well, what was *he* doing here?"

Callie felt something in her chest unkink as she gazed back at Sands' hazel eyes and the warm glow in them. "He has a job here next week and said he was short on time. He told me his firm wanted him to do some pre-measurements or something like that."

"*Had* a job here next week," Sands said firmly, stepping back for a better look at the impressive structure. "This house is officially a crime scene for the time being, at least until we get all the evidence we need. And even then, I don't think a big renovation project will be happening here anytime soon. Any reason to think he had a beef with this teacher?"

"No way," Callie said. "I was the one who went to most of the meetings, if you want to know the truth. Until recently, Hugh didn't live that close to Livvie's school. I don't think he knew her that well, if at all."

Sands nodded and took Callie's hand in his. "I'm sorry about Olivia's teacher. But now, I'd like you to make an official statement with one of my friends over there." He jerked his head toward the two officers who were now speaking to a thoroughly freaked-out looking Hugh. "I've got work to do here." He gestured at the crew who were coming in to take photos and examine the crime scene.

Callie shivered at the prospect of reliving the discovery of Holly Tennyson. "Fine. But will you call me later?"

"Of course I will. Just as soon as I'm free. It might not be for a while, though."

"I know." Callie attempted a smile at Sands. "You know where to find me. I'll be home with Olivia. I have a feeling she's not going to react very well to this."

"Probably not," Sands said softly, glancing towards Olivia. She was sitting in a police car, crying on her father's shoulder. "She's a strong young lady with a great mother. She'll pull through."

"Thanks," Callie said, clearing her throat. She was moved by his words but it didn't make facing Olivia any easier.

***

Olivia sobbed the entire way home in the car, and Callie could do nothing other than murmur soft words of sympathy to her distraught daughter. "I'm so sorry," she kept repeating, feeling completely helpless. The officer on the scene had taken her statement but warned her they may need to question her again. Callie shook her head. Of course, they'd probably call her again. But first things first: she had to take care of her bereaved 10-year-old.

Suddenly, Olivia stopped sniffling and stared at her mother, red-eyed. "The thing I don't get is: why? Why would this happen to Ms. Tennyson?"

"I don't know, honey," Callie said. She'd be wondering the exact same thing.

"Will you try to find out?" Olivia said.

"Try to find out why this happened to Ms. Tennyson?" Callie repeated as she glanced sidelong at her daughter. *Eyes on the road*, she told herself. She'd had a minor car accident last winter, and it had sufficiently shaken her up. She didn't want it to happen again, especially with Olivia in the car.

"Yes. Mom! You can help. You knew her and your boyfriend is with the police. I know you can figure it out!" Olivia sounded near hysteria.

"Olivia, you've got to calm down. I'll do what I can. Now let's just get on home." She kept one hand on the steering wheel and patted her daughter's knee with the other.

"Fine," Olivia mumbled. She leaned her tousled head back on the seat and stared out the window.

Callie was so upset and so focused on maintaining steady driving, that the trip home went more quickly than she had thought it would. She and Olivia staggered into the house, where they were greeted by her Yorkie, Koukla, who ran around in circles and barked excitedly at them.

She sniffed the air appreciatively. Someone was cooking: the smells of melting butter and feta cheese wafted out of the kitchen. Suddenly, Callie was starving.

George sauntered out of the kitchen and into the entry way. "Calliope! Olivia!" His voice was hearty but his expression was solemn. *He must know what happened. But how?*

"Hi Dad," Callie said, suddenly engulfed, along with her daughter, into a large bear hug. "Whatever you're making smells great."

"I heard what happened, and I came right over to make dinner for you." George broke the embrace and clucked his tongue at his daughter and granddaughter. "Such a shame."

Olivia hung her head and choked back more tears. George got down on one knee so he could look her in the eye. "There, there, *hrisi mou*," he said. *Honey*, what he often called Callie, fully grown adult that she was. "*Pappou* is here," George was saying to his weeping granddaughter, "and you'll be all right."

Olivia threw herself into George's arms, and he held her tight. Callie patted her daughter's back gently. George looked up at her, and she mouthed to him "Let's change the subject."

George nodded minimally and stood up, briskly brushing off his hands. "How would you like to help me in the kitchen?" he asked Olivia. "I'm baking *spanakopita* and I brought one of your favorite dishes: *pastitsio*. You can help me heat it up."

"No, *Pappou*. I'm not hungry. I had Tastee Freeze with Dad. Anyway, I just want to go to my room."

"You go then, dear. Maybe you'll eat later, yes?" Bless George, who always worried about an empty stomach, even at a time like this.

Olivia nodded. Her eyes were swollen and red. Callie's heart went out to her daughter and again, she cursed her helplessness at the situation. Why, oh why had she been the one to find Holly?

Did someone plan it that way?

Four

"I can't believe this," George said firmly, once Callie had Olivia settled in her room. The two were sitting at the small kitchen table, sipping an after-dinner coffee. Koukla was fed, but still she sat patiently at their feet, waiting for food to drop.

"You can't believe it? How do you think I feel?" Callie said in a terse whisper. "Let's not upset Olivia any more than she already is."

"Yes, yes, you're right." He lowered his tone as much as he could, not an easy task as he had an assertive speaking voice. George's command of English was excellent, but even after all of his years in Wisconsin, he still had a strong Greek accent, and when he was upset, it got even stronger. "Still, who would want to kill this young woman? This is crazy."

"Who told you about Holly, anyway?" Callie asked.

"Didn't I tell you? I got a police scanner." George beamed proudly. "Since you're seeing this detective, I figured, I may as well know what the police are up to."

Callie groaned. "Seriously, Dad. You didn't."

"I did! Even so, I was just about to call Kathy and tell her there had been another murder in Crystal Bay, but she called me first." Even though Callie wasn't used to George being involved with a woman, Kathy was growing on her. She was petite and bubbly and a snappy dresser. George seemed smitten.

"How did she find out? From another realtor?"

"No. Apparently, she received a call from Raine. One of the people who work with that theater troupe doesn't live too far from where that poor young lady was found."

"Who lives in the neighborhood where the murder happened?" Callie asked, an uneasy feeling in the pit of her stomach.

"A man named Allan Browne. He has big bucks, I guess. That's a nice neighborhood, no?"

"Uh, yeah. I guess so." Big bucks indeed. How much could a theater director make? But then again, he may have inherited his home. Lucky him.

"I'm sorry you had to be the one to find her," George said sadly. "This is a terrible thing. I feel almost silly with the concern I'm about to share, but I need to say it." George's forehead was creased with worry lines.

He smoothed his curly brown-grey hair with both hands. "What about the church festival? Will this affect business? It's one of the biggest fundraisers of the year for the church. And we're counting on tourism, not just our local friends. Another murder could turn people off to visiting Crystal Bay. Which means they won't attend our festival..." he broke off in misery.

Callie patted George's hand. She always enjoyed the festival, but it was the last thing on her mind right now. Still, she knew it was a highlight of George's year and he was right. The church desperately needed this annual source of income.

"Dad, don't worry. The festival will be a hit. Just give us some good weather, that's all we need."

"Eh, I know." He sighed. "No use worrying. I'm also happy you agreed to help me bake all of those *pites*. I know it's a lot of work, but maybe it will help you take your mind off this latest unpleasantness."

"Maybe," Callie said dubiously. Making *pites* and summer fruit pies was soothing work. She just wished the order wasn't so large.

Callie picked at her food and chatted some more with George before going upstairs to check on Olivia. She was asleep, with tears dried in streak marks down her face. Poor kid. Callie kissed her daughter's cheek gently, so as not to wake her, and tiptoed back down the stairs to say goodnight to her father.

"She's sleeping. Thanks again for coming over, Dad." She hugged him tightly. "You really did help me by being here, and Olivia was comforted too. I could tell, even though she wanted to be alone."

"You were the same way, *hrisi mou*," George said affectionately. "Always wanting to be alone when you were upset. You get some rest, and we'll talk tomorrow. *Kali Nihta*."

"*Kali Nihta*. Good night," Callie called. She locked every door and window and wondered when she'd ever hear from Sands. She knew she should call her best friend, Sam.

Callie sat down on the sofa, rubbing her eyes, hoping to get some of the tiredness out of them. It didn't work.

Koukla took the opportunity to jump on her lap and Callie petted her absently, thinking. Sam would surely she'd have some insights. She figured it was useless to keep waiting for Sands' call, as he was probably busy. She could picture him, brow furrowed, hunched over a huge Styrofoam cup of tea as he reviewed the evidence.

Before she could do anything, though, she had to change out of her clothes and take a shower. Her gruesome discovery had made her feel soiled, somehow. She folded up her too-tight jeans and pushed them onto the highest closet shelf. Maybe she should lay off sampling her own baked goods so often before attempting to put them on again.

When she was showered and dressed in a loose tee and cotton shorts, she felt calmer and ready to talk to her best friend. Callie never knew when or if Sam would be available. As a criminal attorney, she kept hours almost as irregular as Callie's. To Callie's great relief, Sam answered her phone.

"Well, well, well. Nancy Drew strikes again," Samantha greeted Callie. "Sorry, it just slipped out," she said over Callie's sputtered protests. "I was just kidding. The truth is, I'm worried about you, Callie. Bad luck seems to be following you around." Sam adopted a tough exterior in times of crisis, especially when she was worried or stressed.

"You think?" Callie answered sarcastically. "How did you hear about Holly Tennyson?"

"Oh, the usual way." Sam seemed to be regretting her previous glibness. "One of my colleagues mentioned it. This is the kind of news that travels fast. As you should know."

"I sure do." Callie sighed. "Well, what do you think happened?"

"I have no idea," Sam said briskly. "How's Olivia taking it?"

"Not well," Callie replied. "And I don't blame her. I'm not taking it very well either."

"Well, what does Detective Dreamy have to say?"

"Ha, ha," Callie answered. "You know he can't tell me everything. Anyway, I haven't talked to him since he met me at the crime scene." She gulped, remembering. "I did find out one odd thing, though. Well, more like a coincidence. Or maybe not. That arrogant theater director, Allan Browne, lives in the neighborhood where I found Holly's body."

"You don't say," Sam sounded thoughtful. "That is a little strange. What do you make of it?"

"I wish I knew. I was hoping you'd have some ideas."

"Not at the moment, but give me some time. Off the top of my head, I'd say that he didn't seem like the nicest guy in the world, but that doesn't mean anything. Some of the 'nicest' people in the world commit the worst crimes. There was this one guy..."

Callie felt a headache forming behind her eyes. "Listen, I'd better go. It's been a long day."

"All right, friend. If I hear anything or think of anything to help, I'll let you know. Let's talk soon." The two rang off.

***

The next day dawned hot, sunny and humid. Callie dragged herself out of bed early and checked on her daughter, who was due at day camp. She wondered if Olivia would be too aggrieved to attend, and wondered also what she'd do with her if she was. The life of a single mom.

Sands had texted late the previous evening with an apology for not calling and a promise to see her that evening. So there was that, at least.

Before she could do anything else, Callie decided she needed coffee and headed down to the kitchen to brew some. Koukla was lounging in her dog bed, but she followed Callie into the kitchen for her treats, fresh water, food and a trip outdoors. Before Callie had finished her first cup of strong coffee, Olivia straggled downstairs dressed in her camp T-shirt and shorts. Her face was scrubbed, her long, honey-colored hair was combed and she looked fairly alert.

"I see that you're planning on going to camp," Callie remarked, folding her into a tight hug. "Good for you."

"Yeah, we're supposed to go swimming today. I'm sad about Ms. Tennyson, but I don't really want to talk about it now, Mom."

You and me both, Callie thought. "No problem," she said to her daughter brightly. "Let's go."

Callie dropped off her gloomy daughter at the YMCA building in town and was in a pensive mood as she arrived at her shop. Max was already in the work room, rolling out what looked like mass quantities of pie dough while Piper handled the customers at the front of the shop. Sitting on the stainless steel countertops were bowls of glistening blueberries, crimson strawberries and dark cherries.

"Hey, Callie," Max said, not stopping his work. His muscles rippled as he rolled out dough and started placing it in pie pans. "The fruit we got from our supplier this morning is off the charts. We've had a lot of requests for fruit pies, and anyway, they're on this week's menu. I figured I'd get a head start."

"Sounds good to me," Callie said. "Thanks, Max." She was touched to see him working so hard, no doubt trying to rectify his previous slip up. She was also charmed to note the small pie cutters he was using to decorate the pies with pastry designs of strawberries, cherries and hearts. Callie's Kitchen patrons would love these extra touches.

"Did you hear about..." Callie began but Max cut her off.

"I did hear. Holly Tennyson is dead." Max looked grim.

Oh boy, Callie thought. Everybody knows. The thought made her feel slightly uneasy.

"Yes, I can't say much about it, other than I was the 'lucky' one who found her." Callie shuddered. "It was just coincidence. Hugh was supposed to be there, not me."

"Hugh?" Max asked. He furrowed his brow, which only serviced to emphasize the piercing on his left eyebrow. "Cripes. I don't mean to be morbid, but he wouldn't have had anything to do with this, would he?"

"I don't think so," Callie said, but this was the second person who'd brought that up, Sands being the first. What connection, if any, did Hugh have with Holly? Maybe she should dig around a little bit, but she was truly sickened at even the thought that the father of her child could do such a thing.

"I'm really sorry," Max said, brushing his hands to get the flour off of them. "Just look out. You keep finding yourself in these ... uh. Situations, shall we say."

Callie stared at him, exasperated. "I know. And I promise you it's not intentional!"

"I know. No offense intended. Hey, why don't you give me a hand, and let's get these babies in the oven."

Happy to focus on fruit pies and not unsolved murders, Callie washed up at the hand-washing sink and joined Max at the table. The two worked companionably for several minutes before Callie heard the unmistakable sounds of Grandma Viv's voice at the front of the shop. Callie wiped her doughy hands on her apron and swung through the French doors that separated the front of the shop from the busy workroom.

"Grandma!" Callie said, happy to see a friendly face. Viv wore a pink oxford shirt over white capris, her feet in white Ked sneakers. As usual, every silvery gray hair was in place, and she looked much younger than her 80 + years. Standing next to Viv was Mrs. DeWitt, local philanthropist and the owner of an opulent waterfront home. She was slightly younger than Viv and was dressed in her usual casual but elegant manner. Callie nodded at her with a smile. She and Viv were old friends, and Mrs. DeWitt had awarded Callie a cash prize in a local business contest through Crystal Bay's Chamber of Commerce.

"Hello, dear." Viv said. "We heard the terrible news about Holly Tennyson. You must be distraught. But I think I have something to get your mind off of it. Gert and I are here to ask you a favor."

"If I can," Callie said, bracing herself.

"It's like this, Callie," Mrs. DeWitt said smoothly, stepping forward. "You probably know that Viv and I are helping the Chamber with our *Beats on the Bay* series this summer. Well, we thought it would be helpful to you, and to our attendees, if we could offer some refreshments each week. You know, just some tidbits and nibbles, maybe some sweets to be sold at a table. Nothing too complicated. We thought of you immediately." Mrs. DeWitt smiled at Callie, clearly unwilling to be denied.

Callie looked at Grandma Viv. "It would be a great business opportunity for you, dear," Viv said encouragingly. "I know you're busy but think of the possibilities!"

"Yes..." Callie said slowly, calculating how many extra hours she would have to put in. The Greek Fest baking was already taking up a lot of her time.

"I can help," Max interjected. Callie stared at him, aghast, and he just smiled and shrugged.

"See!" Mrs. DeWitt beamed at Max. They must really be desperate, Callie thought. Once, Mrs. DeWitt had told her that Max's tattoos and eyebrow ring "weren't appetizing" for someone in food service.

"I guess it's settled," Callie said. It would add to her already stacked workload, but the extra income would be very welcome. She was still trying to dig out financially from the near shut down of her business after becoming a murder suspect not that many months before.

"Wonderful, dear!" Viv was jubilant. "I knew you would help us. Anyway, you should join us sometime as an audience member. It's a lot of fun. You can bring your boyfriend. And it would take your mind off of this latest...unpleasantness."

"I just might do that," Callie said. When she and Sands would have the extra time, she didn't know. But music under the stars sounded pretty good after what she'd been through in the last 24 hours.

After the two women had left, Callie decided it was time for a heart-to-heart with Max.

"Thanks for offering to help me with this extra work, but Max, as you know we are both going to need to work some extra hours. Don't forget, I also offered to help George bake for the Greek Fest."

"I haven't forgotten. But I'm thinking if I show my father how much I'm needed here, he might get off my back about wanting to have me come home and help him." Max looked at his shoes, speckled with flour and confectioner's sugar. "The thing is, he wants an answer really soon."

"And? What are you going to do?" Callie held her breath.

"I don't know yet. I didn't want to tell you this, but there's a chance I might have to leave Callie's Kitchen and help him out, after all."

Five

allie was still reeling from this revelation when a group of three customers burst through the door, laughing and chattering. Max ran out to greet them, clearly wanting to escape the conversation. As soon as Max had left the work room, Callie sat down at one of her stainless steel worktables and put her head in her hands.

Of course, she could always find another employee, but where would she find an employee to equal Max's loyalty? He had his quirks, but he was truly dedicated and a skilled, enthusiastic cook. Plus, he'd stood by Callie when her business was going through a rough patch and had even recruited his girlfriend to do social media work for college credit. No doubt about it: Max was a gem.

Callie measured rice, sugar and whole milk for her rich version of rice pudding, aka *rizogalo*, as she fretted about Max. He'd talked about wanting to take culinary courses and becoming a professional chef, so she'd always figured she'd lose him someday, but she wasn't ready yet.

It didn't matter if she was ready or not. "Someday" may have already arrived.

Food prep beckoned and soon, Callie was mixing cooked rice into a pot of milk and sugar. The comforting scents of rice pudding normally soothed her soul and made her hungry, since it was one of her favorite desserts. Not this time, though. The more she stirred, the more worried she became. What about Piper? Would she leave too?

Once the pudding had cooked into a thick, fragrant porridge, Callie stirred vanilla extract into the pot, placed the pudding into individual containers and sprinkled them with cinnamon. Composing her face into a cheery, customer-friendly smile, she headed out to the front of the shop, her arms filled with that day's main course selections. She planned to restock the take-out refrigerator.

"Hi, Callie," said a throaty voice and Callie looked up, startled. It was Tammy Heckstrom, the woman who scared her half to death the other day when she was pretending to be dead at the murder mystery night. She was also Holly Tennyson's grad school classmate, Callie remembered.

In total contrast to her glamorous get-up at The Harris House, Tammy looked bedraggled in frayed jeans and a pink T-shirt that looked as if she'd slept in it.

"Hi, Tammy," Callie said, concerned for the grieving young woman. "How are you?"

"Not that great. I was wondering if we could talk. About Holly."

Callie glanced at Max, who raised his eyebrows at her and nodded towards the crowded shop. Suddenly, the buzz of happy voices had stopped, and you could hear a pin drop.

"Uh, sure," Callie stammered. "But not out here. Why don't you join me in the work room for a minute?" Callie smiled at Max, who smiled back in relief. Did he think she would be angry at him? Callie of all people knew what it was like to go out on your own in opposition to what family members wanted you to do.

Tammy seemed to regain some of her perkiness as she gazed around Callie's work room, commenting on the goodies cooking and the smells coming from the oven. She glanced hungrily at the rice pudding, so Callie handed her a small cup of it with a generous dash of cinnamon on top for good measure. It was meant to be served cold, but served warm it would probably be even more comforting to someone in Tammy's shoes.

"I haven't been eating lately. This is good," Tammy said, consuming the pudding in a flash. "So, I heard that you found Holly and I was wondering what you could tell me. We were such good friends, and I just feel awful. No one will tell me anything." Tammy's face crinkled up as if trying to squelch tears.

"First of all, I'm really sorry for your loss. I'm also sorry to tell you that I'm not really at liberty to say much," Callie said, thinking of Sands.

There was an uncomfortable silence that Callie decided to break with a question that had been bothering her. "Do you know what Holly might have been doing at the house? It was abandoned, after all. I just wondered if she would have had a special reason for being there."

"I don't know, and it's really been bugging me." Tammy frowned. "I know that she liked the Gilded Age homes, but I can't see her trespassing on someone's property, especially not out of the blue. I thought maybe you would know why she was there." Tammy fiddled with her spoon.

"No idea. I was only there myself because my ex-husband was supposed to have a renovation job there next week. He was meeting me there to drop off my daughter as part of our custody arrangement. It's not our usual agreement. I usually don't pick her up at a work site."

Tammy stood up, her chair making a loud screech as she pushed it back. "Well, I've taken up enough of your time. Sorry I bothered you. Oh, and thanks for the food."

"You're welcome. And you're not a bother at all," Callie said, startled by Tammy's sudden need for departure. "Hey, before you go, I just wondered something. Was Holly close to Allan Browne, the director?"

"Close?" Tammy wrinkled her nose. "What do you mean?"

"There seemed to be some tension there," Callie said gently. "It looked like they were arguing at the murder mystery night."

Tammy blinked at her. "Allan is a jerk to everybody. He's always worried about the bottom line. He was yelling at all of us that night. It seems like he's *always* on edge the night of a performance."

Tammy shifted from foot to foot. "Look, I'm sorry I interrupted your work. I should really get going." In a blur of pink and denim, Tammy breezed through the French doors and was on the sidewalk door before Callie could say another word.

"Darn," Callie said. She'd wanted to ask what Tammy knew about Allan Browne's upscale home that just happened to be near the murder scene but hadn't had a chance.

"What was that all about, boss?" Max asked.

"Nothing. Just someone who knew Holly Tennyson. I'd better get back to work. And Max?"

"Yeah?" Max shifted from foot to foot.

"Don't worry about anything. We'll figure it out."

Max nodded and smiled. Callie went back to the work room. How much longer would Max be calling her "boss?"

And what was up with Tammy Heckstrom, anyway?

***

The afternoon passed quickly. Boaters, shoppers, locals and tourists kept Max and Callie running back and forth throughout the shop. They barely had time to speak, except to discuss food, which was probably a good thing.

It was Max and Piper's turn to work the late shift, thankfully, and Callie was happy to call it a day. After a few last-minute instructions and a promise to be in early the next day to get a head start on all of her extracurricular baking, she bade goodbye to her staff and decided to take a mind-clearing walk around the bay before heading home. She'd already checked with George, and he had driven Olivia to Viv's house after day camp. Callie knew that Grandma Viv would be a good influence on Olivia, so there was no need to hurry back. She needed time to clear her mind. Holly's murder was weighing on her. She couldn't get the images of that terrible day out of her mind.

The shop had been overly warm. Callie welcomed the cool breeze that washed over her as she walked in the direction of the bay. She strolled down to the park that bordered the water and decided to take a look at the bandstand. This was where Viv and Mrs. DeWitt would be working their magic with *Beats on the Bay*.

Callie smiled as she picked her way around kids shouting and running with swim gear and toys, and couples walking hand in hand, their faces dreamy and vague in the beautiful late afternoon. The Harris House loomed, its witches' hat turrets nearly white under the dazzling sun. Gazing out at the shimmering water, Callie wondered if she'd be able to coerce Sands into *Beats on the Bay* or any other leisure-time activity anytime soon.

Turning back to the bandstand, Callie was deciding on the most convenient spot for a refreshments table when she heard voices rising in anger.

Lisa Linley and Tammy Heckstrom were having a loud conversation. It looked like they were arguing. *About what?* They were too far away for her to hear what they were arguing about, but Callie decided to try and get a little closer.

The Harris House was across the street from the waterfront park, so Callie darted through nearly stagnant traffic until she was safely on the sidewalk. Before she could hear the reason for their spat, Tammy had already huffed away and Lisa was stomping up the elegant steps of her hotel.

What to do?

Curiosity won. Callie decided to stop in The Harris House and see if she could find out what was going on. Tammy was acting awfully strange today, belligerent one minute and sad the next. Still, she had lost a good friend in a most horrific way. If there was more to it than simple emotional distress, Callie wanted to find out.

Smoothing back her tangled wavy hair, Callie walked into The Harris House with an excuse at the ready, flimsy though it was. She'd simply ask if Lisa had ever contacted Hugh's firm about renovations. Surely, Lisa wouldn't suspect anything from that inquiry. If anything, she'd think Callie was pushy. Fair enough.

The hotel was cool and hushed in the summer heat, its windows open to the breeze, and the usual group of cocktail and iced tea drinkers seated on the comfortable front porch. A buzz of voices came from diners having an early dinner or a very late lunch. There was no one at the reception desk, so Callie admired an Art Deco lamp while she waited. Had Lisa left work from another exit?

She was just about to ask the bartender where Lisa had gone when the woman herself appeared from the direction of the dining room. Unfortunately for Callie's purposes of interrogation, she wasn't alone. A short but shapely woman in jeans, work shirt and tool belt accompanied her. Her long, light brown hair was in a ponytail, and she had a fresh-faced look. Callie placed her at around 30 years old.

"Oh, hello there," Lisa said smoothly when she noticed Callie. "You're just the person I wanted to talk to. To *thank*, actually. Have you met April Manning? She works for the firm your ex-husband does. They sent her out today to discuss some repairs. She's the project coordinator."

"Great! I'm glad I was able to connect the two of you. I'm Callie Costas." Callie extended her hand to April.

"Hi. Glad to meet you," April said cheerily. She really was adorable, and Callie had a naughty thought; had Raine met April yet?

"Is there something I can help you with? Or are you here for dinner or a drink?" Lisa asked. She seemed calm and professional, with no sign of the distress she had exhibited when speaking with Tammy Heckstrom. Maybe Callie had gotten it wrong.

"Uh, no. Not really. This really is a coincidence. I was just checking to see if you'd called Vintage Reno and you have." Callie was embarrassed.

"Thanks for the recommendation," April said. "You're Hugh's ex?" She gave Callie an appraising look, and Callie blushed.

"Yes, I am. How long have you worked for Vintage Reno? I know Hugh likes it there a lot."

"A few years," April said. "It's a great business to be in. You'd be surprised at how many buildings in Crystal Bay need help, especially these old, historic buildings. They keep us in business, that's for sure."

Lisa blanched a little bit at April's bluntness, and April seemed to realize what she'd said. "You know what I mean" She shrugged and smiled pertly at the two older women. "But don't worry, Lisa. You can count on us."

"I'm sorry," Lisa said, turning to Callie. "I've got to go over some specifics with April. Thanks again. I hope to see you here for a meal soon."

"Nice to meet you, April. See you soon, Lisa." Callie gave a jaunty wave and scurried back out of The Harris House. So much for sleuthing.

So Lisa had taken her advice, Callie thought as she left the two women to discuss repairs and renovations. While Callie was pleased that she was able to help Lisa, she wondered what Hugh knew about work going on at The Harris House. She made a mental note to check in with him about it as soon as she could.

Callie walked slowly down the steps of The Harris House and stopped to admire the waterfront. Kids were swimming, frolicking, and playing on the small beach next to the bay. She vowed to take Olivia for a mom-daughter swim day at the next available opportunity. Summer was far too fleeting in Crystal Bay. You had to embrace every moment.

Deep in thought, Callie had only walked about a block when she found herself staring straight into the white shirtfront of Sands.

"Well, this is a nice surprise!" Callie had been convinced he was chained to his desk somewhere.

"I'm glad you feel that way," Sands said into her hair as he embraced her. "I've been looking for you."

"I promise, I didn't do it," she joked, to hide the fact that she was flustered by his sudden presence. Her heart did a little skip.

"I decided to take a short break, and I thought I'd ask you to an early dinner. How about it?"

"Let me check in with Viv. She's got Olivia tonight." Sands nodded and smiled at her, his hazel eyes warm as she dialed the number on her cell phone. After Viv had given her gushing assent for Callie's dinner date, Sands took her by the arm.

"Can we go somewhere nearby? I don't have a lot of time. I just wanted to see you."

"You did?" Callie was a little taken aback. She hadn't expected Sands to have any time off at all after the tragic incident with Holly.

"Yes, of course." He swooped down to give her a kiss on the cheek. "And if I'm being honest, there are a few things I want to run by you about the other night."

"Ah. So it isn't just the pleasure of my company you want after all." Callie kept her tone light.

"I do, actually. I'd love nothing more than just the pleasure of your company, but I'm quite good at multi-tasking. So, where to?" Sands looked toward The Harris House. "How about there?" he asked, nodding. "It's closest."

"Fine, but I have to tell you, I was just in there. I saw the owner, Lisa, fighting with Tammy Heckstrom. She was the actress who played the murder victim at the show right before Holly..." Callie broke off as images of Holly lying on the grass filled her mind.

"Is that so?" Sands said thoughtfully. "I've met Tammy. She was a good friend of Holly's. We've had a chat with her."

He looked into Callie's eyes. "A murder never stops being painful to contemplate, and you've been involved in more than your share." He gave her arm a squeeze.

"Thanks a lot!" Callie said. "You're right, of course, but what a way to put it!"

Sands raised an eyebrow at her. "Let's go eat. You can put me in my place at dinner. And, you can tell me what you think the fight was about."

Six

Lisa didn't seem surprised by Callie's return, but her smile was a little strained. Her lack of enthusiasm seemed to intensify when she noticed Sands, who had taken a minute to make a quick phone call before joining Callie by the concierge desk.

"I'm back," Callie said brightly. "And this time, I brought a friend, Detective Ian Sands." Lisa hadn't taken ownership of The Harris House the last time Callie and Sands had dinner there, so Lisa had never met him.

"Pleased to meet you," Sands said in his sandpapery voice. "And congratulations on your new purchase. The Harris House is a lovely place."

"Thank you," Lisa said, looking ill at ease. She kept glancing nervously at Sands. Callie looked over at him, but he didn't seem to have noticed.

"Two for dinner? Right this way," she said with a forced smile. Callie followed, perplexed by Lisa's odd behavior.

Lisa sat them near the back of the small dining room, explaining that the larger dining room was closed at the moment. She handed them menus with a stiff smile, and sped away with a promise that a waiter would be right over.

"Hmmm," Callie said taking a long drink from her water glass. "Lisa is usually much friendlier."

Sands studied the menu. "Is she?" he asked. "Well, perhaps she's still upset about this fight you say you saw her having."

Callie shrugged. "I wasn't aware that the two of them knew each other well enough to be fighting. Tammy was one of the performers the other night and that's the extent of it as far as I know. I have no idea why they would be having a heated dispute."

"It could mean something and it might not." Sands finally looked up from the menu and put his hand over Callie's. His hand was warm and Callie was uncomfortably aware that her hands were dry from all of the excessive hand washing she was required to do. If he was looking for someone with perfectly manicured hands, he'd picked someone in the wrong profession.

Sands didn't seem to mind her dishpan hands. He met her gaze, looking thoughtful. "We're obviously interested in this new owner of The Harris House, even though the murder didn't take place here. I'm glad to have a chance to observe her tonight."

"Uh-huh," Callie said wickedly. "So this was all a set up. And here I thought we had a date."

"We do," Sands said, with a smile. He kissed Callie's hand. "I'm happy to grab time with you whenever we can find some."

Just then a waitress came over and Sands released her fingers, reluctantly so it seemed to Callie. He really was a dear, but his job! It was all-consuming.

Like mine, Callie thought ruefully.

The waitress took their drink orders: iced tea for both of them. Callie knew that Sands wouldn't order anything stronger since he was heading back to work, and Callie felt like keeping a clear head with all of the work ahead of her over the next few days.

"So," Sands taking a sip of water. "You said you didn't think your ex-husband knew Holly Tennyson but it appears he did. We checked," he said, interrupting her as she started to ask how he knew that.

Callie almost choked on her tea. "Really."

"Yes, indeed. They briefly dated before he met his current wife."

Callie set her glass down on the table so hard that some of it sloshed over the side. "What? Well, that explains it."

"Explains what?"

"Why Hugh never went to teacher's meetings with me last year. He didn't want to run into an ex-girlfriend while with his ex-wife."

"It appears their relationship was short-lived, and the split was amicable," Sands remarked.

"Maybe that's why I never heard about it. You'd think someone would have told me, though, especially when Holly became Olivia's teacher last year."

"It doesn't appear that many people knew about the brief relationship," Sands said soothingly. "And maybe people were trying to spare your feelings."

Callie chuckled. "Doubtful. You know how everybody loves to gossip at my shop. I guess Holly and Hugh were just very discreet."

"Right," Sands said briskly, clearly warming up to his subject. "Did you know that Raine was also an acquaintance of Holly?"

"No, but that doesn't surprise me as much as what you just told me. How did they know each other, besides working together with the acting troupe?" Callie had relayed Raine's unexpected role as a costume helper to Sands the night of the murder mystery.

"They both attended St. Mary's High School. Raine was a few years ahead of Holly."

"What are you getting at? Does any of this matter?" *Then again, Holly was found at Hugh's new work site.* Was what had seemed a terrible coincidence truly something more sinister?

Sands shrugged, a bland look on his face. "Who knows? I just was checking to see if you could shed some light on any of this, but it seems you weren't aware."

Callie stared at the lacy tablecloth. The prospect of a semi-romantic evening was starting to fade for her. The last thing she wanted to do was to think about her failed marriage, Hugh's dating life and her ex's new wife.

"I knew that Raine didn't go to my high school and that's about it," she told Sands. "I'm a few years older than her, anyway. We probably wouldn't have run in the same circles, even if we *did* go to the same school."

"And as far as Hugh," Callie heard her voice rising and struggled to keep calm. "I know he's not the type of person to do something so violent. True, we didn't get along but he's just not, he's just..." Callie cast around for convincing words but came up short. She knew that Sands was just doing his job, but couldn't he see how serious this was for her? This was the father of her child he was talking about. As for Raine, she was ditzy at times, to be sure, but she didn't seem to have any murderous tendencies.

Or did she? Maybe Hugh did, too. After all, Callie hadn't even known he was seeing their daughter's grade school teacher. It put her friendly relationship with Holly into a whole different light. What had Holly known about her and her personal life? Callie shifted in her chair, suddenly uncomfortable with the entire conversation.

Sands seemed to realize he'd struck a nerve. "I think we've had enough shop talk for one night. Let's enjoy our dinners," he said, gesturing to the food that was now being placed in front of them.

On such a warm day, Callie had opted for the cold leek-potato soup and a chicken baguette sandwich. Artfully diced fruit accompanied her dish. Well, Lisa certainly hadn't let the food standards slip since she bought the place, Callie thought as she dug in. She realized that she was hungry. Soon, disturbing thoughts of murder faded as she sampled the food. Delicious!

Sands seemed to be enjoying his salmon and dill sauce. The two ate heartily as they discussed less toxic topics. Callie brought up *Beats on the Bay* and was surprised to hear Sands was gung-ho for the idea.

"Work is crazy, as you know," he said. "But I may be able to pop down some evening, at least for a little while. I think it's wonderful that Viv is helping out. She certainly never slows down."

"Oh, but I didn't tell you the best part: I'm providing refreshments. At Viv and Mrs. DeWitt's request, of course."

"Ah yes, Mrs. DeWitt. Well, she certainly is a character, but I'll always have a soft spot for her." He gazed at Callie with meaning, and she smiled back at him, her face warm. The two of them had become officially "involved" after a party at Mrs. DeWitt's house.

"I guess you'll be pretty busy," Sands said, taking a swig of tea.

"Well, won't you be?"

"Yes, of course. Especially with this latest case."

Callie sighed. "Me, too. Summer is my busiest season. And I'm not complaining. I need the business."

"You've got Max, though, haven't you? And Piper?"

Callie didn't have the heart to discuss the possibility of Max's departure. "I'll figure it out. Now, before you have to go, how about dessert?"

The two of them shared some bittersweet chocolate sorbet before Sands took his leave. As they exited The Harris House, Sands' arm draped casually around her shoulders, Callie kept her eye out for Lisa, who was greeting more diners as they clustered into the doorway for the busy dinner hour.

"Good night," Lisa warbled, but her smile was uncertain and her previously cheeriness seemed to be permanently extinguished. Callie was determined to find out what had caused the change in Lisa's behavior.

"I'm walking you to your car, so don't argue," Sands said and Callie saluted him. Once they reached her car, she turned to say goodbye, and he swept her in his arms before she could say a word, giving her a kiss that left her breathless. "Gotta go," he whispered, holding the car door open for her.

"See you soon," Callie whispered back. She sat in the car a minute, wishing they both had normal jobs and that everything didn't have to be so rushed. Looking up, she noticed that Sands had stopped and had turned to look back at her. His smile was devilish, and he gave a jaunty wave which Callie returned.

As Callie started her car, she was feeling a little shaky and it wasn't just from Sands' show of passion. She was feeling troubled by their dinner conversation. His mentioning of Raine and Hugh knowing Holly seemed ominous. Callie couldn't believe they were seriously being considered as suspects. However, there was one truth she couldn't escape, uncomfortable though it was for her to contemplate. Everyone had their secrets.

Seven

The next morning, Callie was feeling as mixed up as a bowl of *spanakopita* filling. It helped that Max was working so industriously beside her. The weather had decided to become stunningly beautiful as well.

Sunlight glinted off the polished glass of her display case and sparkled on the stainless steel countertops. The warm, soft breezy weather on her way to work that morning had lifted her spirits, but she still had a lot on her mind.

Callie paused in her food prep for a minute as she looked fondly around her shop. Even in stressful times, she always took pride in its inviting appearance. Fresh daisies in mason jars decorated the tables and a feeling of light and warmth permeated the room. Callie looked at the St. Basil icon that her father, George, had bought for her years ago (St. Basil had once worked as a cook, apparently) and said a small prayer that she wouldn't lose her best employee.

The two of them hadn't broached the topic of Max's potential departure from her employ again, and Callie was relieved not to revisit *that* conversation for the time being. However, she found that she was casting about in her mind for possible Max replacements as she went about her tasks of rolling out pie dough for her famous summer cherry pie, filling display cases with fragrant *koularakia*, the famous braided Greek butter cookie, and baking *spanakopita* triangles to bring to the *Beats on the Bay* refreshments table. Running Callie's Kitchen without Max; it wasn't a pleasant thought.

Max was wiping off the countertop and whistling when Callie emerged from the work room where her ovens were housed. "We sold out of the Greek yogurt coffee cake," he remarked, gesturing at a pan that held nothing more than crumbs. "Want me to make more?"

"Yes, that would be great. Might as well have extra for tomorrow." Callie felt her shoulders slump. Sharp-eyed Max noticed, of course.

"Callie, what is it? You seem really down today. I know you've been through a lot lately."

"Oh, I don't know." Callie didn't know where to start. "Just tired, I guess." Olivia had kept her up half the night with nightmares, and Callie was worried about her, so that was true enough.

"I hope I'm not part of the reason you're upset." Max looked pained. "I'm sorry. I sort of wish I'd never said anything about my dad wanting me to take over the farm. But I thought I had to let you know about my current situation. You know, just in case."

Callie groaned involuntarily, and Max pulled himself up to his full height. He crossed his arms in his usual pose, his huge, tattooed forearms as colorful as ever. "I'm doing my best to stay here. I promise. And if something happens and I can't, well, I'll just help you find someone to take my place. Not that they could," he said, half-smiling at his own joke.

"That's just the trouble, Max. I'm not sure anyone *can* take your place. You're here now, so let's knock out this *Beats on the Bay* food. Remember, you said you'd help, and I need your cooking expertise right about now." Callie smiled at him.

"Yeah, yeah," Max grinned, his face flushing. Any sort of praise made him shy.

"You're right, by the way," Callie continued, picking up the thread of their earlier conversation. "This Holly Tennyson murder is really bothering me. Olivia is devastated, and I don't blame her. I'm not doing so great myself."

"Yeah, I was wondering about that. Poor kid. I wondered how she was doing." Max leaned against the counter and looked outside for customers. "Looks like nobody's coming in, so do you want to tell me about it?"

Grateful for a friendly ear, Callie shared some of Olivia's distress. Then, omitting the part about Hugh and Raine being potential suspects, she blurted out the fact that Hugh and Holly had once been an item, if only briefly.

"No way!" Max looked surprised. "Must have been before his new wife, what's her name, came on the scene."

Callie couldn't help but laugh at his referral to Raine. "Her name is Raine. Remember? And yes, I think it was before she was around. Anyway, I didn't know and just found out about it myself."

"Well, that's just really weird," Max said, frowning. "You didn't even know your ex-husband had a fling with your daughter's teacher? Parent-teacher conferences must have been interesting."

"Hugh generally skipped those last year. I put it down to being busy and moving but now I guess I know the real reason why."

Max gave her an empathetic glance. "Holly was a nice woman. It's a real shame. She seemed a little stressed, though, last time she came in here. Don't you think?"

"What are you talking about?" Callie couldn't remember a stressed-out Holly in her shop recently.

"Oh, that's right. It was Piper and me working that day. You'd already left. Holly was grabbing some food to go and was in kind of a nervous mood. You can ask Piper, she saw her too."

"Go on," Callie said, intrigued.

Max stopped talking as a couple walked by the shop, but they passed by the door and didn't come in. He shrugged and continued his tale.

"Well, it was a couple of weeks ago. She didn't really give specifics. She was in a big hurry, and Piper and I were chatting to her, you know, teasing her about it, I guess. She said she was sorry to be in such a rush, but that rehearsals were getting in the way of some sort of research she was doing for her graduate degree."

"Did she say anything else?" Callie pressed.

Max closed his eyes, trying to remember. He shook his head. "Nope. That's all I remember. Piper might know more. She'll be in tomorrow."

Callie glanced up; the couple had decided to come into Callie's Kitchen after all. "We'd better get back to work. Let me jump back on the baking while you deal with the customers."

Max nodded his head at her as Callie strode back into her work-room, even more mixed up than before. This was another noodle to add to the soup. She resolved to tell Sands about it and shrugging off her many doubts, dove back into her *spanakopita* triangle-making for *Beats on the Bay*.

***

Callie finished her food prep and then realized that she'd need to provide paper plates, napkins and plastic flatware. She hunted through her store room, but her supplies were low, probably from the uptick in customers, so she couldn't spare any.

"Max, we've got to order some more paper plates and stuff," she said, brushing her hair out of her face as she emerged from the storage area. "In the meantime, I've got to run out and get some extra for tonight."

"You're not going all the way to the kitchen supply store, are you? They have the best prices."

"No, there's no time. I'll have to stop at the supermarket."

"You sure? I can go."

"No, it's fine. I'll be back in two shakes of a lamb's tail."

Callie dashed to her car and was soon at the supermarket on the edge of town. Summer people filled the place and, as she sped through the store, she found herself dodging shoppers staring at produce or debating what crackers to buy. Finally she found the paper goods aisle and loaded up her cart, making a mental note to hang onto her receipt for the Chamber to reimburse her.

Callie was just pushing her cart into the one open checkout line when she saw Raine coming her way. As usual, she was dressed in one of her too-youthful outfits: denim short-shorts and a tropical print T-shirt. Her long blonde hair was twisted up into a knot on top of her head, making her look even taller. Out of habit, Callie peeked at Raine's shopping cart. It was filled with thick, marbled steaks, salad fixings, corn on the cob, cans of baked beans and several 2-liters of soda and beer.

"Hi Raine," she said, trying to inject some enthusiasm into the greeting. "Looks like you're barbecuing tonight." Might as well be friendly.

"We sure are. It's been too warm to cook indoors and anyway, you know Hugh loves to stand around a fire!" Raine chuckled immoderately and Callie smiled neutrally back at her. It was strange seeing her after all of Sands' talk of Hugh and Raine being acquainted with Holly. Callie floundered around for a different topic of conversation.

"I meant to tell you how much I enjoyed the show the other night. You did a good job on the costumes."

"You think so? Thanks. Though I have to say, the whole theater troupe is really shaken up about Holly. I am too, especially since I knew her in high school. And it may sound cold, but they're now short an actress."

Callie raised her eyebrows. "Yes, well, I guess they'll have to find somebody new. I hadn't thought of that."

Raine got a funny look on her face. "Everyone is really upset. But you know the saying: The show must go on. It turns out there's another show scheduled at The Harris House in a few days. They booked the troupe for several shows after the success of the last one and before Holly..." Raine broke off, blinking back tears. She took a shuddery breath before continuing.

"They've asked me to be Holly's replacement." Raine wiped at her big blue eyes. "I told them I would, but I just don't know if I can go through with it! It seems...disloyal."

Callie gaped at her a bit but decided to take the high road. "Don't worry. I think it's nice of you to step in." Raine and Holly were physically very different, but maybe that didn't matter, especially in an acting emergency.

"Thanks," Raine said softly. "I just hope I can memorize my lines."

"You will," Callie said absently, a thought dawning on her. She'd really like to get a chance to observe some of the players from the other night, as well as Allan Browne. But it would seem odd to go back when she'd been there so recently, unless she had a reason to be there. "Raine, do you mind if I go to the show?"

"I don't mind one bit." Raine's cheeks flushed underneath her bright pink blush. "I'm going to need all the support I can get." She beamed at Callie.

Callie cringed. She wasn't planning to be there for support, but for more snooping. It was embarrassing the way Raine misinterpreted her every move.

"See you then," Callie said. "I've got to get back to the shop right now, but I'll call The Harris House for details."

"You can also check the website. All the info should be there." Raine seemed to be perking up.

"Will do." Wait until everybody heard this news, Callie thought. Theater might never be the same.

***

"Guess who's going to see their name in lights?" Callie asked Max once she was back at work with her stock of plates and utensils.

"What are you talking about?" Max asked distractedly, his arms full of empty pastry trays. He brushed past Callie and set the trays down on the counter.

Callie looked right and left before answering. Fortunately, only a couple of customers were clustered at tables near the window. It was early afternoon. This was one of the shop's slower times, well after lunch, but right before people started getting hungry for snacks and dinner.

"Raine," she said in a loud whisper. "She took over Holly Tennyson's part in the play."

"Wow," said Max. "That sounds interesting, to put it mildly."

"You're telling me," Callie agreed. "I want another look at the actors and director so I told Raine I'd see the next performance. I didn't get to meet all of the actors, but I did meet one of the other actresses and the director. Let's just say they're both a little...eccentric."

"If I'm not on the schedule, wild horses couldn't keep me away."

Callie smiled at his remark. "Something about that theater troupe has me extremely curious."

"No kidding," Max chuckled. "Now what's on our immediate agenda?"

With all the excitement, Callie almost forgot why she had gone to the store in the first place. "Did you pack up the food for *Beats on the Bay*?"

"Pretty much. Why? It's early."

"I know. I was thinking that I need to have a game plan for getting the food over there."

"Why don't you go ahead and bring it over there in an hour. I can take care of customers and close up here on my own. You want me to call Piper? I know she's not doing anything right now."

Callie frowned. She hadn't figured on paying an extra employee today, but Max could use the help, especially with how busy the summer season had been so far. "See if she's available. Thanks, Max."

"After we close up, I want to check out the band with Piper. One of our friends should be there. He's playing sax tonight."

Max was as good as his word. Shortly after the two of them started serving the late-afternoon rush, Piper flounced in, wearing one of her floaty summer dresses.

"Hi, everybody," she sang. "What have you got for me?"

Max was all smiles as he greeted Piper. The couple exchanged a brief hug before Max shooed Callie away from the front of the shop.

"Go get your stuff for *Beats on the Bay*," he told his boss. "I'll handle things here. You're going to need time to set up, and the last thing you want is people hassling you for food before you've unloaded everything."

Callie had to agree with him. Gratefully, she loaded her car with various sweet and savory tidbits and sped off toward the bandstand in search of nearby parking. At this time of day, parking near the water was nearly impossible.

She was finally able to find a spot near her destination when she spotted a couple of young moms with several wet and weary children departing from a day in the water. Callie waited patiently for several minutes as the two women collapsed strollers, deflated water toys and managed to pack six children into a minivan before vacating the space.

Happy to have found a spot so close to the park, Callie was cheerful as she stacked her insulated food boxes and a cardboard placard advertising her business onto the small collapsible dolly she used for such events. She secured everything into place with cords before carefully maneuvering her goods in the direction of the park.

"You look like you've got quite a load there." Callie looked up at the source of the remark and into the face of the young woman working with Lisa Linley and Hugh. Today she was dressed in jean cut-offs and a white-off-the-shoulder blouse. With her long blond braids, she looked like a milk maid. "April, right?" Callie asked.

"The one and only," the young woman answered with a smile. "Can I help you? Where are you headed?"

"I'm providing the food for *Beats on the Bay*," Callie explained. "But it's OK. I think I've got this."

"I insist," April said, grabbing one of the weightier looking coolers from the dolly. "I lift heavy things every day. And I'll bet you do, too. You and I truly *work* for a living unlike Allan Browne and his acting troupe."

April grimaced as she swung the cooler onto her shoulder. "Most of them are graduate students or they have parents supporting their every whim. I only went to two years of community college before I realized I could make more money doing physical labor. Believe me, this is nothing. Anyway, I'm headed to *Beats on the Bay*, too."

Who was Callie to deny help from a supporter of the working woman? She smiled at April gratefully. "That's really nice of you. Thanks."

The two walked the short distance to the park to the event location. April was quiet. Callie, intent on lugging her heavy wares without jostling them, was grateful that April wasn't the chatty type. She was more out of breath than she would have liked to admit.

"Why, hello, dear!" Viv greeted Callie as they arrived at the bandstand. "You're early." Viv was dressed in a light blue T-shirt with a *Beats on the Bay* logo, khaki shorts and the sturdy trainers she wore whenever she knew she'd be on her feet for a while. "And who did you bring with you?" Viv asked with a smile.

"Grandma Viv, this is April Manning. She was nice enough to help me carry all this stuff."

"Set that cooler down right here, April," Viv said, indicating a spot near the back of the tent. "It's so nice to meet you."

"Nice to meet you, too," April said, bobbing her head in greeting. "I met Callie at the Harris House. I work with Hugh, your son-in-law."

Viv looked questioningly at Callie.

"Yes, *that* Hugh," Callie confirmed for her grandmother in a deadpan voice. "In fact, I recommended him for the job at The Harris House."

April blushed but then recovered with her friendly smile. "Sorry, ex-son-in-law. I'll just put this stuff down." Callie shrugged and smiled at Viv as April scurried to the back of the tent with the cooler. She was gone for mere seconds before she jogged back to Viv and Callie.

"Well, I'd better leave you to it," April said with a flick of her long blonde braids. "I'm supposed to meet up with some friends." Suddenly April grimaced.

"Are you all right?" Callie asked.

"I'm fine. It's just a little muscle spasm. It comes with the territory in my line of work."

Callie felt guilty, but then again, April had offered to help. "Mine too. Long hours on your feet and heavy lifting: that's one thing we have in common. Well, have a good time and thanks again," Callie said. "I hope you'll stop by the tent. I'm known to reimburse people who help me with food."

"Will do," April said. She smiled, waved and headed in the direction of the gazebo.

"Isn't she sassy," Viv commented when April was well out of earshot. "She is darling, though. She works with Hugh, you said?"

"Yes. Much to Raine's chagrin, I'm sure," Callie answered with a wicked smile.

Viv raised her eyebrows at her granddaughter. "You never told me why you're here so early." She frowned. "I hope you're covered at work."

"Don't worry. Max told me to go ahead. He's holding down the fort with Piper." She took an appreciative look around the tent, which was well-outfitted with a long folding table and a couple of chairs. Not that she'd have the chance to sit much, but it was nice to have the option. "You've got a great setup for me here. Who put the tent up for you? And the table? I would have done it."

"Oh, no need. Gert DeWitt took care of everything. Well, her volunteers took care of everything." Viv smiled. "You just go ahead and get settled. We've got a lockbox for your money, along with rolls of change and some cash."

So it was cash only. Well, hopefully no one would throw a tantrum over not having one of those little portable credit/debit card machines. Callie hoped the cash-only policy wouldn't hurt her sales.

Callie finished arranging her food on the table. The array of sweet and salty treats offered something for everyone: *spanakopita* triangles, the Greek butter twist cookies, *koularakia*, cherry pie wedges oozing with dark, sweet juice and some more of her chocolate brownies (she'd found that it always paid to have some chocolate). She was just about to sample a brownie when Mrs. DeWitt sidled up to her.

"I can see that we asked the right person to sell refreshments. This all looks scrumptious. May I?" She gestured to the table of food.

Callie nodded as Mrs. DeWitt grabbed a piece of cherry pie and took a forkful. "Mm-mmm." Mrs. DeWitt chewed contentedly and Callie handed her a napkin. "I was right. Delicious."

Mrs. DeWitt started to take another bite but paused, fork in the air. "I forgot to tell you. Before this tragedy, I spoke to Holly Tennyson at Crystal Bay College. She called and was in what my mother would have called "a state." Apparently, she was trying to find someone in the English department to talk to about her research, but everybody had already left for the day. The next thing I heard, she was dead."

Eight

Callie's blood ran cold. Max had also said that Holly was "stressed" about her graduate school project. "What did she need to know?" she pressed Mrs. DeWitt. "Did she mention any specifics?"

"She wouldn't say. I suggested she call back after the weekend, but then, well..."

"She was murdered," Callie answered for her. "I know she was writing a paper on F. Scott Fitzgerald. But what would that have to do with anything? He's been dead for decades."

Mrs. DeWitt raised her eyebrows. "It's said that he passed through Crystal Bay, back before he was famous."

"Really?" Callie was intrigued. She had enjoyed *The Great Gatsby* and some of Fitzgerald's short stories in high school English class, but that was as far as her interest had gone. "Did you discuss any of this with Holly?"

"No, I tried to make conversation with her but she wanted somebody in the English department, not me." Mrs. DeWitt made a slight frown of disapproval at anyone not seeking her out as an expert source on any problem.

Before Callie could ask another question, she was distracted by a loud crash. It appeared that the band was setting up and somebody had dropped some type of important-looking equipment. Loud curses followed, and Mrs. DeWitt's face flamed bright red.

"Excuse me," she said, handing Callie the plate with a half-eaten piece of cherry pie on it. "I need to go have a word." She stomped off in the direction of the hapless musicians.

Before Callie could process what she had just heard about Holly, she realized that the lawn was starting to fill up with concert goers. Briskly, she ducked behind the table, ready for her first hungry clientele. The lockbox for cash and change had been thoughtfully placed on the table. Searching for Viv, she located her in the crowd and gave her a smile of thanks. Viv's blue eyes twinkled back at her granddaughter just as Mrs. DeWitt took the stage to introduce the band.

"Hello and welcome," Mrs. DeWitt said brightly into the microphone. Callie giggled as she noticed how Mrs. DeWitt narrowed her eyes at the band member with the foul mouth before continuing. "It is our privilege to offer you this lovely *family* entertainment here tonight."

Mrs. DeWitt continued in a friendlier tone. "If you're hungry, Callie's Kitchen is offering some delicious treats for your dining pleasure. Sodas, water and beer are available at the tent located just to the left of the stage. Cash only, please. Now, let's give a warm welcome to The Tundras!"

The Tundras? Callie took a closer look at the band, which used to include her friend Samantha's former boyfriend, Bix Buckman. Although he was a bristly sort, Callie was fond of him. He'd helped her out of some difficult situations in the past.

Bix wasn't there. It appeared he'd been replaced by a lean young man with slicked back blond hair. Callie didn't recognize him.

The band launched into their first song, and it wasn't long before people were lining up for Callie's food. She served customers at a steady pace, shouting to be heard over the band. *Maybe next time, her food tent could be farther away from the main stage*, she thought, as a headache started to throb over one eye.

She looked up as the next customer approached. He looked familiar. He was tall and slim, possibly in his early 20s, with curly dark hair, wearing a black T-shirt and jeans. He handed her a plastic "Tyme Machine" bank card, and she shook her head apologetically.

"Cash only," she said. "Sorry." *Had he not heard Mrs. DeWitt's announcement?*

"Seriously? I'm really starving. You can't make an exception?"

"There's no way for me to do that. I don't have a credit card machine."

"Aww." The guy shook his head in disgust, and Callie realized where she'd seen him before.

"You're one of the actors from the murder mystery play at The Harris House, aren't you?" she asked.

"Yeah, I am," he said, somewhat warily. Then he smiled. "Did you see our show?"

"Yes, I did. You were all terrific."

"Thanks." The young man smiled, showing a set of perfect teeth. Suddenly, his face fell. "It wasn't so great what happened afterwards, though. I'm sure you heard." He gave Callie a look that could only be described as glum. "Everyone is asking me about it."

He must be talking about Holly, Callie thought. She wanted to keep him talking, but they were holding up the line. She heard customers grumbling.

"Don't tell anyone," she said, handing him the *spanakopita* and cookies he'd selected. "You can pay me back. It's only ten dollars. You're good for it, I assume?" she asked with a smile.

"You bet. Thanks!" the young man answered, grabbing the food. "I'm Josh, by the way. See you then, uh ..."

"Callie." She pointed to her "Callie's Kitchen" signage.

Josh nodded and dashed away from the tent, as if he were afraid she would change her mind.

When Josh left, Callie heard the band announce that they were taking a break. A rush of new customers approached her table, and she was swamped for the next several minutes.

While Callie was crouching down looking for extra plates, she became aware of a pair of high top sneakers appearing next to her behind the table. She stood up, startled. "Max. Hi! You made it."

"You look like you could use some help," he said, gesturing at the line of customers.

"Maybe just until the next set. I'm almost out of food. It'll be time to close up shop soon." Callie took cash from the next customer and placed it in the lockbox. It would be nice to have another set of eyes on the money as well.

"You got it," Max said. "I'll take the orders, and you handle the money."

"Sounds good," Callie said, relieved that she had a helper. The two worked the line efficiently and soon, the sounds of the band warming up again wafted over to the tent. The last stragglers paid for the remaining items on the table and went back to their seats on the grass.

"Well," Callie said assessing the remaining items. "We're left with no *spanakopita*, exactly two pieces of cherry pie and a few brownies. All the *koularakia* are gone."

"Nice!" Max was enthusiastic. "It's been a success, then."

"Looks like it." Callie agreed. "I'm glad we sold so much, but I'm a little tired." She looked around, realizing one person was missing. "What happened to Piper? Isn't she with you?"

"Yeah, she is. I left her with some of our friends who came to see the show." He gestured to the crowd. "Our friend, Phil, took over for Bix Buckman" He nodded at the young blonde man Callie had noticed when the band had first arrived.

"Why don't you go and join her?" Callie suggested. "I really appreciate your help, but you're officially off duty. And in a few minutes, so am I."

Max grinned at her before darting off into the crowd in search of his friends.

Before she knew it, the band was taking their final break of the night. Holding onto the cash box in one hand, Callie made her way through the crowd, looking for a place to throw away the refuse that had accumulated around her tent. Evening had fallen and a delightful, cooling breeze was wafting up from the lake, a welcome break from the humidity and warm crush of bodies.

On her way back to the table to retrieve her signage and tablecloth, she narrowly missed bumping into a group of young people. "Excuse me," she said, ready to dart around them and eager to settle up the night's earnings with Mrs. DeWitt. Holding on to so much money was making her nervous.

"Hey, Callie," said one of the young men. Josh. He proffered a ten dollar bill.

"That was quick," she said, surprised and relieved that she had already received payback.

"I went to a *Tyme* machine," Josh explained sheepishly. "That was nice of you to give me food on credit. It was great!"

Callie smiled at the compliment. Her smiled faded when she noticed that the crowd was watching her intently. They all looked vaguely familiar, but it was hard to see their features in the dimming light.

"Are these more fellow actors?" she asked Josh. The small group nodded in assent. Tammy Heckstrom, Callie noted, was not with the group. Did that mean they didn't like Tammy or did she have better things to do?

"Hi," a few of them mumbled, not very interested in a 30-something woman with hair frizzing around her face from the heat. Callie could just imagine what she looked like after rigorously serving customers in this humidity. She'd cut them some slack for their lack of friendliness. They *were* mourning the loss of a fellow cast mate.

Callie tried another topic. "I heard you have a new member of the cast," Callie ventured, curious to know more about the people who had spent some of Holly Tennyson's last days with her. "I ran into Raine, your costume helper. She told me she's stepping in to help out."

"Uh, yeah," Josh was the only one who spoke up. "She is. Should be good."

A few half-hearted voices of assent followed, but Callie could tell she'd worn out her welcome with this group. If the prevalence of empty beer cups around them was any indication, they were probably fading fast.

"Well, see you all at the show. Thanks for the money, Josh."

"You bet!" was his hearty response.

Callie trekked back to her station where she was met by yet another visitor, and a very welcome one at that – Sands.

"Hello, there," he said brightly and Callie responded in kind, but then she noticed he was frowning at her cash box.

"What is that?" he said in an urgent tone. Then, more quietly: "Cash?"

"Yes, well, there was no one to watch it..." she began, but Sands interrupted.

"You shouldn't walk around with cash like that. You could get mugged!"

"You're right. But don't worry: Nobody mugged me." Callie was touched by his concern but realized something must be bothering him. "What's up?"

Sands rubbed his eyes and sighed. "Sorry to be so intense. It's just that there's been a rash of break-ins in Crystal Bay these last few weeks. I guess I'm a little hyper vigilant. Still," he said, coming closer to her and planting a kiss on her cheek. "Don't walk around with money like that. You just never know."

"What kind of break-ins are you talking about?"

"So far this summer, it's been mostly the usual stuff. One or two places have been hit when the summer residents are out of town. But recently, some of the waterfront homes have been targeted. Gilded Age homes, and such. People are coming up for the summer and finding their homes ransacked."

"That's terrible," Callie said, now feeling silly that she'd been toting cash around with her for a portion of the evening. "But don't those places have elaborate security systems?"

"Most do. But when they do arrive at the summer home, so to speak, some people forget to leave them on during the day. And it looks like somebody may have been dismantling some of the security systems, which is extremely troubling. By the way, it should go without saying that you shouldn't repeat any of what I just told you."

"I won't," Callie said faintly. "Sands," she said. "Just tell me one more thing. Where are the homes that have been broken into?"

He looked at her, affection and exasperation in his eyes. "Well, you can read it for yourself online, so I'll just tell you. The neighborhood you found Holly in is the primary area that's been targeted."

Nine

"What's been taken?" Callie asked anxiously. A rash of burglaries didn't sound good. Maybe they'd target local businesses next.

"That's the strange thing," Sands replied, frowning. "It's mainly been small, token items like cash or jewelry. Large items are left alone, but the common denominator is that the houses are generally ransacked. Luckily no one's been hurt."

"Thank goodness for that!"

"Just be careful," Sands said, looking into Callie's eyes. "I suggest you make sure your alarm system at Callie's Kitchen is in top working order."

"Will do," Callie smiled. "And speaking of working order, what are you doing here? I expected you to be working tonight."

"Officially, I am," Sands replied. "I'm here to observe the crowd. You never know what you might see."

"You've got my interest," Callie answered. "Observe anything so far?"

Sands looked pensive but then he smiled at her. "You'll be the first to know."

Callie started to clean up debris from her table. Sands started to help but she waved him off. "You've got your own job to do. I've got this."

"I didn't feel like cleaning. I was just being polite," Sands said, deadpan. Callie laughed and put the last plate away. "OK, done."

Sands nodded and continued to scan the crowd, hands in pockets, eyes darting around. "Looks like a lot of people are here. Anyone you know?"

"Yes, of course. To start, there's Max, Piper, Viv and Mrs. DeWitt. Bix Buckman's band is here but he's not. I guess a friend of Max's took over his spot. April Manning is here: she works with Hugh and is doing some renovations on the Harris House. Oh, and some of the actors from the murder mystery play. I just met them." A slight exaggeration. She'd met Josh officially, that is, but the others hadn't offered any introductions.

"I should tell you," Callie hesitated a minute, thinking of her conversation with Mrs. DeWitt shortly before the concert. "Mrs. DeWitt told me that Holly had called Crystal Bay College wanting to discuss her research with someone in the English department. This was shortly before her murder. However, they'd all gone home for the weekend, so she never got in touch with anyone."

"Yes, I have heard something about that. We're looking into all of her activities and phone calls." He hesitated, so Callie prompted him.

"She's writing a research project about F. Scott Fitzgerald, but that's all I know about it. What about you?"

"American literature is interesting, but I'm certainly no expert," Sands said.

"Mrs. DeWitt also said that rumor has it he may have spent some time here in Crystal Bay before he was famous. Apparently, he had an heiress girlfriend here."

"Lucky chap," Sands said and Callie hit him playfully on the arm. "We're working on it, Callie. I've seen the thesis but it looks like your regular scholarly study for the most part. Also, it wasn't complete. There were lots of notes about citing sources correctly and verifying information. However, the English department head told me that's common. She was only in the early stages of writing, it seems."

"Huh. So she hadn't finished it yet."

Sands gazed at her sternly. "I appreciate the information you've been able to share with me, but you don't have to keep digging. It could get dangerous, as you well know."

"Just one other thing."

Sands sighed. "Yes?"

"Max said Holly was at my shop not that long ago and she mentioned she was stressed about her graduate school research project, so..."

Callie trailed off as Sands took her by the forearms and looked into her eyes. "I know you want this crime solved. And I know Olivia must be suffering about her teacher."

"Yes, she is." Olivia's sad face was crystal clear in her mind's eye. "I promised her I'd help find out who did this."

"That's not a promise you should have made, but it's one that I will. I'm looking into everything, be assured of that." Sands slowly let go of Callie's arms, but his expression belied his concern.

"I appreciate that, but there's just one more thing you should probably know. Raine is taking over for Holly Tennyson in the play. They've got more performances coming up at The Harris House, and she was asked to be the replacement. I guess she has some very minor acting experience." Callie smiled at Sands' openmouthed expression.

"Well, well. That *is* a surprise!" Sands said with a chuckle. "Sounds like an interesting casting choice. I think I may need to attend that show as well."

"I was hoping you'd say that. I told Raine I'd be there and she was thrilled! She thinks I'm there to support her, but really, I'm there to snoop. They're performing the day after tomorrow."

"Looks like we'll *both* be there to snoop. It's a date."

***

Callie spent the next day and a half baking around the clock. She'd been so relieved that her food had gone over so well at *Beats on the Bay* and that her earnings had been safely retrieved once The Chamber of Commerce got their cut. She felt like celebrating.

Then she remembered the pies.

She felt like she was developing new muscles in her arms from all of the rolling of dough and chopping of fruit she'd been doing, Max working feverishly by her side.

And that was just for Callie's Kitchen's clientele, now swelled to twice its normal size with the onslaught of tourists and regular customers. Add to that the pre-baking of spinach-phyllo pie and now, zucchini-phyllo pie that she was whipping up for the Greek Fest. She barely had time to think about Holly's murder or anything else, for that matter.

Still, Callie thought, wiping her forehead, her hair in a high ponytail on this hot and sunny day, she was happy for the business. It was a lot better than having no customers, something she'd learned the hard way just a short time ago. She consoled herself with the thought that she'd get a break later on, giving her a chance to ponder the murder to her heart's content.

And anyway, tonight was the night she'd been waiting for: her second murder mystery night at The Harris House.

Callie's reverie was interrupted by Max, who crashed through the back doors, arms full of empty display trays.

"Everything all right?"

"No," Max said tightly, scooting over to the sink where he placed the trays, more gently than she'd thought he would.

"Uh-oh. We're not out of food again, are we?"

"No, we're good. In fact, I wish it were that simple," Max mumbled.

Callie kept cutting strips for the lattice tops of her cherry pies and let Max take his time. He looked at his shoes and let out a deep breath before continuing. "I really want to keep this job, but my Dad is really pressuring me. He wants an answer, and I don't know what to tell him."

Callie set down her pastry-cutting wheel. She didn't want Max to leave. Over the years, he'd become more than an employee. He was a friend and she hated to see him so upset.

"When does he want an answer?" Callie held her breath.

"Soon," Max said evasively. "Look, just forget I said anything. We've got work to do."

"The good news is that profits have really increased to the point I can offer you a raise," Callie said hopefully.

"Thanks," Max said, smiling at her, but without his usual sparkle. Even his spiky hair looked droopy.

Clearly, Max didn't want to talk about it, and Callie realized she didn't have the time. Working had to take precedence if they were going to get everything done.

An awkward silence followed. Callie decided to try a more neutral topic. "Hey, how did you like the show the other night?"

"It was good," Max said, brightening a little bit. "My friend, Phil did a good job, I thought. He's the one who filled in for Bix."

"Yes, that's what you'd said. From what I heard of the band, they sounded good to me, too." Callie decided not to share her opinion of the headache-inducing high volume. The music had been melodic, even though it was also deafening. "So how long has Phil been with the group?"

"Not long. He just started going to grad school at Crystal Bay College this year." Max helped Callie place a slew of fruit pies in the oven, and she thanked him.

"What does he study?" Callie asked.

"English lit. A real money-maker, as he jokingly calls it. But he wants to be a professor or something like that, so good luck to him, right? Who am I to give career advice?"

English! "Did he know Holly Tennyson?" Callie, stepping over a puddle of water near the sink. She reached for a paper towel.

"Yes, I think so. He knew a few of the people in that play you saw the other day. Turns out that a lot of them have the acting bug and not many local places to perform, so they take what they can get."

***

Max's revelation about the tie between the grad students and the murder mystery play fresh in her mind, Callie set out to her second murder mystery night in as many weeks. She had a queasy feeling, and it wasn't just because she was going to have to witness Raine portraying a flapper.

Perhaps Tammy Heckstrom and her fellow graduate students could shed some light on who may have wanted Holly dead. Did students kill for grades or grants? Callie didn't want to think so, but...

Or maybe it was Tammy who had the academic and acting rivalry with Holly. They were supposed to be friends, of course, but were they really "frenemies"?

Questions plagued her as Callie entered The Harris House.

The first person she saw was Lisa Linley. The hotel owner was surrounded by clientele checking in, checking out and making various demands. Lisa gave Callie a brief smile and wave, before returning to her customers.

Sands had told Callie he'd meet her there, as he was heading over straight from work. To save time, she'd already bought tickets for the two of them so she decided to wait for him in the lobby. As always, the airy space was resplendent in its 1920s glamour and Callie felt herself relax just a little bit in the whimsical environment.

Unfortunately, Max couldn't attend. *Gotta deal with some things at home,* he'd said.

Callie noticed that Lisa had dispatched her clients. Looking around to see if Sands was on his way up the steps – he wasn't – she decided to go have a chat.

"How are the renovations coming along?" Callie asked as she approached the front desk.

"So far, so good. Hugh was here earlier today with April Manning, and they gave me a full estimate. I won't be able to do everything I'd like right away, but at least I have a game plan and can get started on a few things."

"That's good news. I'm glad you found someone you can work with."

"Yes," Lisa replied, her smile looking a little pasted on. "Thank you again for the recommendation." She cleared her throat. "I'm sorry I was a little ... awkward with you the other day. You see, April Manning was a friend of that young woman who was murdered. Holly?"

"She was?"

"Yes, I thought you knew." Lisa raised her eyebrows. As they were speaking, Callie had noticed a young woman standing nearby and dressed in The Harris House's signature hostess gear, a 1920s inspired maid's outfit. Murmuring an apology for interrupting their conversation, she approached Lisa and whispered something in her ear.

"I'm sorry. I have to check something out. Talk to you later?" Lisa hurried into the next room.

Looking right and left, Callie couldn't help but sneak a peek behind the concierge desk that Lisa had just vacated. She saw what looked like an estimate from Vintage Reno and was about to get a closer look, when she heard footsteps behind her. She jumped away from the desk.

"Can I help you with something else?" Lisa Linley asked in a voice brittle with disapproval. She situated herself behind the desk like a sentry.

Callie felt her face turn red. "No, nothing. I was just looking for a pen," she offered lamely.

Without a word, Lisa Linley handed her a pen with "The Harris House," printed on the side. Callie pretended to write herself a note. Blushing furiously, she handed the pen back to Lisa and returned to her seat in the lobby.

The windows were open to the deepening evening and a sunset was streaking pink and purple across the sky. She sat contemplating the view, as well as her brief but illuminating conversation with Lisa Linley regarding the fact that April Manning and Holly Tennyson were friends. They were about the same age, so it was feasible. Holly had never mentioned April to her. Then again, why would she?

Callie remembered back to the day she'd met April. She certainly hadn't seemed like someone in the throes of grief, but maybe she was just putting her best professional face on things. Callie could identify with that. When she was upset, the first thing she did was to focus on something completely neutral, usually work.

Then again, she'd seen April at *Beats on the Bay*, a decidedly social event. April said she was meeting friends, and they very well could have been supporting each other in the aftermath of Holly's murder, despite the unorthodox venue. Callie realized she didn't know April well enough to know how she handled grief. People had all sorts of ways of dealing with it. Who was she to judge?

Just then, Sands arrived with a flurry of apologies about being late, and the two took their seats in the dining room. Callie was somewhat horrified to discover that she was seated at the table right next to Hugh. Hugh didn't seem to like it much, either. He gave Sands a side-long look of resentment, probably because of the questioning regarding Holly.

"How's Olivia?" Hugh asked.

"She's having a sleepover at a friend's house," Callie answered. "She's doing all right. It's good for her to be with friends. She's still very upset about Holly, as you can imagine."

"Uh, yeah, I'm sure." Hugh's face turned a dark pink.

A buzzing sound from Sands' jacket pocket interrupted their exchange.

"Excuse me a moment," Sands said to the two of them and left the table. Callie watched him walk toward the lobby.

Alone at last, Callie thought. This was her chance. "So, when were you going to tell me about you and Holly?"

Hugh turned puce. "*What*?" he asked. He took a sip of water and recovered enough to offer a retort. "There never was a Holly and me, so tell your boyfriend to ease up."

"So you weren't an item."

"No," Hugh said, his voice low. Callie had to lean in to hear him. "We went out a few times, after you and I – you know. After we split up. She was nice enough and all of that. I don't think I was her type."

"Really?" Callie stared at him hard. "And that's it?"

"Yes. But when she became Olivia's teacher, I felt embarrassed. It's stupid, I know. I didn't feel like everyone needed to know about our brief relationship, if you can even call it that. Plus, I didn't want Raine to know."

"Why?" Callie was puzzled. "You weren't with her at the same time, were you?"

"Can't you let it drop?" *That answered that question.* "I didn't kill Holly," Hugh's voice was tight. "Raine didn't kill Holly. Enough already."

Sands slipped smoothly into his seat, just as Hugh and Callie ended their conversation. Callie couldn't tell from his face if he'd overheard.

Fortunately, the show started almost immediately. Allan Browne, Callie was quick to note, introduced the troupe, but didn't say a word about Holly. Well, what could he say? The audience members had come for a staged murder, not a real one.

Callie studied the actors carefully. It was as if nothing had happened to one of their colleagues. They still had all of the sparkle of the previous performance and delivered their lines with panache. The costumes were eye-catching, and the wigs had not a sleek bobbed hair out of place. You wouldn't know that a fellow actor was brutally murdered just a few days before. Still, they were actors. It was their job to stick to the script.

The audience seemed to be enjoying themselves. For once, Allan Browne seemed appeased. He was seated near the stage and laughing uproariously every time one of the actors said anything the slightest bit humorous.

Surprisingly, Raine was holding up pretty well. Even Callie had to admit that she looked beautiful in her costume, and she only stumbled over a line or two. The second time it happened, Callie glanced at Sands, a small smile on her face, but she turned around quickly when she met Hugh's glare. Oh, well.

Callie decided to relax and just enjoy the rest of the show, but she found herself sitting on the edge of her seat as Tammy Heckstrom approached her death scene.

Something was wrong with Tammy, Callie realized belatedly. She was confusing her words and walking with a shuffling gait. Callie glanced uneasily at Sands and he looked back at her, raising his eyebrows.

"Oh no," Tammy was slurring now. "I don't feel so well...." It wasn't a line Callie remembered from the previous show.

"You, you..." Tammy gasped. She tried to steady herself and suddenly her knees buckled. As Callie watched in horror, Tammy fell, face first, onto the lush brocade carpet.

Ten

Sands leapt from his chair and ran towards Tammy. Callie joined him. The crowd went from stunned silence to loud, agitated buzzing in a matter of seconds. Dimly, Callie was aware of a woman screaming and crying hysterically somewhere nearby. *Raine.*

Ignoring the noise, she looked back at Tammy. Her face was pale and clammy with sweat.

"Call 911," Sands said urgently, while checking Tammy for a pulse. Gently, he rolled her over onto her side.

Callie's fingers trembled as she called 911. She was practically a household name with the operators there right now, she thought grimly, as she relayed the situation. Sands motioned for her phone, and Callie handed it to him.

"She appears to be breathing," he told the operator. "But she's having trouble staying awake and her pulse is a little weak."

Callie became aware of the crowd of people leaning over Tammy and realized that the woman needed air, and that people needed to stay where they were until the police arrived. She panicked, thinking that whoever had done this would escape.

Sands must have been thinking the same thing. He was already standing on a chair, cupping his hands around his mouth like a megaphone.

"Everybody stay in your seats. Stand back! The police and an ambulance are on the way. We need you all to remain calm and stay seated."

One by one, the crowd sank back into their chairs. Callie watched as Sands shooed the stragglers from the spot where Tammy lay. Everyone stepped back to make room, except for one person.

Allan Browne stood as if rooted to the spot, his mouth working but no words coming out. Finally, he was able to utter something, but his words sounded garbled.

"What is it?" Callie asked him and finally he met her gaze. His face was alarmingly grey. Was he about to pass out?

"Who...why...?" he stammered. Then he swayed and Callie was by his side in a minute. She took him by one meaty arm and led him to a chair. "Here, sit down," she said gently. She poured him a glass of water from a pitcher on the table and handed it to him. "Drink this."

Obediently as a child, the theater director sipped at the water, slowly at first, then greedily gulping it down. He wiped his mouth and sat there, stony-faced. Out of the corner of her eye, Callie saw that Tammy was moaning and mumbling. *Thank goodness*, Callie thought. She'd been petrified that poor Tammy was dead. Where were the paramedics?

She glanced toward the dining room doors anxiously, but whipped her head back around when Allan Browne grasped her forearm.

"Who would do this to my theater company?" Allan said, his face flushed and his breathing becoming labored. Callie realized with a shock that he wasn't horror stricken over Tammy, as she had thought he was.

Allan Browne was angry.

"Who would do this?" he repeated, his voice gaining volume. Callie jumped as he reared back in his seat and stood, facing the buzzing audience.

"Which one of you did this?" he bellowed, his eyes narrowing and his curly red mop of hair quivering with rage. "I'll find out. So help me I will! And when I do ..." Allan broke off with what could only be described as a roar and stormed towards the restrooms that doubled as actors' dressing rooms.

"Callie, don't let him get away," Sands cried, busy with Tammy and the paramedics, who thankfully, had just arrived.

Are you serious? Callie thought. The guy was clearly unstable. She was just starting towards him, when Hugh stopped her.

"I'll go," he said. "You stay here. That guy is nuts." Callie didn't know if he meant Allan Browne, Sands, or both. Hugh jogged to the back of the room, where Callie could still hear Allan Browne screaming and yelling.

The paramedics took Tammy away on a gurney. Sands said a few words to one of the police officers who had just arrived on the scene, then walked over to Callie.

"They seem to think Tammy might be under the influence." Callie gasped in shock. "They'll do tests." Sands frowned and looked about the room. "Where's the director?"

"Hugh offered to go after Allan, and I let him. It sounded like they were headed towards the 'dressing rooms' aka the restroom."

"Right. Sorry. I didn't mean to put you in harm's way. I just really need to keep an eye on that guy."

"No problem," Callie said. "I've put *myself* in harm's way many a time."

Sands cleared his throat, a small smile quirking up the corners of his mouth. "You certainly have. Right now, I need to get these people interviewed." He gave Callie a rueful smile. "'Murder mystery night' is becoming a bit too realistic for my liking."

***

Tammy under the influence? Callie couldn't quite accept that theory as she submitted to yet another police statement and watched as the play attendees were questioned and released to go home. Why would you get drunk before you were supposed to perform in front of lots of people? Tammy didn't seem like the type to get stage fright.

Callie shook her head. What did she know? Maybe all the actors had a drink together before each show, though it didn't seem like a good idea to her. Raine would know, Callie thought. She knew Sands was most likely planning to question Raine, but Callie planned to ask her a few questions of her own as soon as she had a chance.

Callie scanned the room. Raine was sitting by herself, sniffling into a white cloth napkin, obviously taken from one of the place settings. Hugh was nowhere to be found. Was he still keeping a lid on Allan Browne? Either that or he was being questioned by the police.

Raine looked up as Callie approached, attempting to smile through her tears. "I just can't believe this," she wailed. "Don't think I'm horrible, but I was looking forward to my acting comeback. I guess what happened tonight, plus Holly's death, will just about shut down the theater troupe."

"What makes you say that?" Callie asked in a gentle voice, but inside she was feeling anxious. Hugh would be back any minute and would probably not take too kindly to an interrogation of his wife.

"Allan Browne told all of us that we had to "kill it." Sorry, that's actor talk," she said when she saw Callie's expression. "Let's just say he told us we'd better be excellent tonight or the murder mystery play was cancelled for the rest of the summer. He couldn't afford any more damage to his reputation."

"Nice guy," Callie muttered. Clearly, Allan wasn't too worried about the fact that one of his young and talented actresses had been killed in cold blood.

"He really isn't so bad when he isn't yelling about our acting," Raine retorted. She blew her nose. "This is all such a tragedy. I really can't even believe it."

"It certainly is," Callie agreed. She hesitated. "Raine," she said sweetly. "What about before the show? Do you have any rituals? Like, do you sing a song...say a prayer...have a drink or two?"

Raine put down her napkin/handkerchief and stared at Callie. "Whatever are you talking about? We didn't sing, say a prayer ... or drink. Why would we do that? Especially me? I only just learned my lines!"

"Don't worry about that. I want to know about Tammy. Did you see her right before the show?"

"Yes, I did. She mentioned she thought she had a summer cold coming on, and I told her it was probably stress. She drank a cup of tea to help soothe her throat."

"Tea? She had tea before the show, and that's it?"

"Yes!" Raine narrowed her eyes at Callie. "She drank a cup of tea. That's not a crime, is it? A lot of the actors drink herbal tea and such before performing, sometimes with honey. It helps clear the voice. That's the strongest thing I ever saw anybody drink, by the way. Not booze, for goodness sakes." Raine exhaled loudly, the bangs of her flapper wig blowing upward.

"OK, OK, my mistake," Callie soothed. She noticed that a group of the actors she'd met at the *Beats on the Bay* event were huddled in a corner, whispering. Allan Browne was not among them.

Callie decided to quit while she was ahead. "Take care of yourself." She stood up to leave.

"Sure thing," Raine said solemnly, nodding. "You, too."

After asking around for several minutes, Callie located the room Sands had appropriated for taking statements, but the officer standing outside wouldn't let her see him.

"He's going to be here awhile." The officer was stern.

"Well, can you tell him Callie Costas left and that I'll be in touch?"

The officer nodded, clearly not in the mood for delivering lovers' messages.

Callie's legs felt leaden as she walked to her car, thankful that she and Sands had driven separate vehicles. So much for getting the scoop on Holly. Tammy's medical emergency had blown her plans to dig into Holly's death right out of the water.

Or had it? Callie was deep in thought as she drove home. The night sky was inky black but dazzlingly clear. Stars twinkled as she drove past the bay and the relaxing sound of waves gently lapping the shore calmed her mind.

Tammy being under the influence of drugs or alcohol could have many ramifications, Callie considered. However, if all she had consumed was tea, could somebody have spiked it with a dangerous substance? Say, Lisa, for example? The only question was, why?

Or perhaps Tammy had taken a drug or had a drink without anyone seeing. She could simply be upset about the tragic loss of Holly, her fellow student and colleague, and felt she needed a way to cope. Or was she feeling guilty?

Callie shuddered. She had a hard time picturing Tammy in the role of killer. Then again, she had witnessed some animosity between Lisa and Tammy as well as Allan and Tammy. The questions kept circling in Callie's mind. Why would Tammy have killed Holly? None of it made sense, especially now that she had possibly been dosed with who knows what.

Once again, Callie's mind strayed towards the house where she had discovered Holly's body. Sands had said that homes in the area were being broken into and ransacked. Callie was sure she'd missed something on her first visit to the house. For one thing, she hadn't known what significance it would play in her life, and Holly's death.

Callie slowed down the car and pulled to a stop under an oak tree. She sat for a minute, deep in thought. She wanted to go back to the house where she'd found Holly, but she couldn't do it in broad daylight. It would have to be now. That is, if she didn't want to get caught.

The reasonable side of her nature told her to stay away from the house. If she was found there, she could wind up in big trouble. Sands would be disappointed in her. Still, she argued with herself, Olivia was sleeping at a friend's house, so she didn't have to worry about rushing home to her. She knew she needed to take Koukla out but what Callie wanted to do shouldn't take long, no more than an hour.

Olivia. She had begged her mother to help find out what happened to her teacher and Callie had promised.

That did it. Callie picked up her cell phone and dialed a familiar number with trembling fingers.

"Max," Callie said when he answered. "I know it's late but I need your help. I want to go and check something out and I shouldn't do it alone for safety reasons. Can you come with me?"

"I guess?" Max said, sounding uncertain. "What's up?"

"I can be at your house in 10 minutes. I'll tell you once we're on the road. By the way, do you have a flashlight?"

Eleven

"Are you sure this is a good idea?" Max asked for around the fifteenth time since she'd picked him up at his apartment on the south end of Crystal Bay. He'd produced the requested flashlight without batting an eyelash but had peppered her with questions. Callie had simply explained that she needed to revisit the house where she'd found Holly.

"Have you considered that the killer might be watching the house?" Max sputtered. "Anyway, who knows what Holly was doing there? How do you know the house has anything to do with her death? It was empty, right?"

"The killer can't watch the house twenty-four/seven," Callie argued. "And as far as the house being important, I don't know if it is or not. The whole thing just seems strange to me. Why was Holly even there? I feel like something is staring me in the face, and I just can't see it. Maybe this will help. I'm not breaking in. I just want to look around the grounds."

"Uh, Callie, I hate to point it out to you, but isn't it your boyfriend's job to find the killer? Why the undercover spy routine?"

They stopped at a light and Callie turned to Max. "I know. But I promised Olivia I would help. She's devastated." Max started to interrupt, but Callie put a hand on his arm. "This is probably a long shot, but I feel like this recent rash of break-ins is no accident. Something is going on with these fancy homes, and I want to know what it is. I'm sorry I dragged you into this. If you want me to bring you home, I will."

"If I go home, are you going right back there alone?"

"Yes."

"That's what I thought." Max shook his head and chuckled softly. "Fine. I'm coming with you."

The rest of the drive passed in silence. As they got closer to the house, Callie explained that she would park the car several blocks away in case any neighbors were out and about. She didn't want someone to see a strange car in the driveway and call the police.

The neighborhood was quiet, with a gentle summer breeze and the chirping of crickets the only sounds. A nearly full moon shimmered from behind a wispy cloud. Max and Callie walked quickly but quietly towards the house, Callie leading the way. They kept the flashlight off as they approached the hedge-lined driveway.

"Now what?" Max whispered.

"I'd love to get inside the house," Callie was wistful. "But I know that I can't do that. Let's take a walk around the house and give a look to the backyard. I'm not exactly sure what I'm looking for."

"But you'll know when you find it?" Max asked wearily. He gestured toward the yard. "Lead the way."

The house was eerie in the moonlight. The tall white pillars gave off a ghostly glow and Callie shivered, despite the warm evening.

"Flashlight," she whispered to Max and he handed it to her. Quickly, she pointed the beam of light into the large window on the first floor. The shadowy images of a fireplace and empty rooms stared back.

Turning off the light, she hurried to the front door, Max on her heels, but yellow crime scene tape stopped her. "Darn. I should have known," Callie hissed.

"You aren't thinking of breaking crime scene tape?" Max asked.

"No. Of course not. I told you, I don't want to disrupt the investigation." *And betray Sands* was Callie's unspoken thought.

She motioned to Max. "Let's go around the back and just look around. You never know."

Max seemed to be getting into the spirit of the enterprise now that he knew for certain that breaking and entering wasn't on the agenda. "Yeah, let's go."

They tiptoed to the backyard, Callie trying not to look at the bushes where she'd found Holly. The bushes were surrounded by a small makeshift fence, also covered in crime scene tape. The spearmint scent she'd encountered when she'd found Holly's body brought back the chilling memory with the force of a blow. Callie grew dizzy. She took some deep breaths and forged ahead.

Callie and Max stood looking at the back of the large, elegant house. She turned and scanned the yard. Tall hedges protected her and Max from the sight of any visitors on either side. The lush lawn sloped gently toward the water and the home's private pier, which now stood empty.

"Well?" Max whispered.

"I don't know." Callie forced herself to walk back to the area where she'd found Holly. Max walked toward the back of the yard, where it sloped towards the bay. The spearmint smell made her feel faint. Closing her eyes, she willed herself to remember that day. She remembered seeing the tracks on the dusty floor and the swipes through the dust that had made it look as though Holly had been dragged.

With a chill, she remembered seeing beautiful Holly lying lifeless on the ground.

"What were you *doing* here, Holly?" Callie realized she'd said it aloud.

"Did you say something?" Max was suddenly at her shoulder and she jumped, stifling a scream.

"Gosh, sorry!" Max whispered an apology. "Did you find anything?"

"No. Not yet."

"There's a tool shed back there," Max said. "It's open, but there's not much here. Just a couple of rusty rakes and a snow shovel."

Callie nodded and stepped closer to the house. It loomed over her and despite its elegance, it looked sinister in the shadowy moonlight. She scanned it, waiting for some epiphany to strike. Sighing, she turned to leave.

Wait. *What was that?*

Callie pointed Max's flashlight at the top windows, stopping when she reached one on the far right of the massive house. "Look!" she whispered as loudly as she dared. Max was walking the perimeter of the yard, but he stopped and ran over to her.

"Look!" she repeated pointing, but more quietly this time, training the flashlight on the broken pane just long enough for Max to see it. Extinguishing the light, she peered around to see if the flash had attracted any neighbors, but the tall hedges and trees in the back yard seemed to offer excellent cover. For the killer, too, Callie thought.

"I think that window has a broken pane," she whispered excitedly to Max. "If the police had seen that the day of the murder, wouldn't they have boarded it up?"

"Do you think somebody has been going inside the house through that window? It's one way to bypass the crime scene tape," Max offered.

"Maybe. But why?"

The two of them crept closer to the house.

"What if we just climb up and look inside?" Callie suggested. "We might see something. I'm not sure how we'll get up there, though. There's *got* to be a way."

Max was already running in the direction to the tool shed. Callie followed him, wanting to shout out questions but keeping her mouth shut. Suddenly, Max disappeared behind the small wooden structure.

"What are you doing?"

Max's voice was muffled. She heard the rustle of grass and then the clink of metal.

"Max!"

Callie heard some grunts and groans and an "ouch!" but soon, a sweaty but smiling Max emerged. He was dragging a rusty step ladder.

"Think this might work?" Max asked, clearly triumphant at his find.

"Perfect!" Callie nearly hugged him.

Max dragged the ladder to the house and positioned it underneath the window with the broken pane.

"I'll go," Callie said before he could argue. Carefully, she climbed the rickety ladder as quickly as she could, the flashlight stuck into the waistband of her jeans.

Reaching the top of the ladder, she tensed as she felt it sway, but relaxed when she felt Max steady it. Callie shone the flashlight into the broken window pane. Oddly, it looked as if it had been neatly cut. No jagged edges poked out at her.

The high-powered flashlight revealed that Callie was looking into what looked like a library. She could see empty built-in bookshelves against the far wall.

Callie squinted and shone the flashlight around the room, spotting only a few dusty chairs and a desk.

The ladder gave a violent shake.

"Callie!" Max stage whispered. "Get down!"

"What?" Callie sputtered.

"Just get down! *Now!*"

Callie stuck the flashlight back into her waistband and scuttled down the ladder, her heart in her throat.

As soon as she had reached the ground, Max grabbed her by the hand and started running toward the back of the garden. Callie stumbled along behind him. She stopped for a minute, her breath coming in gasps.

"Max. What is it?"

"Shhh. We have to hide." He pulled her behind a tall hedge. *"Somebody is out here."*

Callie felt like someone had thrown an ice bucket over her. "Are you sure?"

"Yes. I heard somebody sneeze."

"A sneeze?" Callie was incredulous. "Was it nearby?"

Max squeezed her arm like a vise and didn't answer. She wrenched her arm away, but Max grabbed her again and pointed toward a break in the hedge.

A dark figure, of medium height and wearing what looked like a black or navy hooded sweatshirt was walking across the lawn, headed toward the ladder they'd just vacated.

Twelve

Callie and Max looked at each other.

"Let's go!" Callie hissed.

As quietly as they could, they raced behind the hedge and jumped the short wooden fence that bordered the neighboring property. Without looking around or stopping, they looped around to the front of the neighbor's house and made their way back to the sidewalk. Nodding at each other, they ran in the direction of Callie's car.

Callie didn't look back or even speak until she'd reached her car and unlocked it. Max, huffing and puffing was right behind her. He jumped in the passenger seat as Callie started up the motor and pulled away from the curb like a bat out of hell.

"That was a really stupid thing to do," Max said, breathless from his sprint.

Callie was trembling so hard she could barely handle the steering wheel, but she didn't want to stop, just in case they were followed. "You know, Max, I think you might be right."

"Who *was* that?" Max was looking a little green around the gills.

"I don't know. The police?" The police surely wouldn't have any qualms about returning to a crime scene, but would they be wearing a hooded sweatshirt under the cover of darkness? Or it could be the killer. We have to call this in!"

"Callie. We can't admit we were there. We'll be in huge trouble. Are you crazy?"

"I know, but what if it *was* the killer? I'm going to call and just say I was in the neighborhood and thought I saw an intruder. I'll call

Sands." Quickly, she swerved over to the side of the road. Nobody appeared to be following them.

"Great." Max let out a disgusted sigh.

Callie tapped Sands's number into her phone and fortunately, he answered.

"This is going to sound odd, but just bear with me. I was driving by the house where Holly was killed, and there's somebody out there. In the yard. I thought you'd want to know." She grimaced at Max and he shrugged.

"Driving by?" He sounded skeptical. "When was this?"

"Just a few minutes ago."

"Do you have a physical description of this person?"

"Yes. They were medium height and wearing dark clothing. And a hooded sweatshirt. I couldn't see them very well."

"How did you see as much as you did," Sands demanded, "if you were only driving by?"

"I walked around the perimeter of the yard and I spotted it then." It was mostly the truth.

Sands let out a shout. "You did, did you? We'll talk about this later, and I'll need to take a statement about everything you saw. For now, I'll get a patrol car to go over there. Where are you?"

"Driving back towards downtown Crystal Bay."

"I see. Well, I'll want to talk to you later. One more thing."

"Yes?"

"Stay away from there. I mean it. Unless you want to get an obstruction of justice charge and get me fired." He hung up.

Max just stared at her. "Why did I agree to this again?"

Callie felt sick. She put down her phone and resumed driving. "I don't want to go to either of our homes, just in case," she said. "What if somebody is on our tail?"

Max turned around and strained to see outside of the car's rear window. "I don't see anybody, but that's not a bad idea. Let's just head to The Pub."

The Pub, with its prosaic name and comforting atmosphere, sounded good to Callie.

Max kept a lookout for anyone following them, but they seemed to be alone on the road. Callie felt a lot better when they approached Garden Street and Main, Crystal Bay's business district. Many people were still out and about, but they were able to find a prime spot in the parking lot of The Pub.

Max dashed to the men's room while Callie sank down into a booth, letting her breath out with a whoosh. She felt hot, sweaty and dusty, but at least they had escaped detection from the intruder. The adrenaline rush that had sent her running from the intruder was fading, and she realized she needed sugar and maybe some caffeine.

The waitress came to take their order, and Callie ordered fries and Cokes for Max and herself. Not the healthiest options, but the food and drink would sustain them for a while longer. Callie felt her stomach rumble and realized that she had never had a chance to eat dinner. Tammy's sudden illness had halted the deluxe dinner that was being offered along with the murder mystery show. Callie knew how she would feel if she had wasted all of that food. Lisa must be disappointed, furious – or both.

Callie was sipping her icy drink when Max returned. "You got food, awesome," he said, sitting down across from her and appearing to cram half of the fries in his mouth with one huge fist.

"Careful not to choke," Callie admonished, realizing she was treating Max like a child. "Sorry, mom habits die hard," she explained when he gave her a look. "Any ideas about who that could have been?"

"Not a clue," Max said. "I wonder if the person we saw tonight has been going in and out of the house this whole time. I don't know why they would, though. It's a pretty risky thing to do."

"I know." Callie rubbed her eyes. "I wonder who cut the pane. Was it the person we saw tonight? I'm with you. I think somebody is using that window to get in the house, someone who doesn't want the police to know what they're up to. If they use the window, they won't disturb the crime scene tape."

Max picked up a menu and Callie took a long drink from the glass of water the waitress had just set down on the table. "We didn't see anyone go inside, just walk across the lawn, so we don't have definite proof. Still, I find it hard to believe this is the first time the intruder has been there."

"There's one point that's really bugging me. It just doesn't make any sense. Why would anyone want to go inside that house and possibly get caught?" Max slugged down some more pop.

"I wish I knew." Callie put her head into her hands. "Especially because Holly wasn't found inside the house, she was outside." She gave him a rueful half smile. "The house can't have anything of value in it. It's been vacant a long time and the police would have collected any evidence by now. I guess we've got another mystery to solve."

"Yep, it sure does look that way. But we're not going to solve it tonight. Callie, this has all been a blast, but I'd better get going. Food and drinks are on me."

"No, that's not necessary. It's my treat," Callie protested.

"Not this time. I figure I owe you. I haven't had a good scare like that since I went on the biggest rollercoaster at Crystal Bay carnival when I was a kid. Tonight was a bargain!"

***

Max and Callie were droopy during the morning shift early the next day at Callie's Kitchen, which was unfortunate as there were several additional items on the agenda, including preparing more food for the upcoming Greek Fest.

"What's with you two today?" Piper asked as Max and Callie staggered to the back of the shop for yet another cup of coffee. "You both seem half dead."

"It's nothing," Max said, gulping down the hot brew. "I just stayed up too late last night watching a movie." He kept his eyes off Callie, and she started busying herself with food in the freezer.

"Which movie?" Piper asked. She put her hands on her hips and stared at Max.

"Uh...it was an Alfred Hitchcock film fest. I fell asleep somewhere in the middle of *Rear Window* and woke up during *Pyscho*."

"That would make me lose sleep," Piper said, nodding. "I hope it wasn't during the shower scene."

Piper was still chatting away about classic thrillers as she led Max back to the front of the shop. Callie breathed a sigh of relief when they were gone.

She felt remorse for snooping around the crime scene house, especially because she hadn't really discovered much for all the risk she'd taken. However, she did have proof that an intruder had been there. Callie was bracing herself for the conversation she'd have to have with Sands about her nighttime escapades.

Still, she couldn't fully regret her attempts at getting more information. Mainly, she felt bad for involving Max.

She'd deal with all of this later, she thought, facing the packages of phyllo dough thawing on the countertop. In the meantime, she had Greek pies galore to bake.

Working with the food helped to unsnarl some of the tensions that had built up during the last several days. At George's request, she was baking one of his favorite summer "*pites*": zucchini-phyllo pie or *kolokithopita* for the Greek Fest. The seasonal zucchini gave the *pita* a mild but unique flavor that was savory and just a little sweet. The zucchini had to be fully drained or the filling would be too wet, and it would ruin the crispness of the baked phyllo. Better get to work.

The first *kolokithopita* were just going into the oven when Callie heard Max calling her from the front of the shop. Callie set the timer, wiped off her hands, and smoothed her hair before heading out front. Please don't let it be the police, she thought, but no, it was another unwelcome visitor. Hugh.

"Hi, is everything OK?" Callie greeted him with a worried frown.

"Just thought I'd stop in. Can we talk for a minute?"

Callie knew that Max and Piper were listening and customers were starting to trickle in for their lunch breaks. Whatever he needed to say didn't require so many ears.

"Sure. Follow me, but I can't talk long. This is a busy time of day for us."

Hugh nodded and followed Callie into the back room. She offered him a cold drink, but he shook his head.

"I wanted to apologize for how I acted the other night about Holly. I realized that it must have come as a big shock to you."

Callie shrugged, but was inwardly surprised at Hugh's humility. Why did he care?

Hugh continued. "I wasn't trying to put anything over on you, I swear. It's just that it was embarrassing. I wasn't even living in Crystal Bay at the time, so I guess I'd forgotten a little bit about how "small" small towns really are. I should have known better than to date someone who could turn out to be our daughter's teacher. Besides, Raine didn't know."

"I see. Well, thanks for the apology." Hugh didn't budge. "Is there more?"

"I didn't have anything to do with Holly's death," Hugh said, his face turning bright red. "Just because I was secretive about our dating life doesn't mean I had anything against her."

"Now we're getting to the crux of it. Let me guess. You want me to tell Sands to back off." Callie threw her hands up in the air. "You must know I can't tell him how to run his investigation!"

"I know that. If you told Sands you didn't think I had anything to do with it, maybe it would help. This could jeopardize my new job! While I feel awful about Holly, I didn't do anything."

Callie stared at Hugh. She understood not wanting to lose a new job and he seemed sincere. "For your information, I have told Sands that I didn't think you had anything to do with this."

"Really?"

"Yes. Do you think I'd want you around Olivia if I thought anything else? But I can't control the investigation. You know that."

"Yeah, I know."

Hugh turned to leave. "I should get out of your way. I don't want to be late. I'm headed over to The Harris House right now to talk to Lisa Linley." He rolled his eyes.

"What's wrong with Lisa? Or is it the project itself?"

"A little bit of both. April, the project manager, said Lisa's a little difficult to work with."

"How is Lisa being 'difficult'?" Callie asked. She remembered Tammy's argument with Lisa and how strained Lisa had seemed when she had dinner with Sands at The Harris House.

"It's fairly typical stuff. She keeps arguing about how to do the renovations. When she hired my firm, she seemed really open to our expertise. Up to her, of course, but I think we gave her a reasonable estimate. If she does the whole thing now, she'll end up saving money. If she cuts corners now, she may end up spending more later." Hugh shook his head. "I tried to explain this to her. April said she did, too."

"That's strange, but she must have some solid reasons for her logic," Callie remarked. "Maybe she has a limited budget."

"All customers have reasons for their logic," Hugh pointed out. "You should know that."

Callie had to laugh. "I sure do."

Hugh seemed to brighten a little bit. "Overall, though, I really love this job. I get to work on some amazing old homes. Did you know that a lot of the Gilded Age homes on the bay were built when wealthy Chicagoans had to evacuate the city after the Chicago Fire?"

"Yes, of course I know, thanks to Grandma Viv's interest in old homes and real estate. A lot of these homes stay in families for generations." Callie laughed. "It's a good thing, too. Most people keep up the homes and renovate them as needed. It would be a shame if they went to rack and ruin." She was silent a minute thinking of the home where she'd found Holly Tennyson. She gulped, disturbed by the intensity of the memory.

Hugh didn't notice. He was warming up to his topic. "The thing I love about some of these older homes is that they have some really interesting extra features. For example, a few of these business magnates from Chicago had ties to the mafia, and they'd have all sorts of secret compartments they could hide in, if they needed to. I've been really curious to know if The Harris House has anything like that."

"Secret compartments?"

"Yes. And the compartments also came in handy for anyone who was bootlegging back in the '20s. They needed a place to hide their stash of booze. We've found secret cellars in some of these homes, even secret compartments in the walls. They've always been empty, though." Callie stifled a laugh at his wistful tone.

"Nice try, but The Harris House has had several owners. My dad knew the last owner and he never mentioned anything to him."

"Yeah, probably." Hugh shrugged. "Well, it is what it is. I do enjoy my job, even when clients are difficult. Hey, don't repeat that, by the way. I know you deal with Lisa sometimes, too."

"Of course not," Callie said, her mind on Lisa and what, if any, secrets that The Harris House could be hiding.

"Give my love to Olivia," Hugh said. "Tell her I'll see her soon."

After Hugh had gone, Callie leaned back against the countertop, staring at the *pita* ingredients strewn around the kitchen. Everybody had secrets, it seemed.

In fact, two things were starting to become the focus of her life.

Secrets. And pies.

Thirteen

"Olivia!" Callie called for the third time. Yesterday had been a blur of baking, cooking and puzzling out who could have been the "intruder" at the home where Holly was killed. Callie hadn't heard a peep from Sands regarding any news of the intruder, except for a text saying hello and that they would have to talk later. In a way she was relieved. She knew she'd have to tell him the truth about the reason she saw the intruder in the first place.

Shaking off that thought, Callie called up the stairs again. "It's time for day camp! We've got to go!" Whipping out her compact, she put some powder on her shiny nose and checked her lipstick, determined to look fresh-faced for customers despite the heat and her overall exhaustion.

Nothing.

"Olivia!" No response.

Grumbling under her breath, Callie climbed the stairs, Koukla at her heels. Olivia had been at breakfast, but Callie hadn't seen her since she sent her to get dressed.

Olivia's bedroom door was open, but she was nowhere to be found. Callie exhaled loudly and jumped when she heard a soft sound from inside Olivia's closet. She threw open the door.

Olivia was huddled on her closet floor among a slew of shoes and stuffed animals, crying her eyes out.

"Honey!" Callie knelt down and drew her daughter in her arms. Koukla jumped into Olivia's lap.

"I'm just sad about Ms. Tennyson," Olivia said between sobs.

"Well, of course you are," Callie soothed. "I am too." She held her daughter a minute and Olivia stopped crying.

"Is it all right if we go someplace a little more airy?" Callie asked, touching the tip of Olivia's nose. "This closet is a little stuffy."

Olivia half smiled at that. "I guess." Callie heaved herself to her feet and took Olivia's hand.

"Let's sit down," Callie said, gesturing toward the bed. She and her daughter sat down, and Koukla batted their shins with her paws until Olivia pulled the little Yorkie up on the bed with them.

"You don't have to go to camp if you don't want to," Callie said, stroking Olivia's tangled hair. "I can try and get Grandma Viv over here." She glanced at her watch.

"I want to go to camp." Olivia grabbed a tissue and blew her nose. "I'm just sad sometimes. I'm sorry to make us late."

"Nothing to be sorry about," Callie said. "Anything I can do to help?"

Olivia looked at her mother with huge eyes. "You promised you'd help find out who did this to Ms. Tennyson. Have you found anything out yet?"

Oh, dear. "A few things," Callie hedged. "I'm sure the police are finding things out, too. Obviously, they don't share all the news with us, but they're working on it, I assure you."

Olivia nodded solemnly and said nothing.

"Think you can make it to camp?" Callie asked gently.

"Yeah." Olivia got to her feet and stepped into her well-worn sneakers.

"Let's go then. But if you need me, you can call me." She hugged her daughter tight. Koukla jumped off the bed and barked as if in affirmation. Even Olivia had to chuckle a little bit at the Yorkie's antics.

***

Callie was pensive as she dished up *loukoumades* and poured coffee for a stream of customers that morning, Max working busily by her side.

Olivia was obviously suffering. How could Callie assure her daughter that her teacher's killer would be found when she had no idea that was true?

Callie had her cell phone in her pocket in case Olivia needed an early pickup from camp, but she realized if her daughter called, she'd have to bring her to work with her. She couldn't leave her home alone, and there was still so much to do.

She was still fretting about Olivia's mental state, as well as all of the loose ends regarding Holly Tennyson's murder, Lisa Linley's fight with Tammy and the hooded intruder she and Max had seen the other night, when the bell over her door jingled. She looked up to see her grandmother, Viv, striding toward her in cropped khaki pants, a stylish blue cotton top and what she called her "walking shoes."

"Grandma! What a surprise!"

"Yes, well, I thought I'd check in with you, dear. I just, uh, wondered how you're doing." Viv's smile was just a tad sheepish, so it seemed to Callie. Max had disappeared to the back room, so Callie decided to be frank.

"Grandma. What is it? Is something wrong?"

"No, dear. I'm fine. It's just that, well." Viv stood up straighter and addressed Callie. "I may as well come right out with it. You remember that *Beats on the Bay* you helped us with?"

That sounded ominous. "Yes...."

"We need you to provide concessions at the concert again."

"We?"

Viv smiled bravely. "Mrs. DeWitt and I agreed that your food was such a big hit that you should do it again...this week."

"Oh, you did? This weekend is Greek Fest!"

Viv was growing more flushed by the minute. She fidgeted behind the counter and couldn't meet Callie's eyes. With a growing feeling of dread, Callie realized she'd in all likelihood been bamboozled.

"Grandma. Don't tell me you already accepted for me?"

"Well, you know how Gert is. She could sell ice to polar bears! I figured you wouldn't mind the business, but I forgot all about the Greek Fest. I'm sorry, Callie. I should never have agreed to work with Gert. She's just too darned persuasive."

"I thought you were going to feature a different restaurant each week. What happened to that idea? Mrs. DeWitt always likes to feature as many Chamber-affiliated places as possible. Why can't she just have Bob's Brats do it and call it a day?"

"Yes, I know. I tried to sell her on something like that, but she said she wanted you. I don't know where we'll find anyone else on such short notice. I know it's short notice for you, too, dear..."

Viv looked so miserable that Callie's frustration at the whole situation was slightly diminished.

Seriously, though. How was she going to do this? Even with Max and Piper helping out it would be a stretch, on top of her regular summer schedule.

Callie considered. She needed the money. And it would be huge in terms of goodwill with Mrs. DeWitt, who was a good person to have on your side. However, she couldn't go it alone.

Callie smiled at Viv and reached across the countertop to pat her grandmother on the hand. "All right, Grandma. I'll do it. But, I'm going to need some help baking. You up for it?"

"Oh, yes!" Viv clasped her hands in delight. "I'll help. You know I love to bake, even though you'll have to coach me with some of the Greek recipes."

"I will gladly do that. You'll have to work with me right here in my commercial kitchen. Health codes and all. Now, when can you start?"

"Tomorrow, bright and early. I'm due as a library volunteer today but after that, I'll clear my schedule until we've got everything under control."

That settled, Viv left, with far more spring in her step than she'd had when she'd arrived. Callie swallowed the lump of anxiety in her throat. Too bad there weren't two of her. Make that three of her, she thought, as Max showed up for his shift.

Max washed his hands, put on his apron and rang up a few customers before sidling over to Callie as she set out rows of *koularakia*, her braided Greek butter cookies.

"Hey, did you hear anything about the other night?" he asked.

"Nope. Sands said he had to talk to me later. However, we have a more pressing problem. Viv roped me into another *Beats on the Bay* night. This week. Two days from now, to be more specific. Plus, we have the Greek Fest this weekend! I'm already baking zucchini pies to freeze for that, and if I make them fresh the night before, I'll be up all night. Plus, we've got fruit pies to bake. I just got a big order for a party, in fact. And then..."

Max put up a palm. "Callie. Calm down. We've got this."

"We do?" How did Max manage to sound so convincing?

"Sure! Let's get Piper to help make some stuff, and we'll be fine. We've already got a head start on the savory pies. Right? We'll freeze a bunch, and you can thaw them right before the Greek Fest. I'm planning on filling the order for pies today. So that's another job done, and we'll figure out the rest as we go along."

"Viv did say she'd help me bake tomorrow..." Callie remarked. She was feeling slightly more encouraged. "And you know what, I bet even Sam would help me out if she has the time."

"You see?" Max slapped her on the back.

"Ouch," Callie said, but with a laugh. "It's difficult to worry with you around."

"You know who I wish we had to help us out? Sweetie, your aunt, or your dad's cousin...whatever you call her. I could never get it straight."

Sweetie was Callie's aunt from Greece, well, she was really George's cousin, but Callie had always referred to her as an aunt. Her name was really Glykeria, which translated to "Sweetie," which was easier to pronounce for most people.

Sweetie had visited Crystal Bay last winter and been a very welcome guest, and a very *unwelcome* amateur sleuth, in a previous case that had rocked Crystal Bay over the Christmas holidays. The complexity of relations between Greek families was a mystery to Max, but to Callie it was simple. Everyone was an aunt, uncle or a cousin.

"Sweetie would be wonderful to have around here right about now," Callie agreed. Her *spanakopita* is out of this world."

"How is she anyway?"

"She's doing very well. I got an email from her a couple of weeks ago. She misses us and said she'd love to come back for another visit."

"That would be great." Max beamed. "She was funny. I'm sure Viv misses her."

"Oh yes. Those two get along like a house on fire. I'd love to have her help, but it's OK. I've got you."

"Yeah. I may not be an authentic Greek cook," Max smiled, "but I can fake it pretty well."

"No, Max. You've worked here long enough that you're officially the real thing."

Fourteen

"I'd love to see you, but I'm exhausted," Callie was saying into her cell phone the next evening. Her feet ached, her arms were sore and her legs felt leaden. Still, Max, Piper and Viv had baked like they were born to do it right along with her, and she finally felt like she had the *Beats on the Bay* food under control, at least. The Greek Fest food was getting there.

"I'd make it worth your while," Sands was saying in his sandpapery voice. Callie had stopped by the station to give him a statement on the intruder she'd seen the other night, but they'd had no social calls since. He'd been busy on the case and she'd been buried in pie prep.

"Now I *am* intrigued," Callie said with a laugh. "If you don't mind my falling asleep on the couch, you're welcome to stop by. Olivia's here, and we both need an early night."

"Be over in a flash."

Callie looked helplessly down at her rumpled Callie's Kitchen T-shirt and leggings. She wanted to make herself a bit more presentable. She didn't need to look ready for a night on the town, but clean clothes and a hairbrush would do wonders.

Dragging herself upstairs, she changed into a white cotton blouse and scurried around her room looking for a pair of shorts. With a sigh, she noticed her bulging laundry basket. Laundry hadn't been high on her list of priorities lately. Finally, she pulled a pair of jeans from the top of her closet before realizing they'd felt too tight the last time she'd worn them. Sucking in her stomach, she was able to get them on and they even felt a little bit looser. Callie chalked it up to her haphazard eating habits during one of her busiest work seasons yet.

After she brushed her wavy brown hair, she smoothed her hands over the jeans as if she could smooth away excess flesh. As she did so, she heard a funny crackling sound.

With a shiver, Callie realized these jeans were the ones she'd had on the night she found Holly. In her mind's eye, she could picture herself shoving the piece of yellowed paper in her pocket to dispose of later. She'd forgotten all about it.

Holding the note in her hand, Callie tried to read the old-fashioned spidery handwriting but couldn't make it out. "*For...*" was the only word she could read. The other words were blurred with time and the rest of the note had a jagged edge where the paper had been torn.

Grasping the note, she went downstairs as if in a dream, angry with herself for not remembering it sooner. It may mean nothing, but what if it did? She'd give it to Sands right away and explain she hadn't meant to hold onto it.

She flopped onto the sofa, exhaled deeply and placed the note carefully on a side table. Callie must have dozed off because the next thing she heard was the doorbell ringing and Koukla's excited barking. She heaved herself off of the couch and staggered to the front door, Koukla on her heels. Peeking through the peep hole, she saw the smiling face of Sands. He waved, and she opened the door.

Koukla continued her animated barking at Sands as he swept Callie in his arms for a lingering embrace. His warmth and strength were so welcome that Callie felt at peace for the first time in days. She wondered how long the peaceful feeling would last when he found out she was snooping around at the scene of the crime.

"All right, you're next," Sands told the little dog, picking her up so the dog could give him a wet canine kiss.

"Come on in," Callie said, gesturing to her living room. Sands looked more handsome than usual tonight, she noted, taking in his summer tan and long, lean physique, highlighted by his faded jeans and white shirt. Self-consciously, she smoothed the blouse she was wearing and ran a hand through her long wavy hair.

"Can I get you anything to drink?" Callie asked.

"I'll get us something in a minute," Sands replied with a smile. "You're not at Callie's Kitchen right now, remember?"

Callie sank down gratefully next to Sands. "Thank goodness you said that. I don't even think I'll be able to make it to the kitchen right now."

"Tough day?"

"Physically, yes, but enough of my whining. What did you want to see me about? Also, I've got something for you."

"Why do I wish that didn't sound so ominous?" Sands said, pulling her close to him, "I wanted to follow up on that intruder you called about. But first, what do you have for me?"

Gently disentangling herself, Callie took the note from the table and handed it to Sands. "I found this on the kitchen floor right before I discovered Holly's body. I shoved it in my pocket, thinking I'd throw it away later, but I never did. I'd forgotten all about it until now."

Sands took it, holding it carefully by the edges. "*For...*" he started to read. "What does that say?" He squinted at it. "I can't really see anything but the word 'for'. The words are blurred. Or I'm losing my eyesight."

"No, that's what it looks like to me, too," Callie assured him. "It may not be important, but I thought you should have it."

Sands reached in his jacket pocket and pulled out a small plastic bag. He carefully placed the note inside and sealed it. "Could be nothing, but we'll have a look at it."

"Wow. I'm impressed."

"You never know when you might need an evidence bag. Apparently, when spending time with you, it's a good thing to carry." He smiled at her and shook his head.

"Very funny. So what happened? Did anyone track down the intruders?"

"No, by the time our officers arrived, whoever it was had vacated the premises. However, we did find one or two odd things."

Callie's nerves tingled with apprehension.

"Like what?"

"A ladder in the middle of the back lawn, for one thing."

"I see."

"You wouldn't know anything about any of that, would you?"

"OK," Callie said, sitting up and regretfully leaving the warmth of Sands' embrace. "Here's the deal. I went there, just to jog my memory and see if I missed anything. After all, I didn't know it was a crime scene the first time I was there. I didn't go in the house, I promise! But I did look around the lawn..."

"Max?" Sands sputtered.

"Yes, just wait a second. I brought him with me for safety. I figured we could take a quick look around. I figured something about that day might come back to me. We looked in the window with the ladder, but that was it."

"Callie, I don't need to tell you how dangerous that is. Please. We have an investigation, and we can't have people contaminating the scene."

"I know that it was wrong to go there. It's just that Olivia is so upset about Holly. I'm sorry, I really am."

"You always were the adventurer," Sands said, a half-smile on his lips. "But this is serious business, as you well know."

"I do know. And, well, I did see one thing you should know about."

"There's more?" Sands raised his eyebrows at her.

"I peeked in the upstairs window because of the broken pane. It looked to be cut, because I didn't see any jagged edges or anything like that. I guess a pane could have simply fallen out but this looked nice and neat."

Sands sighed, his face lined with weariness. "Yes, we know about that. I'll have to check the crime scene report, but I don't think there was a broken window pane the first time we were there."

"That's what I thought!" Callie was triumphant, until she saw Sands' expression.

He gave her a piercing look. "The other Gilded Age home break-ins I told you about. They had a similar M.O."

Callie gulped. "That's strange."

"It could be. But I try not to jump to conclusions without evidence."

"Speaking of evidence: how is Tammy? Any news on what caused her to faint?"

"Not yet. It could take a while for the lab results to come back. Apparently, she's made a complete recovery."

"Thank goodness for that, at least! She really scared me."

"I can't figure out those theater people. They're an odd bunch. And don't get me started on the director." Sands chuckled softly.

"Allan Browne," Callie said with a rueful grin. "Raine said he's not so bad, except for when he's got a show to produce. He's a little bit hard to figure out, though. One minute he's kind of nice and charming. The next minutes, he's a horrible show-off. Volatile, you could say."

Sands rolled his eyes but didn't offer his own commentary on Allan Browne. "Funny that you mentioned Raine. I find it interesting that Tammy was drugged or poisoned the first night she appeared in the show. Not to mention your ex, Hugh. He was there, too."

A sick feeling was growing in the pit of Callie's stomach. She turned to face Sands. "I just can't believe those two would do something like that. Anyway, Raine said Lisa Linley brought tea to Tammy because Tammy felt like she was getting a cold."

Sands put his arm around her. "Yes, I know. But somebody else could have tampered with the tea," he said. "We'll wait for the tests. Let's drop it for now." He stood up and stretched.

"Where are you going?" Callie asked.

Sands reached into his pocket and brought out the note Callie had given him, now safely ensconced in a plastic bag. "You're a victim of your own enterprising behavior. I've got to get this potential evidence back to the station."

"I was hoping you could stay for a little while longer, but you're right." Callie rose reluctantly and walked Sands to the front door.

"I would like to stay longer." He kissed her cheek. "However, duty calls." He kissed her again and strode down the steps, the set of his shoulders less weary than when he'd arrived. The possibility of new evidence definitely put a spring in his step. It was only a little scrap of paper, but Callie was happy that she may have been able to provide something that could be useful.

Darn it all, she thought. Being helpful sure could make for a lonely evening.

***

The sun was barely up the next morning when Callie arrived at Callie's Kitchen, bright and early. It was, in fact, exceedingly early, but there was no other way to get all of the cooking and baking done. Viv was going to bring Olivia to camp, and then she had to run off to help Mrs. DeWitt with something or other before tonight's *Beats on the Bay* event. She'd offered to come back and help bake, but Callie had told her to skip a day. She thought of the many hours that Viv had spent rolling out dough and whipping up batter the day before and wanted to give her grandmother a break.

Thank goodness she had Max. Today was going to be a hot one, and he had the stamina for hours of cooking and baking.

As she unlocked the door, the smell of hot coffee greeted her, combined with the rich fragrance of buttery pastry and sweet fruit.

"Who's here?" she called.

"Just me," Max replied. He must be in the work space. Callie burst through the French doors that separated the baking area from the front of the shop.

"Max, what in the world..."

Succulent pies with golden brown crusts lined the work area. Max had made inky blueberry pies with lattice crusts, sweet strawberry pies with red juice bursting through the lattice pastry, and dark cherry pies with their blood-red juice bubbling up through the decorative crusts. The fragrance of buttery pastry and sweet-tart fruit filled the air like a heavenly cloud you could almost taste.

Callie noticed the dark circles under Max's eyes. "It's just that pie order I told you I'd work on," he told her. "I'm not even finished yet, but it's a start."

Callie counted at least eight fresh pies on the countertop. "It certainly is. You must have been here early." She glanced at her watch. "It's only 6:30."

"I've been here since about 3 a.m.," Max confessed.

"That's going above and beyond, Max. I mean, thank you, but I didn't expect you to do this."

Max smiled wearily. "I wanted to help."

"You need coffee and so do I," Callie told him. She got two heavy white mugs out of the cabinet and looked around for some *paxemathia* to go with them.

"You go ahead," Max replied, arranging a strawberry pie just so on the counter. "I've been drinking coffee for hours."

"I guess you're fully caffeinated then. Just have a seat and I'll grab a cup for myself."

Max sat down but he couldn't be still. He tapped his fingers on the table while Callie filled her cup to the brim and added just the right amount of milk and sugar. She grabbed a stool across from him and sipped the hot brew for several minutes. Max just looked off into space, then abruptly got up and started washing bowls and spatulas.

"I may not be fully awake yet, but I feel like something is wrong," Callie ventured.

Max didn't answer, so Callie decided to give him some space as she got out phyllo dough, butter and eggs for the Greek Fest *pites*. She figured she could at least start assembling some of the savory pies before her regular morning customers filed into the shop. Max busied himself with the dishes, then started frying *loukoumades*, aka Greek doughnut holes, that he would then drizzle with honey and a dusting of cinnamon.

Callie was cleaning spinach in a colander when Max finally decided to speak.

"The reason I got here so early to bake is because my dad had a fall and broke his hip. There's no one to help out at the farm. Just me. I'm sorry but, today's my last day at Callie's Kitchen."

Fifteen

Callie only realized she had dropped the colander in the sink when she heard a loud clatter. Abruptly, she turned off the faucet and stared at Max.

"I'm...I..." she stammered.

"I'm sorry, Callie. There's nothing I can do. This job means the world to me, but..." Max broke off.

Callie felt like the floor had dropped from beneath her feet. She realized now how much she'd been in denial about losing Max as an employee. Moved by his pain, Callie walked over to him and gave him a hug.

"It won't be the same without you," she said.

He squeezed her back with his big arms. "I have until the end of the day," he said, trying to smile. "Enough with the sappy stuff. Let's get cooking."

The morning rush of customers came and went like a blur to Callie. Mechanically, she smiled, poured coffee, served up Greek pastries, and checked the fridge to make sure she had prepared enough Big (Low) Fat Greek Salads. In the heat, they were flying out of the kitchen.

Max...gone. It was unbearable to imagine. But there it was. Callie couldn't begrudge him helping his father, and she felt horrible that his father was having health problems. In fact, Max was showing his generous, loyal character by helping his family.

But who else on earth would get up so early to bake pies, not only beautifully, but enthusiastically, and without being asked?

As the salty smell of the *spanakopita* wafted from the ovens, a name flashed in Callie's mind unbidden.

George, her father. The man lived to help others, cook, bake and fuss over people.

Did she dare tell George about her dilemma? She would love his help, but she didn't want him to meddle. His experience in food service was valuable, though.

Callie rummaged in the clear glass refrigerator at the front of her shop while she mulled this over. Based on the fact that only two containers remained, it looked like her *rizogalo*, aka Greek rice pudding, was a hit during the heat wave. Cool and creamy, it was served with a sprinkle of cinnamon and a dollop of fresh whipped cream from a local dairy farm. Callie had planned to make a lot more *rizogalo* not only for her customers, but also for the Greek Fest. She had just started cooking a huge pot of rice when she noticed Max speaking in low tones with a young man up near the register.

On closer inspection, Callie realized that the young man Max was speaking to was Josh, the actor she'd helped to feed at the last *Beats on the Bay* event.

"Good morning," she said with as much friendliness as she could muster despite her inner turmoil about losing Max. "What can we get for you today?"

"It's more like, what can he do for us," Max interjected. "Josh is studying culinary arts at Crystal Bay College, and he said he needs another job for the summer. What do you think?"

Josh beamed at Callie. "I'd love to get some hands-on cooking experience serving real customers. I've only worked as a waiter before. I love to cook, and I love people. Max said you needed some help, so maybe you'll be willing to give me a try?"

Callie was completely taken aback. She couldn't simply hire someone off the street! At first, she was angry at Max for going over her head, but then she saw his pleading expression. He was only trying to help.

She had another, more devious thought. Josh might have some insight into the problematic acting troupe and its potential link to Holly's murder. Who knew what she might be able to uncover?

"Tell you what, Josh. Why don't you stop by tomorrow, and I'll give you a trial. In the meantime, why don't you make one of your favorite recipes from culinary school for me to taste? You can bring it by when you show up for your shift. Let's see..." Callie debated what would be the best time for him to arrive. "Can you be here really early? About 6 a.m.? I'd love to see what you can do, but we've been really busy, and nobody but me will be here at that time. Be prepared to stay through the morning rush."

"Yeah, sure! Thanks!" Josh looked a little bit like a puppy with his big brown eyes. Callie couldn't help but smile at his enthusiasm.

"All right. See you tomorrow."

"You bet. See ya! Thanks, Callie. Thanks, Max!" Josh loped out of the shop, grinning.

"Can he really cook?" Callie asked Max once Josh had left. She'd never gone to culinary school herself, but she considered George to be the best cooking teacher of all. He'd taught her to make his favorite traditional Greek dishes since she was old enough to hold a mixing spoon.

"He says he can," Max said. "It's better than nothing. If he's a disaster, at least he can do some prep for you or something. I'd feel better knowing I'm not leaving you totally alone."

"That's true." Callie knew that George would fill in if needed, but maybe Josh would respond better to direction. George was a hard worker, but he tended to dominate in the kitchen.

A feeling of panic washed over Callie. *Max was really leaving.*

Feeling like Scarlett O'Hara, she told herself not to think about that now. She'd think about it tomorrow or she'd go crazy.

***

Unfortunately for Callie, tomorrow was a long way off. Before her head could hit the pillow, she was going to be serving at *Beats on the Bay* again, as well as making sure that she had all of the food ready for the Greek Fest.

Today was Wednesday. Greek Fest started on Friday. Callie took a deep breath and let it out with a whoosh. She could do it. She'd have to.

Maybe Josh was the answer to her prayers.

On that optimistic note, Callie pushed through the rest of the day. Piper came in and Callie could tell that Max had broken the news to her. Exuberant, colorfully dressed Piper was more subdued than she'd ever been.

As Callie was pulling her golden *pites* from the oven, Piper came over to her. "Can I take a picture for our Instagram account?"

"Sure." Callie smiled. "These are for the Greek Fest at the church. Be sure to caption them when you post this."

Piper took a couple of shots of the tantalizing-looking *pites* and then smiled sadly at Callie. "Max told me. I'm not going anywhere. I love this job. And, I love Max, too. I know he wants to stay."

"Of course he does," Callie said briskly, afraid she would start tearing up. "But family comes first. Listen," she said, changing the subject before she broke down. "Can you work here tonight? I need to go to *Beats on the Bay* again. It's the last time I'll be doing it, for a while anyway."

Piper twirled her ponytail. "No problem. I know you can use the help."

"Can I ever, and hey, it will give a nice boost to your paycheck. I may need you to start working more hours."

"Yeah, with Max living forty-five minutes away, I'll have a lot more free time." Piper sighed. Suddenly, Callie remembered something that she'd forgotten in the last few confusing days.

"Max told me that you saw Holly Tennyson in the shop not long before her death. He said that Holly seemed really stressed out and that you would remember."

Piper raised her eyebrows so high they nearly disappeared into her blunt-cut bangs. Piper favored a retro Bettie Page hairstyle and fifties-style clothing. Today was no exception. She wore a sunny lemon-print dress with a full skirt underneath her Callie's Kitchen apron.

"Wow, you're right," she said. "I'd forgotten all about that until just now. Holly was always so sweet, but that day she seemed a little sour if you know what I mean."

"Care to elaborate?"

"Usually she was happy to have some girl talk, and all that. Or sometimes she'd say she was working on her graduate thesis and that it was going better than she'd ever hoped. The reason I remember her so well that day is that she was just kind of snippy with me, and she looked out of sorts. You can tell when somebody is upset. At least, I can."

"Hmm. I wonder what made her stop in here if she was so upset."

"Food, of course! She told me she was starving but that she had no time to go home and eat, so what did we have that was ready to go and didn't need to be heated up. I gave her a Greek salad and she just zoomed out of here. I'm not sure where she was going, sorry."

Piper suddenly broke off and smiled as a customer approached the counter. April Manning. She was dressed in khaki shorts with a tool belt and a long-sleeved denim shirt. Callie wondered if she was taking a break from working on Lisa Linley's house.

"Hi, April," Callie greeted her. "What can we get you?" She remembered what Hugh had told her about Lisa being a difficult client.

April, however, seemed unfazed. "I've heard that everything is good here. What do you recommend?"

Callie was happy to know that her food had been praised. "It depends on what you feel like. Do you want a full meal or just a snack?"

April cocked her head and looked at the menu board on the wall behind Callie. "I'd love to sit down and have a full meal, but I've got to get back to The Harris House. So just a snack, I guess."

"In that case, have some *spanakopita*. It's so filling it's almost like a full meal. Plus, how about a couple of my Greek biscotti to go with some coffee, in case you need a pick-me-up."

"Sounds good to me."

Piper heated up a piece of Callie's spinach-feta pie and put some cookies in a bag while Callie took April's money.

"How's it going at The Harris House?" Callie asked mildly, wondering if April might reveal anything new about Lisa Linley.

"Things are pretty good." April shrugged. "It's probably one of my easier jobs."

Easier jobs? Callie frowned. What had Hugh been talking about, then, saying Lisa was hard to work for?

"April, I understand that you were friends with Holly. I'm sorry I didn't say anything to you before. I didn't know that you knew her."

April flushed and she looked down at the countertop. Finally, she looked up at Callie, her mouth in a tight line. "Thank you," she said softly. "It's been really hard. She was such a vibrant person, and smart, too. I've been trying to keep busy to get my mind off of things. Work helps."

"Yes," Callie said. "Holly had a lot of talents. I hear she was writing a wonderful graduate thesis on F. Scott Fitzgerald, for one thing. "

April shrugged. "Yes, I guess so. I've never been much for reading," April admitted. "I've always preferred working with my hands and things like that. Holly and I used to do outdoorsy things together, like hiking around the lake. Holly was kind of the 'brains' of our friendship, I guess you could say. I'm more the 'brawn.'" April gave a sad little laugh and pointed at her small but well-developed left bicep.

"I enjoy reading," Callie said in a clumsy attempt to change the tone of conversation. The death of a friend was *not* a cheery topic. "But I know what you mean about working with your hands. That's what cooking is all about, after all."

Fortunately, Piper returned with the food, putting a halt to Callie and April's awkward conversation.

"Hmmmm. Smells great," April said, inhaling deeply. She appeared to be cheering up at the sight of the food and Callie felt relieved.

April grabbed the bag and paid for her purchases. "I really should get back," she said, already halfway to the door. "Thanks for the food recommendation. This should hit the spot." She nodded at the two women, waved and walked out of the store, her calf muscles rippling.

Maybe if she, Callie, rehabbed houses all day instead of cooking, she'd have muscular calves as well. And maybe all of her jeans would fit better...

Piper interrupted her thoughts.

"I hope I was helpful regarding Holly. There's not a lot more I can tell you."

"No need. Thanks for sharing. And thanks for your support. I really appreciate it."

"You bet. You can count on me."

***

Those words were still stuck in Callie's mind as she pulled up at the *Beats on the Bay* event several hours later. Max had said goodbye and promised to keep in touch. It was a short exchange. Max seemed determined to leave before either of them got too emotional. Callie had to admit that she'd shed a few tears when he'd gone. It wasn't like he was going away forever. It was just that he'd been her right hand since the inception of Callie's Kitchen. It would seem incomplete without him.

But there was no time for tears right now. Callie straightened her shoulders as she arrived at her designated tent. She spotted Viv yakking away with a group of women, but Viv waved goodbye to the jovial group when she spotted her granddaughter. She rushed to Callie's side.

"How did it go today?" Viv asked. "I'm so happy you could help us. Gert DeWitt is beside herself with joy that you're the one serving food again tonight."

"Hi Grandma," Callie said, giving Viv a quick hug. "I've had better days. Max quit."

"Quit?" Viv took a step back. "Whatever for dear?"

"Family problems. His father fell and broke his hip. Max is needed on the farm, and there's nobody else to help right now. He had to leave today without giving me any notice. Not that I blame him, but it's been a difficult day."

"Oh Callie," Viv said grasping her granddaughter's hand. "I'm just so sorry, and here I gave you even more to do than usual."

"The show must go on," Callie answered, unwittingly echoing Raine's words to her at the supermarket. "On a brighter note," Viv was saying, "everything is ready for you. Since you're on your own tonight, I'll pop back here and help out. Would you like that?"

"You bet I would. Thanks."

Callie unpacked her food from the coolers as Viv set off in search of Mrs. DeWitt to let her know that she'd be behind the tent. The band name wasn't one she recognized, but she hoped they'd be a bit quieter than The Tundras.

Stepping back from the table, Callie surveyed the items she was serving to the concertgoers. Her dismal spirits rose just a little bit as she'd surveyed the food. Wedges of strawberry pie, their crusts sparkling with sugar and berries bursting with thick juice looked like the picture of summer. Crunchy chocolate chip cookies in sets of two beckoned on small white paper plates. Tempting slices of Greek honey cheese pie, or *melopita*, dusted with cinnamon, lay next to the cookies. The pie was like a cross between custard pie and cheesecake, but with a lighter texture and lemony flavor notes.

Next to the *melopita* was a tray of the "emergency *spanakopita*" Callie always kept in the fridge, thawed, baked to golden perfection and cut into appetizing squares. Callie had also brought a few trays of tiny cream puffs. Cream puffs were a Wisconsin tradition. For a couple of savory options, she'd brought home-baked pretzels and feta/olive "*meze*," aka small plates, for people who just wanted a snack. It was quite the assortment of Mediterranean specialties and Midwest summer favorites.

The missing ingredient, Callie realized, was Max. She hadn't realized how much she'd counted on his support. Piper was great, but Max was a whiz in the kitchen. Who else would go on nighttime visits to crime scenes with her?

The sound of the band tuning up provided a welcome distraction to Callie's ruminations. They were a group of dapper older gentlemen who appeared to be much quieter than the noisy Tundras. *Thank goodness.*

The lawn was filling up with people on this mild summer evening, and Callie served a few hungry concert goers who seemed enthusiastic about her offerings. Despite her numerous worries, Callie felt her shoulders relax as she scanned the crowd for familiar faces.

April Manning, wearing cut-off jean shorts and a flowy white top, was chatting and laughing with a group of young men and women Callie didn't recognize. And oh my ... was that Raine and Hugh just a few feet away? They were sitting on a blanket with a two glasses of wine in front of them.

"How's it going, dear?" Viv scooted over to Callie. "Any customers yet?"

"Hi, Grandma. Just a few, so far. I think it will pick up when Mrs. DeWitt makes her announcement. That's what happened last time."

"Everything looks good enough to eat." Viv patted Callie on the shoulder. "I'm so sorry about Max. But I'm here to help. Remember that."

"Thanks. It's just such a shock. The good news is that Max found a friend to fill in for him already, so I guess it could be worse."

"That's wonderful! Who is it?"

"His name is Josh. In fact, he's one of the actors from the murder mystery night. He played a gangster, I think. He's tall, with dark brown eyes and hair."

"Oh, yes. I remember him. Very handsome."

"The question is: can he cook?"

Sixteen

allie and Viv were deluged with customers, anxious to grab a bite before the music started. Callie kept a close eye on the lock box as she served the crowd, remembering Sands' warning at the last *Beats on the Bay* event.

Finally, Mrs. DeWitt made her announcements and the music started. As Callie had hoped, the music volume was much more palatable than last time, making conversation possible without shouting.

"From what I've heard," Callie said to her grandmother, "Holly Tennyson was worried about her graduate student thesis on F. Scott Fitzgerald. Mrs. DeWitt said you knew some history about the author that pertains to Crystal Bay."

"Why, yes. It appears that he courted a Chicago debutante. She was very well acquainted with a family who had a summer home in Crystal Bay. As luck would have it, she married the son of that family. She's said to be the inspiration for quite a few of his characters. That's all I really remember, dear. I read an article in *On the Bay*, but that was a long time ago." *On the Bay* was a local free magazine, filled with historical lore and tourist info.

"You don't happen to remember the name of the person who wrote the article, do you?" Callie asked, thinking that the author of the piece might have some illuminating theories.

Viv frowned. "No, I'm sorry, I don't. I feel like it was familiar, but I just can't put my finger on it. You can find old issues at the library or online."

Mrs. DeWitt rushed over, interrupting their conversation. Her face was flushed with excitement.

"Viv, I need you for a minute." She nodded at Callie. "A reporter is here, and they want a quote from the organizers. I couldn't forget Viv."

Callie was shocked and touched. Mrs. DeWitt usually liked to keep press quotes to herself.

"A reporter?" Viv smiled girlishly and smoothed her hair. She winked at Callie. "Back soon, dear. Hold down the fort." The two older women strode across the lawn toward a young man in jeans and a t-shirt, with black-rimmed glasses and a camera hanging from a strap around his neck.

Callie smiled as she served the next wave of hungry music lovers. Viv would enjoy seeing her name and quotes in an article, provided Mrs. DeWitt actually *did* let her get a word in edgewise.

Food was flying off of Callie's table and the lockbox was filling up with cash. The sight of so much green alleviated some of her existential despair over losing Max as an employee. Callie pulled the box a little closer to her and looked up at the next customer in line.

Tammy Heckstrom stood before her with Phil, Max's friend from The Tundras. Was he checking out the competition? The band tootled along pleasantly enough, but Callie had to admit she preferred Phil's band, even despite their high volume.

"Hi, can we have some *spanakopita* and a couple of those feta-olive plates?" Phil asked.

"You betcha," Callie said. "That'll be $15." She took a $20 bill from Phil's outstretched hand. "How are you, Tammy? I'm so happy to see you up and about after the other day."

"I'm holding up, I guess. They still don't know what happened to me at the show the other night. I thought some music would be a nice change. This is Phil, my boyfriend, by the way."

Boyfriend. "Pleased to meet you," Callie said, handing Phil his change. "I think you know Max, my..." She started to say "employee" but then realized that didn't fit anymore. "My former employee."

"Former?" Tammy asked, aghast. "He quit?"

"It wasn't because he wanted to, exactly. His father had a fall, and he's got to head home to help take care of the family farm."

"I didn't know," Phil said. "I'd better call Max and see how he's doing."

"I'm sure he'd like that," said Callie. "Tammy, can we talk for a minute?" The sounds of the band starting up again wafted across the lawn with a soft breeze.

"I'm going to head back to our seats," Phil said to Tammy.

"You go ahead," Tammy told him. "I want to talk to Callie, too."

Well, well. "Can you give me just a few minutes? I'll serve the rest of these people, and then we can chat."

"Sure. Mind if I sit down?" Tammy gestured at one of the lawn chairs Callie had brought with her in the chance she'd have a moment to sit.

Callie nodded as she dished out food to customers, keeping one eye on Tammy, who was placidly eating feta cheese chunks and nodding her head in tune to the band.

Finally, the last customer had been served, and Callie joined Tammy. "So, what did you want to talk to me about?"

Tammy had finished her food. She put her empty plate on the ground next to her chair before speaking.

"Nobody will tell me anything." Tammy related this news with a disgusted sigh. "My doctor thinks I may have been drugged with a heavy tranquilizer, but the test results aren't back yet. At least, not according to my doctor. I know you date a cop, and I thought you might have some inside information."

"Tammy, I don't. I swear. And even if I did, I'm not supposed to go around giving out information during an active investigation."

"I know," Tammy sounded dejected. "It's just been a really rough week. I'd love to know who did this to me and why."

"I know. The whole situation is frightening, no question about it," Callie soothed. "Let me ask you something as long as we're on the topic. I saw you and Lisa Linley arguing the other day, outside of The Harris House."

"You did?" Tammy replied. Her face was unreadable.

"It looked rather heated. This is nosy, I realize, but can you tell me what it was about?"

"Just dumb stuff," Tammy shook her head angrily, remembering. "She didn't want The Harris House involved in the murder mystery night anymore, for one thing."

"Why not take that up with Allan Browne?"

"I'm not sure if you've noticed, but he's not exactly the type to sweet talk anyone." Tammy's mouth was a stubborn line, so Callie decided to change the subject before the band's set ended and more customers swarmed her tent.

"By the way, where did you meet Phil?" she asked cheerily. "He seems to be a good musician."

Tammy brightened at the mention of Phil's name. "We met at Crystal Bay College. He's a grad student in English lit."

"Does he know anything about Holly's thesis? Has he read it?"

"Not that I know of," Tammy said. "They weren't working together. People generally keep their research to themselves. There's a lot of competition for grades and fresh ideas."

Callie pondered this silently for a minute. "That makes sense. Well, just thought I'd ask."

Tammy nodded toward the register. "Looks like you have another customer."

Callie looked up and saw a woman perusing what remained of the food. "Thanks. Back in a minute." Callie served up her last two pieces of *spanakopita* to the woman and reached for the lockbox to get change.

Except it was no longer there.

Panicked, she turned to Tammy to ask if she'd seen anything. She was gone, too.

Seventeen

The feeling of panic about the missing lock box full of cash quickly turned to anger. How dare anyone take her hard-earned money? And a cut of it was supposed to go to the Chamber of Commerce, headed by none other than Mrs. Gertrude DeWitt. She was not someone you wanted as an enemy.

Callie hesitated. She had to report the theft to the police, but did she really want them showing up right now, disrupting the night for Viv and Mrs. DeWitt? Having a reporter here complicated things.

Also, hadn't Callie's Kitchen been the subject of enough infamy recently? Reports of a theft could diminish the credibility she'd worked so hard to repair over the last year.

Callie couldn't bring herself to believe that Tammy had taken the lockbox, basically, from right under her nose. But maybe she'd seen something. Gritting her teeth, Callie vowed to track down Tammy then and there.

One thing was for certain. She was shutting down her food tent.

Callie swept refuse into the garbage and the remaining food into her cooler, so quickly that she probably resembled a video on fast forward. Stomping off into the crowd, she kept her eyes peeled for Tammy, but the crush of people had worsened, and it was slow going through the crowd. She didn't see Hugh and Raine, thank goodness. Maybe they could only take so much outdoor music in one evening. April Manning was still with her group of friends. All of them were laughing and holding plastic cups of wine and beer. April gave a wave as Callie pushed past.

Finally, Callie pushed her way to the front of the audience and scanned the crowd in line at the beverage tent. Feta cheese was salty and could make a person thirsty.

Bingo. There was Tammy, waiting with Phil, near the front of the line. Callie snaked through the throngs and confronted Tammy.

"There you are! Please, don't broadcast this, but my lockbox has been stolen. Did you see anything? When did you leave?"

"*What?*" Tammy looked close to tears. "I'm sorry! I figured you were busy, and we were finished talking anyway. I didn't see a thing!"

"You should call security," remarked Phil. Callie nodded at him in weary assent as he stepped forward to place his drink order.

"If you remember anything," Callie addressed Tammy, "be sure to let me know."

"I will. I'm sorry I can't be of more help."

You and me both, thought Callie as she went in search of Viv to break the bad news about the night's food earnings.

***

When her alarm went off the next morning, Callie was tempted to throw her clock out the window. She'd spent a restless night. Despite her desire not to make a scene, she'd contacted the police about her stolen lockbox. After leaving Tammy and Phil, she'd found a uniformed officer on duty and had quietly explained the situation to him. He'd checked her tent and taken a report. He'd questioned Tammy, Phil, Viv and a few others, but no lockbox had been found.

Callie rolled over and put the pillow over her head. Her sleeplessness had prompted her to do an online search of the *On the Bay* article regarding F. Scott Fitzgerald and the young Chicago woman that Viv had mentioned. Frustratingly, the magazine didn't post all of its articles on its website. Strike one. She'd have to find the article another way.

Koukla jumped up on the bed and started trying to burrow under the pillow, rooting out her owner. Callie laughed at the Yorkie's antics and staggered out of bed.

It was time to make the doughnuts, or rather, the *loukoumades*. Josh was starting work as her apprentice today, and it wouldn't do for her to be late.

Because she knew she would be working late at *Beats on the Bay*, Callie had arranged for Olivia to spend the night with George. So it was just Callie and Koukla in the pre-dawn light of the kitchen.

Strong coffee, a stronger shower and an internal pep talk finally galvanized Callie. She was even capable of feeling mildly optimistic about Josh as a prospective employee as she unlocked the door of Callie's Kitchen at 5:45.

The building had an empty feeling to it, as if it missed a presence that was no longer there. Callie smiled at her whimsy. A building, after all, couldn't miss a human.

Fortunately, Callie was saved from further gloomy ruminations by Josh's arrival, five minutes early. That was one check in the "plus" column for him.

Callie greeted Josh warmly and provided him with a cup of her strong coffee before offering him a tour of her shop. She showed him where the extra aprons were kept, what was in the freezer, and what the menu's weekly offerings were. She was chattering away in a dismal attempt to fight off the gloom about Max's departure, when Josh stopped her.

"Don't you want to see the dish I brought for you to try? You wanted to test my cooking skills."

"Yes, yes. Of course! I'm sorry that I'm such a chatterbox this morning. Too much coffee, I guess." Belatedly, Callie remembered

Josh placing a covered dish on a nearby table near the door before she had offered him her frenzied tour of Callie's Kitchen.

"Great. I'll go get it. You're going to love it."

Josh returned carrying a foil-covered rectangular dish. It smelled good. Josh peeled back the foil to reveal what looked like a baked egg dish. It looked golden and tempting. Callie's spirits rose.

"Since you had me arrive so early, I thought a brunch-style dish would be nice to try. This is my herbed onion tart." He cut a square out of the plate and handed it to Callie. "See what you think. It's still warm. I got up early this morning to bake it."

Saying a prayer, she took a bite. She chewed and swallowed, then took another bite. The dish had an odd taste she couldn't quite place. Reluctantly, she tried another forkful. The dish was sweet where it should be savory: that was the problem.

"Josh, this is...interesting." She set the plate down. "It looks good and smells divine. But I'm sorry to say that something is just a little bit off. Is it supposed to have a sweet taste?"

"Sweet? No way. It should be a little salty, if anything. Let me have some." He grabbed a chunk of the tart out of the pan with his fingers, eliciting a gasp from Callie. Where was his hygiene? Didn't he learn that at culinary school? *Max, where are you when I need you?*

Josh swallowed his bite of food and pushed the rest of the dish away. "Oh, boy. DARN IT."

"What's wrong?" Callie was losing patience with this entire enterprise. Maybe she'd be better off alone.

"I must have used SUGAR instead of SALT. How could I do that?" Josh hung his head for a second and then looked back at Callie with a hangdog expression. "I guess I mixed up the two. But I swear that is the first time I've ever done that, and I want to assure you that it will be the last. I must have been nervous or something. I'm so sorry."

Callie didn't know what to say. It was tempting to order Josh out of her kitchen, never to return. She simply did not have time for basic cooking mistakes at this juncture. Callie pictured Josh accidentally using salt for the large amounts of sugar in her delicious brownie recipe and shuddered. Salted chocolate was one thing, but...

On the other hand, she hated to prematurely dash the hopes of a culinary newbie. He could be trained. And, he *had* been five minutes early. Plus, he was part of the murder mystery night theater troupe, and would have lots of valuable insider information. She hoped.

Oh, who was she kidding? She was desperate. It was this kid or the loony bin had better have a free room.

"I'd like to give you a chance," Callie told Josh. "But please, whatever you do, keep any ingredients that look similar completely separate at your work space. Label them, if you have to. Mistakes happen, but we have to make sure they don't happen too often. In fact, right now, I need as much perfection as I can get."

Josh appeared receptive to her spiel, so she continued. "I've got the Greek Fest tomorrow, so Piper will be holding down the fort and our Callie's Kitchen menu will be more limited. I've made most of the food for Greek Fest, but not all of it. I'm going to need you to help with our regular Callie's Kitchen dishes today, plus, you can bake some of the stuff that's already in the freezer. I won't try to overload you on Day One."

"Thanks!" Josh whooped. "This is great news." He shook her hand, pumping it up and down. "I won't let you down again. I'm your man."

***

Despite Josh's enthusiasm, the pace at Callie's Kitchen was considerably slower. It wasn't really his fault, though. Callie had to walk him through steps that Max could do in a flash. However, that was after years of experience, Callie kept telling herself.

Piper showed up at 8 a.m. and that made the morning rush go a little bit easier. Callie noticed that the exuberant Piper was "coaching" Josh in the ways of Callie's Kitchen, so that helped. "Ordering him around," might be a more accurate assessment, but Josh was so eager to please that he didn't seem to mind.

If he didn't confuse the salt with the sugar or the baking powder with the cornstarch, they just might be O.K.

While Josh was in charge of the rice pudding pot in the back room, Callie sidled over to Piper to see how she thought things were going.

"Josh is serious about cooking, that much I can tell," Piper said, a worried frown puckering her forehead. "But he is really slow. I have to get used to how he does things."

"It's his first day," Callie pointed out. "He seems to take direction pretty well."

"He's a really nice guy," Piper said, nodding slowly. "But he's no Max."

Callie had been trying very hard not to think about that. She was digging about for an optimistic comeback, when the phone rang.

"I'll get that," Callie said, relieved not to have to talk about Josh or Max any longer. "Just make sure Josh doesn't burn the pudding."

Piper saluted her and walked through the French doors. "Don't stop stirring," Callie heard her order Josh in stern tones.

Callie grabbed the phone. "Callie's Kitchen. How can I help you?"

"You can start by telling me why I never hear about the exciting crises happening in the life of my best friend anymore." Callie breathed a sigh of relief. The sound of her friend Sam's voice coated her spirits like a balm.

"Which crisis are you talking about today? I've got several."

"Let's see. How about that you had money stolen at *Beats on the Bay*? Or the fact that you watched Tammy Heckstrom drop like a sack of potatoes at The Harris House the other night?"

"Yep. Those are two exciting crises all right. How did you hear about this stuff?"

"Now, now. I can't reveal all of my sources. Let's just say I have spies everywhere. On another note, I thought you might like to know that they found the lockbox, *sans* cash, in one of the trash cans at the park last night. I heard about it this morning."

"Seriously?"

"Sure am. I'm really sorry about that."

"Not as sorry as I am. I needed that money, and I certainly don't need any more bad publicity. And I am absolutely dreading telling Mrs. DeWitt about it. Despite everything, I really appreciated the chance to provide food for the Chamber events. I guess that's over now."

"Not necessarily. Besides, we've got bigger problems. I happen to have a report in front of me that confirms that Tammy Heckstrom was given a strong dose of muscle relaxant the other night. That's why she passed out."

"Muscle relaxant? That's weird."

"Some of them are pretty strong. It's definitely not a drug you'd want to take before an acting gig."

"Definitely not. I wonder who did that to her and why?"

"Well, you didn't hear any of this from me. I just wanted you to know that people are getting nasty. Be careful."

Feeling her face burn with the memory, Callie thought of her escapade at the crime scene the other evening. Sam hadn't brought it up, so Callie hoped she didn't know about that "crisis" at least.

"I will. I don't have time to do anything but cook for the next couple of days. Remember? Greek Fest is upon us!"

"I know, I know. And I also heard that Max has left Callie's Kitchen. Wasn't he supposed to help?"

"Yes, he was." Callie sighed. "I'm sorry I haven't had much time to catch up with you lately. How did you hear about Max? Or should I even ask?"

"No mystery there. Your Grandma Viv bumped into me at the dry cleaner's. I got the whole story, very colorfully presented, let me tell you. I'm very sorry to hear that his dad is having health problems, but Max isn't going to be easy to replace. What are you going to do?"

"I've got a temporary replacement right now," Callie whispered. "I can't really talk about it." She heard a yelp from the kitchen and realized she needed to wrap up the phone call. "I've got to go."

"So do I. But not before I tell you this. You've got a new assistant for Greek Fest. Me."

Eighteen

Friday, the day of Greek Fest dawned sunny and warm. Callie peeked out the window and was thankful to see a clear, blue sky dotted with just a few puffy white clouds. Nothing was worse than huddling under a tent with soggy *souvlaki*.

She'd been up until 2 a.m. baking additional savory Greek pies for the festival. Better too many than not enough, was George's motto, and in this case, she had to agree. The Greeks among the festival attendees would be horrified if they didn't get a piece, or two, of *pita*.

Thoughts of the busy day in front of her almost helped to drive the story of Tammy Heckstrom and her muscle relaxant dosing out of Callie's mind.

Almost. Because now it looked like any one of a number of people who could have spiked Tammy's tea: Raine. Hugh. Lisa Linley. Allan Browne. Any of the actors, really.

Even Josh, heaven help her.

It was too much to process right now. She needed all of her positive energy today and then some. Callie smiled as she thought of Sam and her generous offer to help out at Greek Fest. Her busy friend had promised to leave work early and help Callie get through the evening crowd. Sam was no cook, so Callie planned to put her in charge of something simple, like selling cups of rice pudding or plates of *spanakopita* while Callie handled the frying of the *loukoumades*, the one "fresh" item that needed to be prepared.

Sometimes Callie ran the "frappe" station, providing traditionally Greek frosty coffee drinks to overheated Greek Fest attendees, but

142

this year, a couple of women from the church had taken over that duty. Callie was glad to surrender the task.

On a brighter note, Sands had promised to try and meet her at the Greek Fest that evening.

After checking in with Piper to make sure that Callie's Kitchen was up and running, Callie figured out her game plan for the day. First, she had to visit Callie's Kitchen and get her *pites* and other goodies. Then, she had to dash over to the event location to claim her refrigerator space, a highly valued commodity. Jockeying for refrigerator storage was typical, so Callie made a note to bring some of her own ice-filled coolers as well.

Fueled by coffee and adrenaline, Callie drove to her shop just long enough to load up her foodstuffs. Piper was not her chipper self, missing Max, no doubt, but she was doing a competent job of serving the customers for the morning rush. As if in mourning, she was dressed more conservatively than usual, in a navy blue blouse with a Peter Pan collar and black capri pants, instead of one of her brightly colored, cinched-waist dresses.

Josh and Piper had baked the frozen *pites* the day before, and now, the delicacies were spread out in golden brown rows. Callie hoped the sight of that buttery goodness would tempt festival attendees to eat up and spend. Combined with the fresh-baked *pites* that she had slaved over the previous evening, the food situation seemed to be under control. Callie recalled Max's frenzied efforts at baking and cooking over the last several days. *I couldn't have done it without him*, she thought.

Packing up the food and ensuring that it was securely fastened in the coolers took longer than Callie had thought it would, and it was nearly 11 a.m. before she was pulling into the parking lot of the public park rented out by the church. Because of the small size of the Greek Orthodox community in town, the church hall and grounds weren't large enough to hold the hordes of Crystal Bay locals and tourists who turned out for authentic Greek food and music. Luckily, the park was a green and open space, with a view of the water and fortunately, ample restroom access.

Across the bay, the elegant silhouettes of the beautiful Gilded Age homes were just visible in the distance. Narrowing her eyes at them, Callie was gripped by a feeling of something important eluding her. It was the same feeling she'd had ever since she and Max had pulled their spy mission the other evening. She made another mental note to research the article Viv had mentioned as soon as possible.

White tents were set up on either side of the park, creating a walking path that led directly to a small dais at the far end of the park, right near a thick copse of trees. Several picnic tables and smaller tables covered in white paper tablecloths surrounded the stage. This would be the space for the Greek band to perform. Callie smiled as she thought of George kicking up his heels in a traditional Greek folk dance, something he dearly loved to do once he'd served his time grilling *souvlakia,* aka kebabs, at his food tent.

"Calliope! Over here!" The hearty, Greek-accented voice of her father called to her. Smiling, Callie lugged her rolling trays of food a few tents down the "lane" towards her father. He waved at her impatiently.

When she was just a few feet away, George couldn't wait anymore. He barreled over to her and embraced her in one of his signature bear hugs. "*Hrisi mou.* Calliope! I thought you'd never get here. But now you're here, so let's get to work!"

"Don't worry, Dad, I've been working on the food for the festival for days. It's going to be good. And look! The sun is out! It's going to be a great success."

"Are you joking? I'm not going to stop worrying until the last *souvlaki* has been grilled. Then and only then will I sit back with *ouzo* and maybe a lamb chop with some *tzatziki.* But that's hours away. No use thinking about it now."

Callie smiled warmly at her father as he bustled about, helping her to unload her food. Despite his self-deprecating tone, she knew this was one of the most joyful and much-anticipated days of his year. Dimly, she remembered Greek Fest as being an anchor to George when he'd lost her mother so many years ago. Perhaps it was a symbol of how he'd remade his life since then. Greek food and camaraderie had a way of being life-affirming.

Exclaiming excitedly over each item as he removed it, he nonetheless couldn't help himself from a visual critique of each item. Fortunately, most of it seemed to meet with his favor, even the food baked by Josh.

"So, I hear young Max has left Callie's Kitchen," he said, putting his nose to a covered dish of *spanakopita* and pronouncing it just a little under baked.

"Yes, he has. How did you hear about that? Viv?"

"No, a regular at the Olympia mentioned something." The Olympia was her father's diner, and he'd harbored dreams of her taking it over one day, a dream that had been dashed when she'd opened Callie's Kitchen.

"A friend of Max's father told me all about it," George was saying, shaking his head. "So sorry to hear about his father's tragic accident, but what will you do without Max? It's summer season, *hrisi mou*. So many tourists!"

"I know, I know. The thing is I've got this new guy, Josh, helping me out. And Piper's still there, so we'll manage. Samantha is going to help me out today. Max was supposed to be here, but obviously he has to be where his family is."

"Of course. Family is the most important thing of all." George puffed out his chest and Callie was ready for a pontification to begin, but he only held out one meaty forefinger and pointed it at Callie before pointing it at himself. "You and me. We're family, and we will stick together. I'm happy to help at Callie's Kitchen while you find a permanent replacement."

He stowed a couple more *pites* before adding "I'm surprised you haven't asked me already. Especially with this latest murder in Crystal Bay. Don't be afraid to ask me for help, you know. It won't kill you."

Uh-oh. George was warming up for a lengthy discussion, Callie could feel it.

"I admit: I may very well need your help and I thank you for the offer. Right now I've got Josh and I will see how he works out at the shop. He's young and not an experienced cook, but he seems to enjoy food, so that's half the battle." She decided not to mention Josh's tie to the murder mystery night troupe and Tammy's unfortunate muscle relaxant dosing while performing.

"The things I could teach him in the kitchen!" George had a light in his eyes, and Callie remembered him as her cooking instructor, showing her how to brush just the right amount of butter on the phyllo dough, or that a squeeze of lemon improved the flavor of any grilled meat dish.

Callie was saved from having to respond by the arrival of more Greek Fest volunteers, George's buddies from church and The Olympia. Their biggest concern was that one of the deluxe grills they'd brought to the festival didn't seem to be working. With apologies to his daughter, George rushed off to attend to the problem. Several minutes later, cries of *"Opa!"* told Callie that the grill was fixed, and that somebody may have dipped into the *ouzo* earlier than they'd said they would.

The next 15 minutes were a blur of talking to her fellow festival workers and setting up food. After she had unloaded everything, Callie took a quick trip around the festival, peeking in on each tent and saying hello to her fellow festival hosts. She was charmed to see so many crafts, including some by young girls not that much older than her daughter Olivia. One father and daughter were offering their own handmade jewelry and lush-looking olive oil soap. Callie made a mental note to stop by later. Perhaps next year Olivia could join her mother in the tent. She would be just as old as Callie was when she started helping her father, George, with the annual Greek Fest.

The first attendees were due at 1 p.m., and Callie could already see that the parking lot was filling up with everything from trucks to sleek sports cars. Fleetingly she thought of Piper and wondered how the shop was doing without Max, but she shook off that thought.

Callie had just decided it was time to put the first of the rice pudding into disposable cups when her cell phone rang.

"Callie, it's me." Sands' voice was warm, but wary.

"Oh, hi! Don't tell me you're not coming to the Greek Fest today. I can use every bit of moral support. Plus, you haven't lived until you've watched my dad do his Zorba routine on the dance floor."

"You sound a little stressed, my dear. Of course I'll be there. I wanted to tell you that we found your lockbox but without any cash. I would have called sooner, but I was tracking down some information about something else."

"Sam told me. I don't know how she found out. I appreciate the news. I just wish we had the cash."

"Sam told you? Hmm. I wish we'd found the money as well, but we usually don't in cases like this. I just thought you would like to know."

"Thanks for the call. Let's chat some more tonight. I've got hungry people approaching me right now."

Sands laughed. "I bet you do. See you later."

Callie sprinkled cinnamon on her rice pudding cups and was startled when a young man suddenly joined her behind the table.

"Josh!" she cried. "What are you doing here?"

Nineteen

"I wanted to redeem myself," Josh said.

"There's really no need..." Callie started to say. Today of all days, she didn't have time to deal with training anyone on her team. Plus, she realized she didn't know if her food was safe around Josh, and not only because he'd confused salt with sugar.

"No, I insist," Josh said. He found an extra "Callie's Kitchen" blue and white apron lying across one of the large folding tables and tied it on.

"Well, that's awfully nice of you," Callie said, trying to hide the uncertainty in her voice. "I can't really pay you today, you know. This is volunteer work that I, we, do for the Greek Fest. The proceeds go to the church, mostly. I only get a small cut of the profits."

"Yes, that's what Piper said. It's OK. I just want to show you what I can do."

That's what I'm afraid of, Callie thought.

"Wait a minute here, what do you mean, Piper said? Did she tell you to come here and help me out? I swear I never mentioned a thing to her." Callie fumed a bit, wondering why Piper was so anxious to foist Josh upon her today of all days. Was Piper trying to remove Josh from Callie's Kitchen so that she could have some peace and quiet herself? Or was Josh truly just an eager-to-please, would-be chef?

Josh blushed, and Callie felt bad for scolding him. "Yeah, she did mention something. Don't be mad at her. Seriously." Josh gazed at Callie with wide eyes. "I want to help."

"Thank you for showing up," she said, collecting herself and feeling badly that she was behaving in such a bad-tempered way. "I do need someone to help. But I have to warn you this isn't glamorous work. I'll need you to be versatile. That means maybe even basic stuff like getting ice for coolers or moving tables. It's not all food related. Are you up for that?"

Playfully, Josh flexed a bicep. "What do you think? Just tell me what you need done."

Callie stood with her hands on her hips. "First things first. I need all these rice puddings from this cooler to be placed in one of those portable refrigerators in the refrigeration tent. Make sure the food is labeled Callie's Kitchen." She handed him an indelible marker. "It's getting hot and the puddings are perishable. Use sharp elbows to get in there if you have to. Fridge space is limited and highly prized!"

"No problem." Smiling, Josh took her tray of puddings and walked off jauntily in the direction of the refrigerator tent.

Callie turned back to her work, making sure she had enough plastic spoons, paper plates and paper napkins with her blue-and-white Callie's Kitchen logo on them. She carefully placed all of her baked goods out on the tables and put out signs stating how many tickets each item cost. Thankfully, the Greek Fest used tickets instead of cash transactions at each tent. Callie made a mental note to suggest this system to Mrs. DeWitt for the next *Beats on the Bay* event.

The gates would open soon and the literal feeding frenzy would begin. Callie looked around. Where was Josh? Had somebody bested him in the refrigerator space wars, and he was afraid to report back to her? He'd better not; she couldn't have her desserts spoiling in the hot sunshine.

Callie peeked outside of her tent and saw that several attendees were already checking in and getting their tickets. Her heart soared for her father. If these early birds were any indication, the Greek Fest should be a success!

After scanning the growing crowd for several more minutes, she finally spotted Josh. He wasn't carrying any rice puddings, thank goodness, but he was speaking to a portly gentleman with wild red hair. Allan Browne.

"Good news, Callie," Josh said proudly. "I got all the refrigerator space I needed. The women in the tent called me something that sounded like "pethas." What does that mean?"

"Pethas? Oh, you mean *"petharos."* Callie couldn't help but laugh. "I guess you're home free, then, Josh. *'Petharos'* is a Greek term that means 'handsome, strapping young man.' "

"Really?" Josh gulped and smiled sheepishly at the two of them.

"You lucky boy. Or should I say *'Adonis?'* Another of the strapping, Greek young men." Allan Browne smiled benignly at the two of them before continuing. "Before I offer up my tickets that will allow me to sample some of your delicious-looking food, I want to apologize for the other day. I was supremely upset. I'm sure you can understand."

Callie tried not to show her surprise at this apology from the blustery Allan Browne. "It was an upsetting evening. I saw Tammy, though, and she's made a full recovery."

"Yes, I know. I'm so relieved. Losing Holly was just..." Allan's face crumpled, but he regained his composure so quickly that Callie wondered if she had imagined it.

"In any case, what a wonderful day this is for such an event!" Allan slapped Josh on the back. "You know that the ancient Greek actor, 'Thespis,' is considered to be the creator of the theater, in particular, Greek tragedy. That's where the term 'Thespian' comes from. Though of course, you know all about that, Josh." Apparently, Allan Browne relied on pomposity to see him through the difficulties of life. *Well,* Callie thought, *whatever helps.*

"Yeah, sure," Josh said uncertainly. "Listen, you're our first customer today. What would you like?"

Rubbing his hands together, Allan turned to the food, choosing pieces of savory zucchini pita, *spanakopita* and a cup of rice pudding. He gave Josh the allotted number of tickets and stacked his plates precariously on one meaty forearm.

"What is that delightful smell?" Allan asked Callie. Sniffing the air, Callie knew he was most likely speaking about the *souvlaki* that George was cooking in the tent right next door. Pork was the traditional meat used in Greek souvlaki, so that's what they cooked at the festival. Tradition was everything today. The *souvlaki* got a squeeze of lemon after they came off of the grill, and they were served with cool, creamy *tzatziki*, the luscious cucumber-Greek yogurt sauce.

"*Souvlaki*. Also known as kebabs. My father, George, is in charge of those today, and he is a master. I'm sure he'll be happy to serve you some fresh from the grill."

Allan nodded at the two of them and stuck a piece of *spanakopita* in his mouth before shuffling off to the next tent. Callie could hear him say, "And of course, you know that Thespis, an ancient Greek, is considered the father of theater..." She shook her head and smiled.

"Did you know Allan Browne was a Greek food fan?" Callie asked Josh.

"Not really. Though, he does seem to enjoy talking about Thespis, so I should have known."

"I do believe my dad may have just met his match," Callie said.

***

As the bright afternoon sun faded into a gentle dusk, Callie realized that the crowds were growing exponentially. So far, she'd seen quite a few Callie's Kitchen regulars, as well as many friends and acquaintances. Tammy Heckstrom was there with her boyfriend, Phil. April Manning was walking around with Raine and Hugh before disappearing into a crowd of young twenty-somethings, just like she had at *Beats on the Bay*. Josh had served quite a few of his fellow murder mystery players who teased him about "making the doughnuts."

Tourists milled around eating and shopping at the craft market. Children screamed on the Ferris wheel that had been set up just for the event. Callie was happy to see quite a few of her fellow business owners from Garden Street. They must have come over after they closed up shop for the day. Overall, it looked like half the town had shown up, not to mention tourists. Callie couldn't help thinking about Max and how much he usually enjoyed this annual event.

Callie wondered if Josh had regretted his brave vow to volunteer. He was speeding back and forth to the refrigerators, for more puddings and batter for her sweet *loukoumades*, the fried Greek doughnuts that were always such a hit at every Greek Fest she'd ever attended. Small balls of dough were fried in oil as festival-goers watched, then drizzled with honey and cinnamon. The fried treats were a morning mainstay at Callie's Kitchen, too. After a short tutorial, Josh had taken over the *loukoumades* preparation to the delight of the teenage girls and twenty-somethings that crowded around his work station, watching him work.

Petharos, indeed.

Callie wiped her hands on her apron and glanced at her watch. It was time for Samantha to show up for her shift. She'd planned to send Josh home when Sam arrived, but as she watched girls squeal for the *loukoumades* and hand over several tickets, she wondered if she could convince him to stay longer.

"How's my favorite Greek goddess?" said a voice behind Callie. Sam must have swept into her tent as she'd stood contemplating the *petharos* who had taken over so much of the burden today. Sam looked smashing as always, in a pair of sleek khaki shorts and a loose royal blue top.

"Sam! I'm so happy to see you. Grab an apron so you don't get anything on that cute outfit." She noticed a new group of people clustering near her food. "Let me get these customers squared away, and I'll put you to work."

Callie's heart was lighter than it had been in days as she provided plates of food to the hungry hordes. George had to be thrilled! She'd been so busy that she'd only had glimpses of him and heard his booming laughter for several hours. The festival had been such a success that breaks had been nearly non-existent.

Her rumbling stomach told her that she needed a break, and soon. The *souvlaki* that had tempted her appetite all day were calling, and besides, she was awaiting the arrival of both Sands and Viv. Viv had planned to show up with Olivia, who wanted not only food, but a chance to ride the Ferris wheel and play some carnival games.

The sounds of Niko and The Grecian Keys, the band scheduled for the fest, was starting their jaunty Greek folk songs. Cries of "OPA!" rang from George's tent, and Callie laughed.

Suddenly, over the sounds of the band and the joyful cries of the dancers, Callie heard other, more unwelcome sounds.

"You..." expletives filled the air as Callie listened in horror. Then there was a crash, and somebody screamed.

The next words Callie heard turned her blood to ice, despite the heat.

"I'll KILL YOU!!"

Twenty

"Stop that man!"

Callie heard a voice with a heavy Greek accent bellowing above the rest. Callie ran from her tent to have a look, praying that George wasn't caught up in the melee.

Instead, she was treated to the sight of Allan Browne being body-slammed to the ground by three older Greek gentlemen. Callie recognized one of the men as Sotiris Giannopoulos. A short, balding man with impressive muscles for a man in his sixties, Sotiris sat on Allan Browne's back while the other two men knelt next to Allan and tried to hold his writhing body in place.

Without thinking, Callie rushed to Allan's side. "What is going on here?"

"Callie?" Allan Browne's voice sounded out of breath as he called to her from the ground. "This is an outrage. Tell them to let me go."

"What is it, Sotiris?" Callie asked, determined to find out why these mild-mannered men had seen fit to tackle someone to the ground in the middle of Greek Fest.

"He steal from the cash box! I see him!" Sotiris shouted in his non-native English.

From the ground, Allan Browne roared in either disapproval or guilt. At this point, Callie didn't know which one. By this time, a large crowd had gathered. Callie looked around desperately and before she knew it, Sam was by her side, grasping her arm protectively.

"He stole? Are you sure, Sotiris?"

"Of course! This is money for the church. Church money, he stole! Then, when I try to stop him, he say he'll kill me!" Sotiris's cohorts nodded their heads, glaring with menace at Allan Browne.

"Just an expression, I assure you," Allan's voice was sounding strangled. "I was very upset at the accusations."

"You can't keep him on the ground," she told Sotiris. "Let him up. Please. I know him. It's all right."

Sotiris shook his head stubbornly, and Callie decided she'd pull him off if she had to.

Just then, George appeared. In rapid Greek, he told his friend to let Allan go. He repeated himself once more, and Sotiris nodded reluctantly. He and his gang released Allan, but stood closely around him in a semi-circle as if daring him to escape. Allan stood up laboriously, brushing dust from his clothes.

"Are you all right?" Callie asked him. Even if he was a thief, and possibly a thief that had stolen from her as well, she didn't want him to have a heart attack on the premises.

"I am not!" Allan Browne bellowed. "This is an outrage!" he repeated, appearing to relish the fact that he now had an audience. "Allow me to explain."

"Explain to police!" Sotiris shouted, and several people grumbled in agreement.

"Callie, you have to believe me!" Allan Browne turned to her with a look of despair. "It was a simple disagreement about tickets. I was sold too many tickets, and the young woman at the ticket counter wouldn't take them back. So I handed her my extra tickets. I returned them, you see. Then, when she wouldn't give me my money back, I took it myself." He glared at Sotiris and George. "How can you steal your own money?" If he was acting, it was awfully good, she had to admit.

"Allan, I don't know what to think. Couldn't you have come to me? I would have helped you get your money back."

"Thank you, Callie, but this situation did not have to come to this." He brushed more dust off of his clothes. "I never had such treatment in all of my life!"

"Sure," Sam whispered. "He's a real friendly guy, gets along with everyone." Callie stifled a giggle before hushing Sam.

Josh suddenly appeared, gesturing nervously at the group of men. "I was in the refrigerator tent. What did I miss?"

"I'm not exactly sure," Callie whispered back. Was Allan telling the truth? If so, then he was something of a bull in a china shop. If not, then he was the type of guy to steal church funds. Neither one was a great look for him. If he had stolen any money tonight, then had he stolen from her as well?

George's voice rang out over the angry buzz of the crowd. "OK! It's time for Niko and the Grecian Keys. Everybody, go and dance! Nothing to see here."

George nodded towards the stage. The band was standing motionless watching the mini brawl. After a couple of seconds, they took up their instruments again and started playing loudly. The crowd began to disperse, and people glanced curiously at George, Allan and Callie. Callie felt her cheeks burn. She just couldn't seem to stay out of drama, no pun intended.

George took Allan by the arm. "Let's sit down," he said kindly, but firmly. "I'd like to talk to you some more, clear this up. Maybe that way, we don't need to call the police."

Allan looked at Sotiris and crew who were still standing guard, then he glanced at Josh who was standing with arms folded, giving him a stare-down.

"Fine. Let's talk. I did nothing wrong."

"Then you have nothing to worry about," she heard George say as he led Allan to a chair.

"We'd better get back to our tent," Callie told Josh and Sam. A good old-fashioned fight was bound to make people hungry.

A few minutes later, Callie had her head down, deep in thought as she cut up more squares of *spanakopita*. Suddenly, she felt a pair of strong arms grasp her firmly around the waist. "Hey!" she protested, "I've got a knife here, you know!"

"Yes, you *are* dangerous," was the reply from Sands. Callie was laughing as she turned around to embrace him.

"Break it up, you two," Sam said with a smile, as she walked over to join them. "You certainly missed a good show," Sam continued, with a twinkle in her eye as she gazed at Sands. Callie didn't blame her friend for being the slightest bit flirty. Tonight, Sands looked tan and handsome in a white t-shirt and well-worn jeans.

"No! Wait, don't tell me, don't tell me..." Sands pretended to ponder the possibilities. "George already did his Greek dance!"

"Unfortunately, no," Callie said, smiling at his quip. "We had a potential attempted theft...maybe. It's unclear. It may just be a misunderstanding."

"What? Where's the culprit?" Sands wanted to know.

"The 'culprit,' if he actually is one, is talking to my father at that table over there. Allan Browne? You know him well." She pointed to the duo, who were having an animated conversation.

"Yes indeed. He keeps turning up, doesn't he? I'll just have a little talk with him." Sands nodded at Callie and strode towards Allan with a deliberate, long-legged stride.

"I like a man who takes charge," Sam teased once Sands had left the tent.

"Oh, stop it," Callie said, laughing. "Anyway, he's just talking to Allan. I hope." She glanced anxiously over at them, but the conversation seemed to be calm enough.

"Sorry to interrupt, but do you want me to make more *loukoumades*?" Josh asked, stumbling over the long Greek word. Callie smiled. Josh had been surprisingly competent tonight. She thought warmly of Max who had provided her with help when she needed it, even though he was dealing with his own problems. Was it possible that Josh could be as helpful someday?

"How much batter do we have left?" Callie couldn't bear to think of Max any more tonight.

"Not that much. We may as well kill it."

"I agree. Sam, would you like to put the honey and cinnamon on them after they're fried?"

"You trust me with that?" Sam asked, her long-lashed eyes wide. "Just kidding," she said when she saw Callie's expression. "You got it. Come on, Josh."

Callie finished cutting up the last pans of *spanakopita*, zucchini pita and Greek cheese *pita*, while she watched the conversation with George, Sands and Allan Browne wrap up. The smells of buttery phyllo dough and salty cheese were too tempting to resist. She put a piece of *pita* on a plate for herself.

Allan was a confusing person, Callie thought, digging into a piece of cheese *pita*. On the one hand, he could be very pompous. On the other hand, there were times that he seemed bumbling and relatively harmless. He did seem to have a temper, as he'd proven on many separate occasions, including this one. Then there was the fact that his home was in the same neighborhood as the one where she'd found Holly Tennyson. She wondered what Sands thought of him and planned to ask him later.

Callie was just finishing the last few bites of *pita* when she saw Sands walking back towards her. Allan Browne was stomping off in a huff, and George was presumably heading back to his grilling station.

"Well?" Callie asked.

"He gave me his explanation, the one I believe you already heard. While bullish of him, I didn't see any evidence of a theft." Sands appeared thoughtful. "True, his judgement was off, but I asked him to leave, and that should do it for now." He stared after Allan Browne who was walking off toward the parking lot, looking like a man with the weight of the world on his shoulders. "Still, I may just keep an eye on him. For fun. Know what I mean?" He smiled at Callie.

"You have a weird idea of fun," Callie replied, a gleam in her eye.

"Then how about this: Let's dance."

"That's better," Callie said, taking his hand.

Niko and the Grecian Keys had the crowd in a full circle Greek folk dance by the time Callie and Sands pushed their way through the crowds. Sam had offered to help serve any remaining food lovers, so Callie was happy to take a few minutes and just get away from food for a minute. She wasn't even hungry any more.

She and Sands joined the circle, and Callie was charmed to see George in the center of all the dancers, whirling and kicking his legs to loud encouragement and cries of "*Opa!*" Sands grasped Callie's hand and chuckled as he tripped along in the complicated Greek folk dance steps. Callie felt a tug on her other hand and looked down to see her daughter Olivia joining her in the dance.

"Hi honey," she greeted her daughter. "Where's Grandma?"

"Over there, with Kathy." George's girlfriend. Callie looked over to see the two women beaming at them and clapping their hands to the beat of the music. She nodded and smiled at them, feeling better than she had in days.

"Well, hello there!" Sands called to Olivia. "I'm guessing that you're better at these Greek dance steps than me."

"I sure am!" Olivia agreed, and they all laughed and danced in the circle, Callie and Sands smiling at each other over Olivia's tousled, honey-blonde head.

Like a family.

Twenty One

"Well, Piper, sending Josh to the Greek Fest was a pretty good idea after all."

It was the next day at Callie's Kitchen, and Piper and Callie were working side by side. Callie was setting out food and Piper was ringing up customers.

Today, Callie had taken some prebaked *koularakia* from the freezer early that morning to thaw, and they'd been a hit. Along with several of her Greek yogurt coffee cakes, she'd also made several Big (Low) Fat Greek Salads, and stocked the fridge with several other dishes. Hummus, pita wrap sandwiches and other light fare were the perfect foil to the summer heat. The smell of lemons, dill and feta cheese filled her shop with a fresh, summery scent.

Callie had told Josh to take a break that day, and she'd get back to him, but she was leaning towards giving him a chance at Callie's Kitchen. His performance at the Greek Fest had been excellent overall, and his people skills were good, too. Callie wasn't sure if she trusted him to create recipes from scratch yet, but he just might be the kitchen savior she so desperately needed.

"I sent him over there because I knew you'd be busy, especially without Max," Piper said, innocently blinking her lashes, thick with mascara.

"Are you sure there weren't any ulterior motives?" Callie couldn't help but ask her employee.

Piper looked flustered. "Yes. I admit it. Josh was getting in the way. Believe it or not, I felt like I could do a better job without him hovering around, asking questions. I miss Max." Piper sighed gustily and then turned back to the register to help a customer.

Don't we all, thought Callie. Still, Josh had gone a long way towards redeeming himself. Maybe things were looking up.

"It was a good call, Piper, but Josh may be someone I want to work with. You can't send him out of the shop instead of training him. We need more than just you and me working here. You of all people know that."

Piper had the good grace to blush. "I'm sorry. You're the boss. If you like him, I'll learn to work with him. He's a nice guy. He's just not..." she trailed off with a sigh.

"He's just not Max," Callie finished for her. "I know." She decided to drop the subject.

Callie was still rattled from the altercation with Allan Browne. For some reason, his story rang true to her. Taking money from a cash box because he wanted to return pre-paid tickets seemed like exactly the overdetermined sort of thing he would do. At least there hadn't been any casualties, except maybe Allan's pride when he'd been tackled by three older men.

She hadn't even had a chance to research anything about the Fitzgerald debutante and the article that Viv had told her about.

Soon, Piper and Callie had no time for conversation or speculation of any kind whatsoever. The shop was mobbed with tourists and locals, clamoring for Callie's Greek pastries, salads and sandwich wraps. She and Piper ran back and forth, serving and re-stocking for at least an hour. It was exhausting and worse yet, food wasn't being prepared. No Max meant no food prep while Callie was otherwise occupied, an unacceptable state of affairs.

When just a few customers remained, seated at tables and enjoying their food, Callie made a decision. She went to the back room and called Josh.

***

"Callie, I'm glad you called. Last night was a blast! I'd love to keep working here with you, and with Piper, of course," Josh said, nodding graciously at the young woman. Piper simply dipped her head at him, and when he looked away, she gave Callie a meaningful glance. Callie shook her head at Piper, who shrugged and went back to laying out cookies in the display case.

"Josh, I'd like to show you how to make some *avgolemono* soup. This is a customer favorite, even when it's warm outside. It goes great with our salads and breads. Have you ever heard of it?"

"Sure. It's that egg-lemon soup. Right? Kind of creamy, with those little pastas in it? Or is it rice?"

"You're thinking of orzo, the Greek rice-shaped pasta, and you're correct. *Avgolemono* has lemon and eggs, and it can include orzo or rice. I prefer to use rice in my soup, though. It's the less soggy option, in my opinion." She beamed at her pupil.

Working quickly but carefully, with Piper holding down the fort in the front of the shop, Callie showed Josh how to add the egg-lemon mixture to the hot broth. The trick was in blending some of the hot broth into the egg mixture, before adding the whole thing back into the pot. The heat had to be just right or the eggs would be scrambled, instead of providing the creamy base that was the hallmark of this classic soup.

Josh seemed to be listening intently to her directions, and she even had him accomplish some of the tasks himself. He was definitely enthusiastic in the kitchen, but still a little uncertain. He worked very slowly, which was not a plus when you were making *avgolemono* and trying to avoid scrambling the eggs.

"Josh," Callie said, stirring. She motioned to Josh, and he added several tablespoons of fresh lemon juice to the soup. "That thing with

Allan Browne was very strange last night. What do you know about him?"

Josh raised his eyebrows. "Besides the fact that he takes himself way, way too seriously? I know a little bit. For example, this thing with the murder mystery theater troupe suspending our shows has got to be bugging him. I know he's been having financial difficulties."

"Really? Enough to want to steal from a church?"

Josh's face reddened. "Oh, I don't know about that. But I know that he's been trying to raise money for something. I think he had family money, but he's spent a lot of it by now. He's started so many businesses and pursued so many careers. A lot of them have flopped. I'm sure all of that has taken a financial toll on him. I think he thought that the murder mystery night had a lot of commercial appeal and he thought that was going to be a great source of cash for him once it got going. Doesn't look like that's going to happen now."

Callie froze, spoon in hand. "I thought he lived in one of those big Gilded Age homes? You need money for that, surely."

"I heard he inherited that house. It's probably paid for."

"Where did you hear all this stuff, anyway?" Callie asked.

Josh's face reddened again, but then he laughed and shrugged. He turned to look at her. "Callie, you've obviously never been involved in an acting company. When we're not rehearsing, or dating each other, we're gossiping."

Callie was thoughtful as she pondered Allan and his dreams. Despite the fact that he was a blowhard, she could sympathize with him. Wasn't she following her own dreams? It wasn't easy.

"Josh, you go ahead and finish the soup," she said before she could indulge in any more sympathy for the pompous Allan Browne. "Add the chicken and rice and make sure it doesn't thicken too much. We don't want it to seem like glue. Use more of the hot broth if you need it."

Josh carefully followed her instructions, and Callie thought he had it figured out well enough. She couldn't stand over people like a mother hen, now could she? Suddenly, she had a terrible thought. Maybe that was what had made Max want to leave Callie's Kitchen. Maybe his father's health was just an excuse!

No. Max wouldn't lie, especially about something like that. Still, she had to learn to delegate. Having been raised by George and watch him keep watch over The Olympia, his diner, like it was one of his children, Callie realized where she had gotten her controlling gene from.

Still, in her heart, she knew she was being too hard on herself. Max had free reign in the kitchen for the most part. She had trusted him, and she knew in her heart that he knew it.

Callie cast a sidelong glance at Josh, who stood, with an intent but happy look on his face, stirring soup and adding a little more broth.

She decided to take a chance.

"I'm going to run an errand. I'll be back in half an hour. Don't stop stirring that soup!" She smiled, waved and left.

***

Callie didn't intend to stray very far. She only wanted to find the article about the Chicago heiress who had been courted by the author F. Scott Fitzgerald. Since her online search had come up empty, she decided to head straight to the *On the Bay* office. The article might help her to give her an idea of what Holly might have been working on.

The office was located just a few short blocks from Callie's Kitchen, so it was a pleasant walk. She figured that they had to have several years of past magazines stored somewhere, since the magazine was still published in print, and not digitally. She took a deep breath and relished the fresh air and bright sunshine. It felt good to be out of the kitchen, if even for just a short time.

In a stroke of luck, the tiny, cramped office of *On the Bay* was open.

"Hello," she called as she swung open the door, blinking as her eyes adjusted to the dimness. The office was filled with stacks of magazines. It was almost as if somebody had created a paper fortress.

"Hello! Be there in a sec." Callie's greeting was returned by a muffled voice from what sounded like a back room. Patiently, she waited. And waited. While she waited, she looked around the latest stack of magazines, flipping idly through and wondering if her Callie's Kitchen ad should be bigger in the next issue.

"Sorry about that." A man that looked to be in his late sixties with graying hair and glasses emerged from the back of the office. He wore a white shirt with rolled up sleeves and baggy khaki pants. "I was just organizing some files," he told her. "Or trying to. Now, what can I do for you?"

"Hi there. I hope I'm not interrupting anything, but I figured you could help me. I'm Callie Costas, the owner of Callie's Kitchen. I advertise with your magazine, but that's not why I'm here. I'm looking for an article, and I'm not sure of the issue where it appeared. It's about F. Scott Fitzgerald and an heiress from Chicago, who used to visit friends with a home in Crystal Bay."

"Ah yes," the man said. "I thought I recognized you. Jerry Anderson." He put out his hand and Callie shook it. "So, you're a Fitzgerald fan, are you? Fascinating figure. I'm partial to Midwest authors myself. He even used this part of the world as the setting for some of his stories."

"I'm interested in him, yes," she said. "Well, what I know of him." No need for Jerry to know that she was interested in him because of a recent murder.

Jerry Anderson nodded with enthusiasm. "So you'd like to read the article. That's not one we have online, I take it."

"I couldn't find it. I thought you'd have it here."

"Normally, I could put my hands on it immediately. But I'm doing inventory, and I think that article was written a while ago. I can't recall the exact issue. When you get to be my age, your memory can be, shall we say, selective." He smiled kindly at Callie. "In any case, it's a mess in here today. Do you have time to hunt around for it? I can let you poke through past issues."

Callie looked despairingly around the small office, which was stacked nearly to the ceiling in spots. "I appreciate the offer, but I have to get back to my shop. Right now I just don't have the time."

"Tell you what, then. I'll look for the issue, and if I find it, I'll drop it off at Callie's Kitchen. How does that sound?"

"Oh would you? Thank you! I really do need to be getting back."

"Anything for a fellow reader. People today spend too much dang time on their phones." He gave her a wink.

Twenty Two

When Callie got back to her shop, she waved to Piper and immediately went to check on Josh and the delicate soup.

The sight that greeted her could only be a bad omen. Josh was standing over the soup pot shaking his head and mumbling to himself. When he saw Callie, he banged the lid back on top.

"How's it going?" she asked him, walking over to the pot and lifting the lid. "Josh! It looks like scrambled eggs!" The eggs in the soup had curdled. It was ruined.

"I – uh, I don't know." Josh appeared genuinely puzzled. "I kept stirring, just like you said."

Callie looked down and noticed that the blue flame under the blue soup pot was so large that it looked like it was engulfing the bottom of the pot.

"I think I see the problem," Callie said, turning off the flame. "The heat was turned up way too high! No wonder the eggs scrambled."

"I did that," Josh admitted. "The soup didn't seem hot enough. I thought it wouldn't matter, once the eggs were mixed in."

"Unfortunately, it does matter. We'll have to start over." Callie was dismal at the waste of food. It was costly, too, but she didn't feel like telling Josh that right now.

"I'm sorry!" Josh pleaded. "I didn't mean to ruin the soup! Let me try again."

"I don't think so." Callie stood firm. She couldn't afford to waste any more expensive ingredients on another failed pot of soup. Josh looked crestfallen, so Callie cast about looking for something for him to do. "Why don't you cut up those cucumbers and chop that fresh dill for the *tzatziki*?" she suggested.

"OK, sure," Josh replied glumly. He went over the walk-in and started gathering the vegetables and herbs for the sauce.

Callie realized she agreed with Piper. Josh was a nice guy, but he wasn't Max. She was going to have to take more drastic measures, such as asking George for his kitchen help. Glancing at her St. Basil icon, she said a small prayer.

***

Callie wrestled with her conscience that night at home, but she found she had no choice but to replace Josh with George, for a short time, at least. Sugar instead of salt. Curdled soup. She didn't want to know what kitchen mishap would happen next.

Still, Josh was excellent with the customers and certainly seemed to be personable. The ladies at the Greek Fest had loved him. They were a tough crowd and difficult to please. Still...

She drank a glass of iced tea. She ate three cookies. Finally she realized she could put off her decision no longer. She had no choice but to scale down his Callie's Kitchen role. Was this what Allan Browne felt like when he gave an actor a less than stellar part?

After calling Josh to ask him if he would mind being *sous chef* and given the most basic kitchen tasks for the time being, he had reluctantly agreed, saying he needed the work. Then Callie phoned a delighted George to see if he could fill in with some kitchen help. He was happy to oblige. That task done, Callie finally was able to sleep.

As she rolled into work the next morning, Callie was surprised to see the shop was already open and filled with good cooking smells: honey, cinnamon, brown sugar and dark roast coffee. The scenario was so reminiscent of when Max worked for her that her heart leapt. Maybe Max had made a surprise return!

However, it was not Max, but George who greeted her when she entered her kitchen work room.

"Calliope! I got here early, so we can get an early start. Now, what else do you want me to do?" George looked dapper in a fresh blue and white Callie's Kitchen apron, his curly brown-grey hair smoothed down and his brown eyes crinkled at the corners from the huge grin on his face.

Arranged on the countertop was an assortment of ingredients, so many, that Callie suspected George had brought some of his own supplies. Smiling, she went over to George and hugged him tightly.

"Dad, I forgot that you still had a key to this place."

"Of course I do!" George huffed. "What if you have an emergency like today?"

"Hmm. Good point. Well, I'd love it if you'd make some *avgolemono*. We had a little mishap with it yesterday."

"You bet. I'll start right now." George started gathering eggs, lemons and chicken broth. "What happened?" he wanted to know.

"Josh did a good job of stirring, but he turned up the flame. The eggs scrambled, and the soup ended up curdled."

"No!" George hated a curdled *avgolemono*. "Callie, he's not Greek. It's not in his blood to make this soup. You can't be too angry at him."

"Oh, Dad, come on," Callie laughed. "Anyone can learn how to make the soup. It just takes practice. Max made it all the time, and it turned out very well."

"Between you and me, I think Max has some Greek blood he doesn't know about." George started slicing lemons and their sweet, citrusy fragrance filled with kitchen.

Callie decided to take advantage of George's early-bird tendencies and help herself to a cup of his rich coffee. George always made the coffee very strong, just the way she liked it.

Just as she was taking her first sip, she heard the bell ring over the front door of her shop. Piper greeted the customer and Callie went back to her coffee, but then she heard Piper say "Yes, he's here. Kathy, you can go right back."

Kathy poked her blonde head into the workroom. "Hello? It's Kathy. Can I come in?"

George set his wooden spoon down with a clatter and ushered Kathy into the room, offering her coffee and a place to sit. Callie took it upon herself to get the coffee and she sat down next to Kathy.

"I hope you don't mind my barging in like this," she began. "I just was on my way to the gym and I heard George was here so I thought I'd say hello."

"Good, good!" George answered. "I'm busy making soup for Callie, but can I get you something? Some *loukoumades* to go with your coffee?"

Kathy nodded and laughed. "Maybe just a few. I'll burn them off during my workout." Callie took in Kathy's slim-fitting workout pants and tank top.

"Kathy, you look great. Maybe I'll join you there someday." Callie didn't have the greatest luck sticking to workout routines.

"Oh, please do. I'd love the company." Kathy took a bite of her Greek doughnuts. "Delicious!" she pronounced. "I'll only stay a minute," she said to Callie. She scanned the workspace, which was littered with foodstuffs.

"Stay as long as you like," Callie said. A lightbulb went off over her head. She turned to Kathy. "I was wondering. Do you know who bought the house where Olivia's teacher was found?"

George *tsked-tsked*. "That is such a sad business."

Kathy stirred her coffee before answering. "I'd heard a couple from out of state. I didn't handle the transaction, of course. I don't have the specifics on the couple, only that they are new to the area."

"Hmm. You don't know who used to live there, do you?"

"That house hasn't had too many owners." George chimed in. "The people who lived there before had it for many years. Before that, I think the house was kept in the same family for at least a couple of generations. That's what they're saying at The Olympia, anyway."

"I believe George is right. If I hear anything more, I'll let you know." Kathy took a sip of coffee. "Things have been really busy in the real estate market ever since sales have picked up. For example, I wish I'd had The Harris House listing."

"I'll bet," Callie answered. "It must be worth a lot."

"Oh, it is. And the location is ideal. It does need work, though. The new owner got a good deal. But," Kathy leaned in conspiratorially. "I heard the new owner used up her life savings for the purchase!"

"No wonder she was complaining about the cost of the upkeep," Callie remarked. She felt for Lisa, since she'd done the same thing with Callie's Kitchen just a few years before. The scale was much smaller, but still, owning *any* size business was a daunting financial challenge.

"Callie, that's enough detective work for now. I have an idea that I know you will love. I'm going to teach Josh how to cook. But first, he needs to learn the basics. Nothing tricky, until he gets the basics." George nodded his head firmly as Callie started to interrupt. "I have the time, and you don't. You give us some dishes to make, and he will learn to make them. I promise!"

Kathy and Callie exchanged a look.

"Time for me to go," Kathy remarked and stood up, resplendent in her Lycra exercise attire. Obviously, she didn't want to witness any father/daughter fireworks regarding work-related matters.

"Thanks for the coffee and treats!" She gave George a kiss on the cheek and waved to Callie. "See you both soon."

Kathy looked at George and gave him a wink. "Be good," she said.

***

"No, Josh. That's not nearly enough butter," George's voice interrupted her thoughts.

"What? I thought too much will make it soggy."

"No, no. The butter will make it crisp and flavorful. It only looks soggy now. Just wait until we bake it."

Callie looked up in time to see Josh roll his eyes, but George didn't notice. He was already busy melting more butter for the phyllo dough *pites* he was making with Josh. Josh froze when Callie saw him make a face and immediately put his head down, clearly trying to appear fascinated with melting butter.

She couldn't blame Josh entirely for his impatience. Earlier that day, George had attempted to rearrange Callie's entire walk-in refrigerator, and he argued with her about several menu items she'd planned for the week.

Rotating her head to get the crick out of her neck, Callie took charge. "Hey guys. When you're done with that, I think you can take a break. Dad, you've helped so much today, and you were here so early, you must be tired. I think you're work day is over. I can't thank you enough," she repeated as George started to protest.

She went over to him and gave him a kiss on the cheek. "Josh learned a lot from you today." Josh smiled sheepishly at this remark but thankfully didn't say a word. "Maybe you can come back later in the week," she told her father.

George's smile lit up his craggy face. "I'd love to. I'll make a list of all the things that need improvement here. This is a wonderful chance to help you get organized, Calliope." He kissed her back, on both cheeks.

Grinning, he patted Josh on the back. "You'll learn, young fella. Don't give up." He surrendered his apron and left. Callie could tell he was tired, but he also looked like a man who wanted to take control of a new kitchen. She sighed. She loved George, but there was no way he was taking over her kitchen. That wouldn't be good for anyone.

The rest of the day inched by, with Josh relegated to chopping vegetables and filling display cases. It was still helpful to have him do that, but Callie realized she needed a permanent expert in the kitchen. Piper wasn't it, and she wasn't available to work full-time anyway.

As Callie shut herself into the workroom to finish prepping and cooking dishes for the next several days, she was almost happy to be alone in the kitchen. As always, cooking restored her equilibrium and gave her time to think about the last few days.

There seemed to be too many loose ends and unanswered questions related to Holly's untimely murder. Her gut told her that somebody affiliated with the murder mystery night had something to do with Holly's death. Lisa Linley, Allan Browne and Tammy Heckstrom were all potential suspects. Motive still unknown. In fact, the entire theater troupe was suspect, especially after Tammy's run-in with a muscle relaxant.

What if Tammy had done that herself in an attempt to throw suspicion off of her? Callie shuddered at the thought of Tammy being so diabolical, but right now, she didn't feel like she could rule anyone, or anything, out.

They were many other "players," to use theater-speak, who may also be involved: Hugh, Raine, Phil, Tammy's boyfriend, and even April Manning, who worked with Hugh. Not to mention, Holly's fellow grad students, and even her fellow teachers. What about parents of Holly's students? Could it be that Hugh wasn't the only parent that Holly had dated? Maybe she had run afoul of someone that Callie didn't even know about.

And then there was the hooded figure that she and Max had seen running across the lawn of the abandoned home where Holly was killed. Who *was* that?

Callie finished preparing that evening's pita wraps and carefully replaced them in the walk-in to stay fresh until she put them out later that afternoon.

She knew one thing. She was going to re-visit The Harris House. Lisa Linley was hiding something. *What?*

"Callie." Piper's voice nudged her out of her thoughts. "I've been calling you for five minutes. Some guy just delivered this envelope to you."

"Huh? Oh, OK. Thanks." Callie took the envelope. "What did he say?"

"Just to tell you that this was what you've been looking for." Piper shrugged. "I'd better get back out there. We're starting to get busy again."

"Fine, I'll join you in a minute." Piper nodded and rushed back to the front of the shop. Could this be a delivery from Jerry Anderson? If so, it was quick. Callie promised herself she'd reward him with *koularakia* if that was the case.

A prickly feeling descended over Callie as she opened the plain brown envelope. A glossy copy of *On the Bay*, dated 2014, slid out. Callie could see a neon-yellow sticky note, and she quickly flipped open the magazine to the indicated page. "*Lady of the Lake: F. Scott Fitzgerald and His Crystal Bay Muse*" was the flowery title. The byline made Callie catch her breath.

The author of the piece was none other than Allan Browne.

Twenty Three

llan Browne. Callie had been sure it had been one of the graduate students who'd penned the article, maybe even Holly. However, it did make a strange sort of sense that Allan Browne would have written the article. He certainly seemed to be interested in the arts and in origins of things, if his commentary about "Thespis" was any indication.

Quickly, she skimmed the article while simultaneously making sure that her soup didn't curdle.

The article was interesting, especially for people who liked to know about the "real lives" of writers. "Genevieve" had been a wealthy Chicago beauty who had spent a fair amount of time in Crystal Bay. Apparently, Fitzgerald was so taken with her, that he used her as the inspiration for some of his characters. Her family was based in Chicago and her father was some type of business magnate.

Eventually, Genevieve married into a family who had owned one of the most stunning homes of its day. The name of the family was Linley.

Linley! Callie sat down on a stool, deep in thought. Were these Linleys any relation to Lisa? She would be sure to find out. Why didn't she inherit the home? If she had any connection, she'd certainly never mentioned it. There had to be a reason.

The other running theme throughout this entire murder investigation, besides the acting troupe, seemed to be F. Scott Fitzgerald and his mysterious muse. Holly had clearly been onto something with regard to this theme.

Putting the magazine aside, Callie was filled with a burning curiosity. Besides Lisa Linley, there was Allan Browne and the mysterious money-making scheme alluded to by Josh, but also what the graduate students and teachers at Crystal Bay College might know about Holly's research.

Isn't your boyfriend supposed to be investigating? Max's admonishment the night they'd traversed the crime scene rang in her head. Yes, of course, and she was sure he was doing a fine job. However, people clammed up around police. Hadn't she witnessed that with Lisa Linley, the night that she and Sands had enjoyed their impromptu date at The Harris House?

Now all she needed was a reason to go barging into Crystal Bay College, but of course, she already had the perfect excuse.

Food.

***

"Hi, Dad. Can you do me a favor? I have to drop off some marketing materials and make a few other stops. If your schedule allows, can you spend just an hour or two at Callie's Kitchen? I just need someone who knows the food inside and out while I'm gone." Callie fidgeted as she gripped her cell phone to her ear. She didn't want George to attempt a kitchen takeover but desperate times called for desperate measures.

"Hello, *hrisi mou*! Let me check." She heard George flipping pages, probably in his old-fashioned paper calendar. Truth be told, Callie preferred an old-fashioned paper calendar herself, at times.

"Good news, Calliope! I can help today. I'll just ask Gus to stay a little longer. You know I like to be at my place of business, but if you need me, I'm there. That's what I've always taught you. It's good that you're marketing yourself, though. Where are you going?"

"Here and there. It shouldn't take too long," Callie said, determined to stay vague. No need for anyone to know what she was up to. "Dad, can you be here in half an hour? Josh and Piper will be here, but I've instructed Josh to simply act as *sous chef* for the time being. He won't be creating anything from scratch."

"Take your time, Calliope dear. I can teach Josh to make something to add to his repertoire. He seemed to really enjoy it last time!"

Callie smiled to herself. "If you have time, otherwise, just hold down the fort. I'll make a list of all the foods I'm working on. You could probably finish these dishes with your eyes closed."

"All right. See you soon!" George sounded elated, and Callie felt a twinge of guilt. He clearly loved feeling needed by her. In her zest for creating her own life and business, had she shut him out too much?

Never mind. He was welcome with open arms today. She only hoped he would be so busy he wouldn't have time to discuss or attempt to implement any more of his "improvements" to Callie's Kitchen. Right now, the number one improvement was getting another cook in the kitchen.

George fairly danced into Callie's Kitchen at his appointed time. Josh seemed wary of George at first, and he looked worried when George told him he hoped there was time for another cooking lesson.

"Calliope, your shop has a nice 'buzz.' Lots of customers out front!" George beamed. Today he wore a blue polo shirt with The Olympia logo on the chest pocket and ironed khakis. George hated to iron and Callie wondered if perhaps his new girlfriend, Kathy, had taken on that task. They certainly seemed inseparable nowadays.

"Yes, it does. I'm glad about that too." She leaned forward and whispered to her father. "Lots of people have asked where Max went. I haven't broken the news yet to the regulars. I guess I'm hoping he'll still come back."

George looked sympathetic. "I understand. But put this young fella in front of the register for a while. I hear the ladies at the Greek Fest called him *'Petharos.'* "

Callie had to laugh. "That they did. Thanks again, Dad. I'll be back soon."

As she was leaving, she heard George say, "Josh. You're not chopping those cucumbers the right way. Here, let me show you." *Oh, boy.* Quickly, she left before she would be compelled to change her mind and stay.

As Callie made the scenic drive to Crystal Bay College, she hoped Josh wouldn't take offense to George's "coaching" techniques. Even though he wasn't as experienced in the kitchen as she'd like, she realized that she was coming to rely on his help. And with so many more customers flowing through the doors of her shop, she didn't really have a choice.

The water on the bay glistened invitingly in the sunlight. Fleetingly, Callie realized that she'd had hardly any time to enjoy the warm summer weather. Last winter, Sands had offered a warm weather vacation, but neither of them had the time. Would they ever?

These sorts of romantic ruminations would have to wait for the time being. Callie was soon cruising down the long, tree-lined drive that led to Crystal Bay College. A deer poked its head out of the woods before it bounded back into the greenery. Callie slowed down. When you saw one deer, there were usually more. However, they must be too shy today. No friends joined the beautiful creature, so she kept going until she reached the parking lot.

Crystal Bay College had a small campus but it boasted a gorgeous view of the water. The well-preserved, early twentieth century buildings were designed in classical style that somehow blended beautifully with the more rustic surroundings. The buildings were grouped in a semi-circle around the grounds of the campus. With school out for summer, there was ample parking. Callie found a spot close to the campus welcome center. She collected food samples and marketing materials and exited the car slowly, careful not to drop anything.

Scanning the campus, she inhaled deeply. What a clear, beautiful day! Puffy white clouds floated across the sky, and she could see a few children playing on the small beach at the water's edge. Boats and jet-skis dotted the choppy, white-capped waves. Across the water, the trees dotted the shoreline in a symphony of green not apparent at any other time of the year.

It was a picture-perfect scene, and Callie dearly wished she could sit at the end of the pier and catch a few rays instead of trying to dig up facts about people who were deceased: Holly, Fitzgerald and his Crystal Bay girlfriend.

Finally dragging her gaze from the water, Callie approached the campus welcome center, one of the more modern-looking structures on campus. In fact, it looked brand-new. Opening the door, Callie smelled the undeniable scent found in a brand new building: new wood, new carpet, new paint.

A young man sat behind the desk, wearing a white oxford shirt with a Crystal Bay College insignia. He was exceedingly clean cut with rosy cheeks that made him look like a much younger man or like someone who was permanently embarrassed. He gave Callie a welcoming smile.

"Welcome to Crystal Bay College. I'm Brian, one of the reps. What can I do for you today?"

Callie put on her most charming smile. "Hello, there. I'm Callie Costas, the owner of Callie's Kitchen here in Crystal Bay. I wondered if I could leave some of my marketing materials here. I have many student customers and I'd love to get some more. Ready-made Greek meals and baked goods are my specialty, but I also carry many classic American dishes." She held up her brochures and business cards.

The young man smiled again. "I would have to ask the dean if you can leave these things here, but it sounds good to me. I love Greek food!"

"Wonderful. Well, I'll tell you what. Let me leave a couple of things for you just in case. I can always come back with more. And here are some complimentary things for you to try." She handed him a white box that she'd filled with *spanakopita* triangles, as well as another box she'd filled with a couple of slices of her customer-favorite cherry pie. "Here are two pies for you: One is a savory Greek *pita* and the other is cherry pie. Feel free to share with your co-workers."

The young man's cheeks flushed an even deeper crimson. "Wow. Thanks. We're always starving!" He accepted the white boxes eagerly and placed them gently behind the counter.

Callie smiled. "Now let me ask you one more thing. Which way to the college advisory building? I was hoping to speak to one of the English graduate advisors."

"I'm sorry. Most of them are on vacation. Only a few graduate students are still on campus, finishing up research or what have you."

Uh-oh. Callie recovered quickly. "All right. Then I'll just drop off some off my brochures in the office and I'll be on my way."

Brian pulled a map out from behind the counter. Taking a pen, he circled the building closest to the water. "This is it. I'm not sure if it's open, though. Like I said, most of the advisors are gone, though a few do keep hours now and then in the summer. You can always leave whatever it is at the front desk. The graduate students and advisors also have mail boxes." Brian shrugged.

She thanked him and left, smiling and waving as she left the office. Whew. She was in. Now, it was onto the next part of her admittedly flimsy plan. Hopefully, she wouldn't run into Mrs. DeWitt or anyone else she knew.

Holding the map firmly in hand, Callie walked down the curving path until she found the brown-shingled building that Brian had pointed out to her.

Callie tried the front door. It was locked, but the lights were on. Callie peered through the window and saw a man walking through the hallway. After a beat, she realized it was Phil, Tammy Heckstrom's boyfriend. Excitedly she knocked on the window, and he peered at her more closely. She motioned to him to come to the door.

Phil looked right and left, but then he appeared to sigh as he walked over to Callie. He opened the door and stared at her.

"The office is closed for lunch. I'm about to leave. You should check in at the campus welcome area."

"Phil, it's me. Callie Costas. Don't you remember me?"

Finally, Phil's face relaxed. "I'm sorry. It was so dark the other night when we met. And I was still so worried about Tammy, I didn't recognize you at first. What are you doing here?"

"I wanted to drop off something for one of the advisors."

"I can do it," Phil offered.

"That's OK," Callie said, thinking quickly. "Between you and me, I'd love to have a quick chat with one of them, or even the office secretary. Maybe some of the departments would like me to provide some of the food for some of the smaller student events this year."

"That would be great, actually. The food is usually pretty awful. People don't usually get back until around one, though. Is anyone expecting you?"

"Not exactly." Callie smiled sheepishly. "Sometimes my, uh, marketing attempts work better if they're unexpected."

Phil nodded appreciatively. "Gotcha. Well, most people return around one."

Callie looked at her watch. "It's 12:30. Is it all right if I come in and wait?"

"I don't see why not," Phil said, stepping aside to let Callie enter the building.

"I already checked in at the main campus office," she offered.

"Well, that's fine, then. Is there anything else? I've got to run."

"I'd like to leave some marketing flyers. Brian said the advisors and grad students have mail boxes. Can you show me where they are?" Callie figured it was a good idea to look like she had a legitimate reason to be in the building and Phil, a grad student, was the perfect cover in case anyone else remained.

Phil nodded and motioned to her. "Follow me."

He led her past a short hallway, with offices on both sides. Some of the offices were open, with the lights on, but many of the offices were closed, with only darkness showing through the small windows at the top. Phil gestured to a wall with several cubbies that had envelopes and pieces of paper sticking out of them.

"Do you have many people on campus right now?" she asked.

"There are always people around. Some of them might be in here just cleaning out their offices before the coming year and a few of us are working on our research all summer long. It really just depends on the person."

"Phil, who was Holly Tennyson's advisor? The graduate advisors have offices in here, right?"

"Yes." He stopped walking and gave her a quizzical look. "Why do you need to know that?"

Callie hemmed and hawed a bit before answering. "I just wanted to offer my condolences. I know she was a very promising graduate student."

Phil stared at her. "I know what you mean. You found her, didn't you? Holly?" Callie didn't like the way Phil was looking at her.

"Yes, I did." There was an uncomfortable silence.

"That's what Tammy said. Anyway, Tammy and Holly had the same advisor. His name is Keith Dyson." Friendly Phil had suddenly turned stone-faced.

Suddenly, Callie felt that it would be a good idea if she was no longer in a darkened, deserted hallway with Phil.

"Thanks, Phil," she said, following him back to the lobby. "I'll just wait here." She sat down, doing her best to look innocent.

Phil walked to the door and turned the knob, but then he stopped and faced Callie. "We all feel terrible about Holly, you know."

"Yes, I'm sure," Callie answered. Phil nodded once and finally left.

Callie exhaled loudly. *Way to go.* Phil knew something was up, he just didn't know what. Giving him a minute to leave the area, Callie ran to the door. She saw Phil striding up the hill and didn't relax until she saw him get in his car.

"Anybody here?" she called out but all she heard was the low hum of office machinery. She'd have to do her snooping quickly and before Mrs. DeWitt busted her.

Callie scurried down the hallway and tried the door for Keith Dyson. Of course it was locked.

"Darn." She exhaled with a frustrated whoosh. Then she remembered the cubbies.

The cubbies didn't have names on them, but they were numbered. Maybe by office number? She raced back down to Dyson's office, which was marked not just with his name plate, but with the number 204.

"204, 204," she repeated to herself. Looking right and left to make sure she was unobserved, she grabbed the envelopes out of his cubby.

Rapidly, she flipped through his mail. The Modern Language Association had sent him something. He also had what looked like a fundraising letter from The University of Minnesota. Maybe that's where he'd gotten his advanced degrees. Then there was a flyer from a pizza place on the water. A couple more handwritten envelopes followed, but unfortunately, no return addresses. Letters from students?

All of the envelopes were unopened and Callie fairly itched to rip them apart, but she restrained herself. Tampering with the mail was a federal offense and she had no idea what she expected to find, in any case.

She wondered if she could find a way into Holly's advisor's office, but realized that wouldn't work. Time was running out. It was already 12:50 and people would be returning from lunch any minute.

Not willing to call her visit to the college a bust-out just yet, she rummaged as quickly as she could through the rest of the cubbies. Since it was summertime, the cubbies didn't offer much of interest: junk mail, educational brochures and the like.

Callie was tempted to call the whole thing off. Tossing her tangled waves out of her face, she dug into one of the last cubbies and pulled out what looked like a Xeroxed article.

Her heart pounding, she saw that it was the Fitzgerald article penned by Allan Browne. A sticky note on the first page read: "I thought you should see this."

That was it. No name, no signature.

Twenty Four

Callie replaced all of the papers back into the cubby and zoomed to the front of the building. She felt chilled and it wasn't from the overactive air-conditioning blasting through the office. Why did people want to be so cold in the summer? It was cold enough in Crystal Bay during the winter months. Callie shivered and looked around.

She was still alone. Apparently, summer was the time for a leisurely lunch hour. Head down, she nearly ran out the door, but froze when she spotted Mrs. DeWitt making her way down the hill. She looked crisp and cool in a pink linen shirtdress and she was headed in the direction of the advisory office.

Callie raised her eyes heavenward. She really didn't want to run into her right now. She'd wonder what Callie was doing there and rightly so. Anyway, she'd fibbed enough for one day.

The office had a back door next to a large picture window that framed a picturesque view of the water. Callie scurried outside, but all too late realized she'd better hurry if she didn't want to be seen, in case Mrs. DeWitt was headed for the graduate advisors' offices.

Walking as fast as she could, she quickened her pace even more as a haven beckoned: the waterfront walking path, partially obscured by a thickly wooded area. In the hot sun, the trees provided delightfully cool shade. The tall pines and maples would also provide enough cover for her to escape the notice of anyone inside the graduate advisors' office.

Callie race-walked over to the path and kept walking until the tall shoreline trees shielded her from office onlookers.

When she was a safe distance away, she peeked out from behind an oak tree. The campus had regained its deserted look, save for the children splashing at the beach. Taking the long way around, Callie managed to avoid most of the campus offices before darting back across the parking lot to her car.

***

It had felt like forever, but Callie was pleased to learn that she'd been away from her shop for less than an hour. Smiling, she walked through the door, pleased to see a happy crowd. Several customers were perusing her ready-made meal display cases and others seated at tables and enjoying a salad or piece of *spanakopita*.

Piper had a harried look when Callie approached. Callie's smile faded. "They've been at it the whole time you've been gone," she whispered. On closer inspection, Piper appeared near tears.

"What are you talking about?"

Loud arguing suddenly erupted from the back room, and Callie gasped. "That?" she asked.

"Yes. That. Arguing. I can't listen to any more! I mean, is there really a right way or a wrong way to cut vegetables?"

"Sorry." Callie's heart sank. George meant well, but... "I'll take care of it," she told Piper, sounding more confident than she felt.

"Thank you," Piper said in a beleaguered tone, but she smiled brightly as a customer approached.

Telling herself to stay calm, Callie went to the kitchen to see what was what. Josh, looking flushed, was chopping onions, but George was standing over him, shaking his head. "No, not like that. I need a fine dice. Like this." Grabbing an onion, George started chopping rapidly, onion dice flying out everywhere.

"So, how's it going?" Callie asked through clenched teeth.

Josh just looked at her and didn't say anything. George looked up from his onions, seemingly unfazed.

"It's going fine! I've already started several dishes for you, and now I'm teaching Josh how to chop. If you chop vegetables too big, you might as well feed them to a horse or donkey, not a human. He's getting the hang of it."

"No, that's just what I'm not getting," Josh said. To Callie's horror, he tore off his apron and threw it on the counter. "I don't think I'm cut out for cooking after all."

"No pun intended?" Callie tried to make a joke but it fell flat. "Listen, Josh, I think with a little practice, you'll be a great asset in the kitchen. I appreciate all you've done already."

"Thanks, Callie." Josh looked at George. "But I think this might be a case of too many cooks in the kitchen. And I don't think I'm the right one."

He walked over to Callie and shook her hand. "Thanks for the opportunity. I do appreciate it. If you think you need me on my own, just let me know." He nodded to George. "Goodbye, George. I'll be out of your hair now."

"Now, Josh, everyone has to learn..." George protested, to no avail. Josh was already gone.

Callie stood there, slowly registering that she was now the only full-time cook in her kitchen.

"Calliope, I'm sorry!" George implored her, hands outstretched. "I only wanted to show him so that he could be a help to you. I didn't mean for him to leave."

"Dad, I know! I know. But you come on a little strong at times, and this is one of those times where it turned out to be too much." She felt overwhelmed, but she refused to cry. Why, oh why had she left the two of them together? She should have known.

"Callie, I'll make this up to you. I promise I will! Let me help you until you find another cook."

Callie felt torn between anger at her father, love for him and simple desperation about needing someone to help her cook. She walked over to her father and took him by the hand. "Dad, I would love you to help. On one condition, though. In your kitchen, you do things your way. But here, it's my way. That's the only way this will work. Remember, you always taught me to be in control of my own kitchen. Well, that's what I'm going to have to do."

George looked down at the diced onions, then back at her. "Calliope Costas...'" he began.

"Yes?" Callie braced herself for yet another argument.

"You're absolutely right. Your kitchen...your rules."

***

In the wee hours of a sleepless night, Callie had made a decision. There was someone she had to see, and it couldn't wait any longer. As Callie made an early morning drive the next day, to say that she had "butterflies" in her stomach was a misnomer. At this point, it felt more like pterodactyls.

Olivia was staying with Hugh, so Callie was free to drive without making child care provisions. In addition, George had agreed to open Callie's Kitchen for her. In fact, he'd been overly solicitous, probably in his eagerness to make up for the disaster with Josh. George had even promised to bring some of his signature *baklava* from The Olympia as a special treat for her customers.

First things first. If she was terminally short-staffed, she wouldn't be able to keep things going at Callie's Kitchen. Hence, her crack-of-dawn drive. Earlier, really. It wasn't officially dawn until the sun came out.

The sky was fading from inky black to dark blue when Callie finally arrived at her destination, about an hour outside of Crystal Bay. She parked her car in front of a tall, weathered-looking red barn, got out and took a look around. Callie was glad she'd worn her oldest sneakers. No telling what you might step in on a farm.

Callie could hear the hum of machinery coming from one of the outbuildings. As she looked more closely, she could see a single light burning in one of the windows. Gathering her courage, she headed towards the building.

Sure enough, Max was inside, overseeing the milking of his father's cows. It was a tiny dairy farm, but Callie knew from Max that it required a lot of work. No wonder his father had wanted him home.

Max must have heard her walking towards him because he spun around, startled.

"Callie! What are you doing here?" His face was scruffy with beard outgrowth, and he looked more haggard than the last time she'd seen him.

"I'm sorry to sneak up on you like this, but I thought what I have to ask you required an in-person meeting."

Max stepped forward and hugged Callie. "I'm glad to see you. And there's nobody here right now except me and the cows. Come on." He led her to a pair of stools. Nearby, a black and white cow with huge brown eyes watched them placidly.

"What's up? Is everything all right? I mean, something must be wrong or you wouldn't be here."

"I'm fine, Max. I'll tell you why I'm here in a minute. How's your Dad?"

"He's doing better. Still can't move around much, though, so he's been as grouchy as a bear rousted out of hibernation. My mom is great, though. She just laughs at him when he acts up." He half-smiled. "I wish I could follow her example."

"I'm glad to hear he's doing better. Max," Callie hesitated. "I was wondering if there's any possible way you can help out at Callie's Kitchen, just until I can find somebody else. Even a few hours a week would help. You could set your own hours."

Max was silent a minute, thinking. "Josh didn't work out, huh?"

"He probably would have, eventually. It's just that, well, George kind of took charge of my kitchen, and I think Josh got the wrong idea. He left."

"Oh, boy. That does put you in a tough position. I'm sorry, Callie." Max shook his head.

"I know you're busy here, but I thought that maybe you could see your way clear to helping out even two or three days a week? Just until I find someone."

"Yeah, Piper said things were rough, but I thought she might be exaggerating. Now I see she wasn't." Max shifted on the stool.

"Max, I wouldn't ask but I'm really stuck. You know my business and you know my food. What do you think?"

"I don't know. My life has become surreal. Look at this place!" He opened his arms wide as if to include the entire dairy barn. "I'm hanging out with cows at five in the morning instead of getting ready to bake and greet customers. I've hardly seen any humans besides my parents since I came out here. At the end of the day, I'm so tired I can't even make it to Piper's to see her. If that keeps up, she'll probably dump me." He sighed. "I wouldn't blame her."

"Max..."

"I know what you're going to say. Don't feel sorry for me. I don't mean to complain. This life would be perfect for some people. It's a fine way to make a living, and I do love the animals." He nodded at the cow, and she blinked her long eyelashes at him. "I miss working with food. Plus, I miss feeding people, dealing with the customers, the whole thing. I miss Callie's Kitchen." He smiled. "But I'm so busy here. I just don't think I can do it." When he saw Callie's face, he added "Well. I'll think about it."

"Max, we miss you, too. All of us, the customers included. I understand what you're saying and I shouldn't have come. I didn't mean to put you on the spot."

Max chuckled softly. "Well, you are one for getting to the root of a problem. Any more sleuthing regarding Holly Tennyson's murder?"

Callie blushed. "A little bit. Well, maybe more than a little. But look, I should get going." She stood up. "I have to get to work."

"Don't go just yet. Come have a cup of coffee at least, for the ride home. I can leave the girls here for a few minutes. Let me finish up a few things, and we'll go in the house. I think my mom even made some zucchini bread. It's even made with Greek yogurt."

"Sold."

Max finished making his rounds of the milking machines and made sure each cow had enough water before securing the barn and leading Callie back to the large, white-washed frame house located at the edge of the property. Max wiped off his boots and took them off before entering the sunny kitchen, which was full of good cooking smells. Callie took her sneakers off, too, just to be on the safe side.

The homey scents of coffee, bacon and cinnamon floated through the air. Entering the kitchen behind Max, Callie was startled to see an older man already seated at the kitchen table. "Hey, Dad," Max said. "This is Callie Costas." Max cleared his throat.

Max's father was sitting with a mug of coffee in front of him and what looked like the remains of scrambled eggs and bacon. He looked up in surprise, but then smiled kindly at her, and Callie could see traces of Max's features. "Another one?" he asked, looking at his son and slowly shaking his head.

Another one? Were women visiting Max on a regular basis at the farm? Oh, dear. Did this man think she was interested in his son *romantically?*

"Dad, not now. Please," Max said through clenched teeth.

"It's nice to meet you Mr. Evans," she said, extending her hand in the hopes of setting him straight. "I'm Max's boss. Former boss, that is." Max gave her a grateful look.

"Call me Henry," Max's father said, shaking her hand with a firm grip. "Nice to meet you too, after all this time. What brings you out here?"

Callie and Max looked at each other. "I was just checking on Max," Callie finally spoke after an awkward silence. "You know, to see if he needed anything."

"Is that so?" Henry took a bite of toast. "Well, that's nice. He's been a big help." He beamed at his son. "Couldn't do it without him."

The tips of Max's ears reddened. "Thanks, Dad. Uh, Callie, how about that coffee?"

While they were fixing their coffees, a tall woman with short blonde hair and pale blue eyes walked into the room. "I thought I heard voices in here. You must be Callie."

Max's mother. She wore a t-shirt and shorts with an incongruous flowery apron over them. Her youthful appearance was enhanced by a spray of freckles over her nose.

"Rose Evans." She extended her hand to Callie. "I was just baking some more of that zucchini bread that Henry here likes so much." She said, nodding at the oven. "You know how it is with zucchini in the garden. There's always so much and you just need to use it up."

"Yes, this is Callie."

Callie remembered Max saying his parents were so busy on their farm that they rarely made it to town, much less her shop. She wondered if there were other reasons they hadn't visited their son at his former workplace. It was intriguing to finally meet them and get a peek inside of Max's life.

Max was hiding behind his coffee mug, making Callie wish once again that she hadn't shown up out of the blue. However, Mrs. Evans was smiling warmly at her, as if it were commonplace to have a strange woman in her kitchen first thing in the morning.

Max put down his mug and addressed his mother. "Callie came out to check on me, and see how I'm doing. I'm giving her a cup of coffee before she heads back to work."

"Well, now isn't that sweet of you. Max sure loves Callie's Kitchen. In fact, he gave me a tip to use the Greek yogurt in this zucchini bread, and it makes it just so good! Max is such a wonderful cook, and he said he's learned so much working for you."

Max glanced at his father nervously as if he were worried about his mother's enthusiastic words offending him.

"Great, Mom. Thanks. Uh, Callie, here's your coffee. Milk and sugar are on the table."

The quartet sat in silence for a few minutes, the only conversation arising when Callie complimented Rose on the texture and flavor of the zucchini bread.

"So Callie, Max tells me you're involved in a murder," Rose said and immediately turned pink. "That didn't come out right, did it?" She gave a self-deprecating smile and Callie smiled back. She liked Max's mother more by the minute.

"It's all right," Callie reassured her, looking at the clock. It was later than she'd thought. "I found the body of a teacher. Holly Tennyson. She was my daughter's teacher, in fact. I've taken an interest in the case because of the personal connection."

"Oh my goodness. That's just horrible. Where did you find her?" Rose put a hand over her mouth in shock.

"At one of those Gilded Age Homes on the bay. I was meeting someone there. It was supposed to be renovated by a firm that employs my ex-husband. You know the type of house I'm talking about. They're on the mansion boat tours. This particular house could be an absolute beauty, but it had been abandoned for a long time." She hesitated. "I heard that it once belonged to a family named 'Linley.' There's a Linley currently running The Harris House but I haven't had a chance to ask her about any connection."

"Henry." Rose turned to her husband. "If it's the house that I'm thinking of, I think I know it. And so do you. It had some sort of scandal associated with it, didn't it?"

Max's father took another sip of coffee and shifted in his chair. He grimaced. "Sorry, hip's acting up again." He swallowed a pill and continued. "I think that house was owned a long, long time ago by a Chicago family. I guess it was the Linleys. Don't know about a scandal, but I think the son may have married a young woman who had some type of affiliation with the 1920s."

"Yes," Callie answered casually. "That's what I heard, too."

Rose frowned and tapped her fingers on the table. "Yes, but I'm thinking of a different thing. More recent." She turned to Callie. "You see, the Linleys were very wealthy, but they didn't get along. We went to school with some of the family," she said, nodding at her husband. "There was some kind of battle about a will and who would inherit the mansion."

"I hadn't heard that," Callie replied, stunned.

"It was a shame. The family ended up losing the house and it went through a series of owners. I always felt bad about it. Those types of homes should stay in the family. I'm sure they never wanted to give it up."

Twenty Five

Callie gulped. "So you're sure this is the Linley family?" She did a little math. "Did the Linley's you know have any children?"

Max's mother frowned. "Yes. I think just one, though I'm not certain of that."

"Lisa," Hank Evans said decisively. "They had a daughter named Lisa."

"Are you sure?" Callie held her breath.

"Sure I am!" Hank said with a low chuckle. "Pain meds haven't kicked in yet. Anyway, the name stuck with me for some reason."

Callie felt as if every nerve was humming like an electrical wire. Lisa Linley really did have a tie to the house! Was this why she had come back to Crystal Bay? Had Holly somehow stood in the way of that?

And what about Allan Browne? Had he been involved, too?

It was too much information to process all at once. She'd analyze it to death later. In the meantime, George was at her shop and she needed to get over there.

"Would you look at the time," Callie said. "I really appreciate the food and hospitality this morning, but Callie's Kitchen calls. I've got to go." She stood up, brushing crumbs off her lap. "Delicious bread. Maybe you'll give me the recipe someday."

"Why certainly, hon. You can have it right now." She went to her recipe file, and Callie took a picture of the card with her phone.

"The miracles of the modern world," Rose quipped, and Callie nodded and smiled, barely hearing her. Her mind was racing.

Max walked her to the door. "You OK, there boss? You don't mind if I still call you boss?"

"No, not at all. And I'm fine. I just have to get back." She gave Max a quick hug. "Your parents may have just given me an important piece of the puzzle regarding Holly's murder."

"Really?" Max was aghast. "What do you mean?"

"I'll tell you when I've had a chance to check out a few things. Please keep in touch, all right? And let me know if you can help out."

"Will do, Callie. It was real good to see you. Give everybody my regards and tell Piper I'll be sure to see her soon." He cocked his head at her. "One more thing: be careful."

Max waved at the car as Callie exited down the long driveway. Despite her preoccupation, Callie couldn't help noticing he kept standing there, watching the car until she couldn't see him anymore.

***

"Piper, how's it going?" Callie asked briskly when she returned. She was determined to visit The Harris House and Lisa Linley, but unfortunately, the kitchen needed her attention first.

"He's back there, cooking up a storm. Everybody loved his *baklava*."

"Good," Callie said. "By the way, I saw Max this morning. That's why I'm late."

"You did!" Piper's eyes lit up like a Christmas tree. "What were you doing out there?"

"Trying to get him to come back to Callie's Kitchen, I'm afraid. I feel guilty about going to his parents' farm. It's obvious that his dad is still in a lot of pain."

"Did he say he'd come back?" Piper asked eagerly.

"He didn't." Piper's smile faded. "But he did say he'd think about it," Callie added.

"That's a start," Piper said, brightening.

Callie yawned. Her early morning journey had been emotionally tiring. "We'll see what happens. In the meantime, thanks for your hard work, Piper. I'm going to check on George."

When Callie entered the kitchen workspace, George had his head down, chopping vegetables. She had no doubt that he was chopping them the *right* way.

"How are things, Dad?"

"Excellent." George was flushed with heat or happiness at being needed, Callie couldn't tell which one. "I've made *yemista* for you. Greek stuffed peppers, one of Callie's favorites. Also," George was saying, "my *avgolemono* is perfection."

Callie went over to him and put her arm around him, giving him a squeeze. "Thanks, Dad. I knew I could count on you." She felt tears start. She was having so many feelings: gratitude that her father was helping her, sadness at how much she hated leaving Max behind, and an overwhelmed feeling about her new insight into Lisa Linley and her family.

"Calliope! Tears? What is this?"

"It's nothing, Dad. Really. Thanks again. I'm just overtired."

George looked at her evenly. "In that case, there's lots of coffee. Go have some."

Callie knew the jumpy feeling in her stomach would only be worsened by coffee. "I'll take an ice water instead," she said, grabbing a bottle from the fridge.

Work was staring her in the face, but Callie couldn't keep still. She wanted to give Sands a call and ask if he'd heard anything about the Linley family and their tie to the murder scene. She was just about to head to the alley behind Callie's Kitchen for privacy when the phone rang.

"Callie!" called Piper from the front of the shop.

Sighing, Callie picked up and said a weary hello.

"Thank goodness you're there!" It was Mrs. DeWitt. "I need a favor. And I do realize you've done quite a few for me lately. But this could be big for you. They're doing a feature in this week's Crystal Bay Courier about the restaurants who've been contributing to *Beats on the Bay*. I told them all about you, and they want to do a feature on your summer pies! Isn't that wonderful?"

"When?" Callie asked, her heart in her throat.

"Can you have the pies ready to be photographed by tomorrow? I know that it's short notice. But think of the exposure!"

Callie hung her head, but then she looked over at George, humming away as he chopped lettuce and spinach. He'd help her. Anyway, after all she'd been through, what were a few pies?

"I'll do it," Callie said. "I'd like a chance to feature my Greek-style *pites* and American fruit pies. All right?"

"Of course, of course. I'll tell them. Now, I'd make about a half-dozen pies at least. They'll be at your shop tomorrow morning, between 8 and 9. Congratulations! This will be some good publicity for Callie's Kitchen!"

Callie couldn't argue with that. She signed off with Mrs. DeWitt and looked around the kitchen.

"Dad, can you help me? In addition to finishing our regular menu items, I just got a pie order. It's kind of special. We need at least six picture-perfect *pites* and fruit pies for *The Crystal Bay Courier*. They're doing a feature on Callie's Kitchen."

"Of course, I'll help! What wonderful publicity! In fact, I can get started on some *spanakopita* right now."

"Thanks, Dad. Remember, they have to be picture perfect."

He raised his eyebrows. "I've been making *spanakopita* before you were a twinkle in your mother's eye!" He cleared his throat. "She'd be so proud of you, *hrisi mou*. Just like I am."

Callie felt guilty for resenting George's bossy kitchen ways. True, he had cost her an employee, but he had a heart of gold. Maybe she could get Josh back, if she ever finished making pies, that is.

George and Callie set to work. As she baked, stirred, conversed with George about food, and interacted with customers, her mind churned with all of her new knowledge. She didn't quite know what it all meant, but she knew she needed to tell Sands what she knew.

There was no privacy to call Sands right now, either, so she decided to do the next best thing. Wiping flour from her hands, she texted him and asked him to call her later.

She also made a plan. As soon as she locked up for the day, she was heading over to The Harris House under the guise of asking about the murder mystery night and when it might resume. Perhaps there was a way to work Allan Browne's Fitzgerald article into the conversation. If Lisa's ancestry had anything to do with the topic of his piece, she would have to know something about it. Maybe she could even get some information about the family feud, though that would be tricky ground to cover. She didn't want to offend Lisa.

Callie had been convinced that the day would stretch into an eternity, but it flew by in a flurry of activity. That was one good thing about being busy: Time certainly didn't drag.

Callie couldn't have stood it if it had. Once the last customer was gone, and she'd locked and cleaned up with George's enthusiastic help, it was late for her shop to close, but early for festivities at The Harris House: 8:00.

Now fueled purely on adrenaline after her early morning and busy workday, Callie slugged down another bottle of water and set off the short distance to The Harris House. In the dusk, the building's witchy turrets sparkled and blinked with the tiny white strings of lights that adorned it year round.

Brushing back the wisps of wavy hair that had fallen from her ponytail, Callie heaved her tired body up the steps. The dining room was semi-full, but the bar was crowded with tourists seeking a summery cocktail and a sunset view. Callie approached the concierge station, but Lisa wasn't there. She waited several minutes and was finally greeted by a harried-looking hostess wearing The Harris House signature vintage waitress uniform. She looked like someone out of Downton Abbey, but when she spoke, her accent was pure Midwest, flat vowels and all.

"Can I help you?"

"Yes, I'm looking for Lisa. Is she here tonight?"

"She is, but I think she went to her upstairs residence for a minute. She should be back soon, if you want to wait."

"She said she was definitely coming back?" Callie persisted.

The young woman looked impatient to get back to her customers. The drinkers in the bar were getting rowdier by the minute. "That's what she said."

"All right, then I'll wait." Callie sat in a chair in the hall outside the restaurant so that she would have a clear view of Lisa when she returned.

The longer she waited, the more the plan seemed like a weak one. With the place being so busy, Lisa wouldn't really have time to talk to her. She'd resent the intrusion and rightly so.

Young women in their Downton Abbey style uniforms and young men in white shirts with black trousers held up by old-fashioned suspenders rushed back and forth. Several asked her if she'd like a drink, and Callie had to compliment Lisa on the efficiency of her staff.

Getting desperate now, Callie watched the first young woman who had told her Lisa was in the residence upstairs. She went down a hallway, and Callie decided to follow her. Was Lisa back there? She couldn't wait forever. If she didn't see her in a few minutes, she promised herself she'd leave and call Sands.

As Callie hung back, her body partially obscured by heavy velvet drapes, she saw the young woman take a key from her apron pocket and unlock a door. She put her head in and called to someone. "You've got people asking for you! It's crazy down here! What do I tell them?"

The waitress called again to no response. Callie heard her muttering to herself. As she heard footsteps coming back towards her, she raced back towards her chair and sat there, out of breath, waiting for the young woman to take her place once again at the concierge desk. Only, she never appeared. Could she have gone straight into the bar without Callie seeing her?

Several minutes passed, but the desk remained empty. Before she could lose her nerve, Callie scurried down the hallway, her heart in her throat. She tried the door that she'd seen the waitress/hostess unlock and to her surprise, it opened.

The stairway was steep and narrow. Rich flocked wallpaper in a brocade-style print lined the walls. This must be the residence. Did she dare enter?

"Lisa?" Callie called uncertainly. "Can I come up?"

Silence. Callie tried again. "Lisa?"

Hesitating for just a moment, Callie straightened her shoulders and started up the staircase.

She cast about for an excuse for her intrusion if, say, Lisa stood at the top of the stairs. She could always fib and say that the hostess sent her up to check if she was returning to the restaurant for the evening. Feeling calmer now that she had a cover story, Callie climbed the steep staircase with a surer step.

When she was out of breath, heart fluttering at her audacity, the stairs finally culminated in what was once known as a "sitting room." The dimly lit space was filled with lush antique furniture and heavy draperies, just like the rooms downstairs. Gleaming dark wood, high ceilings and rich colors gave the impression of luxury to the surroundings.

On closer inspection, though, Callie could see that the furniture was threadbare with age, and the wood was scarred from decades of use.

"Lisa!" she called again. Still, the place could definitely be brought back to life, provided someone had enough money.

Callie took a quick walk around the room but saw no signs of Lisa's presence: no half-filled water glass, no teacup, and no sounds of a television or radio.

Just off the sitting room, was a small hallway illuminated by wall sconces, alight with a soft and somewhat ghostly glow. Callie's curiosity got the better of her. She entered the hallway, which was bordered by a white subway tile bathroom and claw foot tub on one side, and what looked to be a master bedroom on the other. So Lisa wasn't simply in the bathroom. That answered *that* question.

The bedroom door was ajar, so Callie knocked and called Lisa's name. When no one answered, she cautiously pushed the door open, half-expecting to find something horrible.

To Callie's relief, the room was empty. It was slightly less shabby than the lounge, but the furniture was at odds with the rest of the décor. Lisa's bedroom, if this is what it was, had furniture that more closely resembled something you'd find at IKEA. On this floor, the heat was more intense and there was the smell of musty corners and old plumbing.

Callie saw something lying on a desk near the doorway.

Allan Browne's article.

A noise from behind her made her jump. Her blood turning to ice water, she turned around, ready with her flimsy excuse on her lips.

When she saw who it was, she was nearly weak with relief. Callie let out her breath with a whoosh.

"Hi, there," Callie said cheerily, hoping to bluff her way through. "I didn't expect to see you here."

Twenty Six

"**I** could say the same thing of you," April stood, her arms crossed in front of her. She didn't sound so cheery now. Callie took note of April's clenched jaw.

"The hostess sent me up to see where Lisa had gotten to. It's getting busy downstairs, and I was just checking to make sure she's all right," Callie explained, wincing at her lame excuse.

"Lisa is in the dining room. They're getting so busy here, they can't even keep track. I followed you up here."

"Why would you..." The words were barely out of Callie's mouth before April lunged.

Callie ducked and ran to the opposite corner of the room, but she panicked when she saw that April had closed the bedroom door and was standing in front of it. There was no way out.

Callie didn't wait for April to lunge again. Screaming for help, she did the first thing that occurred to her. Spotting the slightly open door of Lisa's bedroom closet, she sped inside and pressed her body against the door, hoping to keep April out.

The closet was a roomy walk-in, exceedingly large for such an old house. Perhaps it was once a small bedroom. Callie cast about wildly as April started banging on the door, trying to open it. Using her muscles daily for home renovations had made April strong, and she was proving it now.

April? Callie could hardly believe it.

April rattled the doorknob as Callie's eyes grew used to the dimness. A heavy-looking antique dresser was to her right. She nearly cried in frustration. She could use it to barricade the door, but how? April would crash into the closet the second she moved an inch.

April shouted and beat her fists on the door. Holding her breath and saying a prayer, Callie turned around so that she faced the door and pressed against it with all of her body weight. Stretching out her arm to reach the dresser, she saw now that it was a heavier than it had looked. She gritted her teeth and was able to pull it halfway in front of the door.

Unfortunately, Callie's movements allowed April to make some headway. Muttering threats at Callie the whole time, the young woman pushed at the closet door until it opened about a quarter of the way. Callie was already on the other side, pushing the dresser in front of the door. With one huge shove, the closet door was barricaded, if only temporarily.

Callie heard her own ragged breath. She was really in a pickle now. Effectively all she had accomplished was to box herself into a closet. She grabbed her cell phone and dialed 911 with trembling fingers. The call wouldn't go through.

She tried again, but it was no use. There was no cell phone reception.

Callie gripped the phone so tightly she felt she could nearly break it. Of course there was no cell phone reception inside the closet of such an old home. Back then, the walls were built to last.

It sounded like April was throwing her body against the door. Why didn't somebody hear her? Callie used her back to brace the dresser more firmly against the door. It hurt. Her eyes scanned the small space wildly for some small sign of hope.

In the dark, she hadn't noticed a strange detail when she'd first walked in. One part of the wall looked odd, like it had been painted over. Squinting, she saw a square, raised area.

Recalling Hugh's words about the old homes with their secret compartments, Callie used one hand to hold onto the dresser, keeping her makeshift barrier in place. With the other hand, she pushed as hard as she could on the strange, square area of the wall. To her surprise, her hand burst through, creating a window-like opening. Without stopping to think, she pushed her body through the smallish space and fell with a thud on the other side.

Callie scrabbled to her feet and replaced the panel. It fit as neatly into place as a puzzle piece. However, if April had sharp eyes, she would be sure to notice it.

April was making progress on the other side of the wall. Breathing hard, Callie scanned her surroundings.

Callie was in what looked like a long, narrow hallway. Could this be one of the "secret compartments" that Hugh had discussed with her? Where did it lead?

First stopping to grab her phone from the dusty floor, Callie raced down the hallway, just as she heard April crash into the closet. There had to be another way out of this secret passage. There had to be!

No such luck. The hallway ended in a brick wall.

Callie pounded on the wall hoping that another secret compartment would magically appear, but to no avail. This wall must be the "hotel" side of The Harris House, and of course, it was sound proof. Panic rushed through Callie.

Her only hope now was the cover of the dark. She heard April stomping around on the other side of the wall. She'd figure out Callie's hiding place any minute.

In the shadowy corner of the "secret passage" Callie spotted what looked like several dusty glass bottles. She ran over and picked one of them up, coughing as she dislodged what was probably decades of dust. Callie held her breath as she brushed at thick layers of dust and grime. The bottle had no label, only an amber liquid.

Could it be. . .bootleg? Thinking of Jay Gatsby and F. Scott Fitzgerald who had gotten her into this mess in the first place, if you really thought about it, Callie was suddenly grateful for the lawlessness and ingenuity of bootleggers. She held the bottle loosely behind her back and dropped to the ground, as close to the wall as she could. Maybe she could hit April before she noticed her.

There was no time. With a scream of triumph, April was suddenly in the secret hallway and face to face with Callie. "Nowhere to run, now, is there?" she asked. She beamed the light of her phone directly into Callie's face.

Callie blinked and stood up on shaky legs. She stared in puzzlement at what April held in her left hand: a feather boa, like the one Tammy Heckstrom had worn when she played a flapper.

"I picked this up in the dressing room after the last murder mystery show," April sneered. "Now you can die looking just like a flapper. Since you seem so interested in that whole time period, it's fitting don't you think? What's more, no one will even find you in here, once I reseal the wall. I know how to make it airtight."

Adrenaline fueled by anger coursed through Callie. "Don't be so stupid, April. Don't you think people saw me come into The Harris House? They'll wonder where I am."

"Stupid?" April spat, walking a step closer. She shoved her phone into her front pocket and produced a sharp-looking screwdriver in its stead. She held it loosely in front of her, the point facing Callie. So now April had two weapons. Which one would she use?

None, if I can help it, Callie thought. She felt like she was in a boxing ring, the way that the two of them were circling each other. It was only a matter of time before one of them made the first move.

"*Stupid?*" April repeated with a wicked gleam in her blue eyes. "The stupid one was Holly. But you know that already."

"What did Holly do, April? Weren't you friends? You told me you thought she was *smart*." Callie felt sick.

"*Friends,*" April repeated in a disgusted tone. "That's what I thought. I found a manuscript in the Linley house and brought it to my good friend Holly because I knew she'd be able to tell me its value. That's right, a manuscript from F. Scott Fitzgerald. A never-before-seen, never-before-published manuscript. Worth more than you can imagine. And *I* found it. *Me*."

"Why...how..." Callie stammered.

"You'd be surprised what you find in these old houses."

"Yes, but this is...an unusual discovery," Callie sputtered, stalling for time. How was she going to get out of here?

Callie shuffled her feet, wondering if she could dart around April. "Seriously, how did you stumble on something like that?"

"Ha. This is the best part," April said proudly. "Hugh gave me the idea. He was like one of the Hardy Boys, always wanting to talk about "secret compartments" and mobsters hiding things. Then, when Holly showed me Allan Browne's article as part of the research she was doing, things just clicked. I was thrilled to have the chance to look inside the house where you found Holly, the one that used to belong to the Linley family."

Callie gripped the bottle tightly and shifted her body slightly to the left of April, weighing her options.

April's eyes glittered with excitement and greed. "I had the perfect explanation for doing it when we were hired to renovate it several weeks ago. We had to wait for the paperwork to go through, but I snuck in before the rest of the workers and found a fake wall behind a built-in bookshelf. No one had ever removed the shelf in any type of renovation, probably because it was beautiful, original wood. Lo and behold, that's where the manuscript was stashed. It had a note attached, with the author's signature. That alone will get me big bucks."

Callie steeled herself. She had to keep April talking until she figured out an escape. "Did you rip that note? I think I found a portion of it."

"Whatever," April shrugged. "I still have the part of the note with his signature, plus I have the manuscript and I'm keeping it. That's the important thing." She inched closer to Callie and Callie felt her blood run cold.

"What about Lisa Linley?" she stammered. "Didn't she have some claim to that house?" Callie felt her arm tense as she gripped the bottle, gathering strength for what she was about to do.

"Not a chance. While I was working with her one day, she gave me some sob story about legal battles. The gist of it was that she and her family wound up with *nada*. However, she felt like owning The Harris House was one way to make up for that. Whatever."

April narrowed her eyes and stepped closer. "If you must know, the new buyers are some rich couple from Minnesota who made the purchase a couple of months ago. I had to act fast, before anyone else got there." April choked out a laugh. "It turned out to be the best move I ever made."

"But what about your friend..." Callie blurted out.

"Are you kidding? I could make a fortune selling this manuscript to a collector. Why shouldn't I make money? Holly didn't even think about that. She was selfish, self-absorbed. She'd led a privileged life and her parents had helped her pay for everything."

With a shudder, Callie remembered the day that April had helped her to lug food items to the *Beats on the Bay* event. April had made a comment about *people who had to really work for a living, unlike Allan Browne and his acting troupe.* Callie gulped. She hadn't known the depths of April's resentments. How could she have?

April narrowed her eyes and Callie was chilled by the animosity in her tone. "I didn't read them, but Holly said the stories were excellent. She couldn't figure out why they hadn't been published before. Holly said the breakup was probably messy. The author was famous for girlfriend troubles, and maybe he wasn't able to retrieve the manuscript from her. Or maybe he started working on something else and just forgot about it. We'll never know why or how the manuscript wound up there."

Callie scanned the room looking for a way around April. She needed to catch her off guard. "So why did Holly need to die? You couldn't have worked something out?"

"Holly tried to tell me that the manuscript belonged with the author's estate, or at the very least, in a university library somewhere. But first she wanted to use it for her Master's Thesis. She said it was 'the right thing to do for the literary world.' But she would have become a literary superstar! So where was the money in that for me? The money could be huge! I'd have enough for a nice nest egg to build my own business. You of all people should understand that."

Callie couldn't believe what she was hearing. Poor Holly. How exciting for her to have access to such a manuscript! So *that* was the secret research she was doing, and that was why everyone was interested in the article: Tammy and her graduate advisor included. Maybe Holly had told them she was researching this notion, without telling them about the valuable item that her "friend" April had brought to her.

Callie was getting angry. Holly had been a wonderful person, and this woman was only interested in herself. "You were the one who took my cashbox at the music festival, weren't you. Why?"

April smirked, and Callie couldn't believe she'd ever believed this woman to be either charming or attractive. "To upset you. To throw you off your game. You kept sniffing around, and I figured you needed something to distract you. Same thing with Tammy. That little ploy had the added bonus of casting suspicion on Allan and the rest of the troupe. I have a strong muscle relaxant prescription for all of my work-related aches and pains. It came in handy."

"I still don't get why you killed Holly at the Linley House." Callie took a cautious step to the side. The hallway was too narrow. She wouldn't be able to dart past April.

"It was the perfect meeting place." April took a step closer, and Callie tensed. "Nobody had moved in yet, and the workers hadn't started the renovation. I asked Holly to meet me at the house to discuss how we were going to deal with the manuscript. She had been keeping it for her research, but now I wanted it back." April's eyes narrowed and her voice grew raspy with the memory. "She wouldn't give it to me and kept saying that we had to share it with her college advisor. I realized then that she wasn't going to stop being a problem."

"So you killed her." Callie said calmly but inside she was frantic. The narrow passageway and darkness seemed to be closing in on her. Time was running out.

A sudden rush of movement made Callie duck. April lunged, holding the ridiculous feather boa taut, trying to lasso it around Callie's neck. In the commotion, the screwdriver clattered to the floor.

April grabbed Callie around the waist and pushed her towards the wall, but Callie pushed back as hard as she could. In one smooth motion, she whipped the bottle from behind her back and smashed it onto April's head.

The bottle of bootleg whiskey had done its job. April abruptly released her before falling to the ground with a thud. She laid there, motionless, blood trickling from a gash on the back of her head.

Callie didn't wait to see any more. She hopped over April, pushed out of the secret passageway and back out into The Harris House.

Twenty Seven

"**C**alliope! What were you possibly thinking?" George wailed as Callie relayed her story for what felt like the hundredth time, several days later. "Going to that house when you knew there could be danger? Going upstairs and snooping around. Secret passageways!" George threw up his hands. "That place always felt like a haunted house to me. Now I know I'm right!"

The two of them were working together in Callie's Kitchen, the sun streaming brightly through her sparkling glass windows (painstakingly washed by Piper), and the huge breakfast crowd having just left. Truth be told, the crowd was even bigger than usual. Callie had made the news once again, and this time it didn't have to do with pie or *pita* making. Her adventures had made front-page news. The splashy article even included a sidebar about her business. "You can't buy publicity like this!" Sam had exalted. Mrs. DeWitt and Viv had agreed.

True, you couldn't buy publicity like this, but Callie wouldn't want to have to relive that frightening evening at The Harris House. She'd been shattered by the knowledge of what had happened to Holly. It had been tough breaking the news to Olivia, and she had kept it as simple and PG as she could. Olivia was going to need a lot of love and support. Thankfully, she had people eager to give her just that.

Surprisingly, Sands wasn't the first to arrive at The Harris House following her escapades. She'd dealt with several of his colleagues before he finally emerged from a car and began his slow, long-legged

211

walk over to her. For what seemed like a full minute he stood, shaking his head at her. "What are we going to do with you?" he asked.

"Get me out of here?" she'd said, not being facetious. "That's all I want."

"You were brave," he said. "As a friend of Holly's, we were investigating April." He sighed, long and gustily. "I guess you just accelerated matters, didn't you?"

"You could say that."

"Are you sure you don't want a job on the force? Then you'd actually have a reason for getting into these kinds of death-defying scrapes, and you'd sure make my life a lot easier. Wait, no. I take that back."

"No worries, Sands. I'm sticking to food."

"Right. Pardon me, but you don't have a very good track record of sticking to food. By the way, did you keep any of that bootleg whiskey?" A smile quirked the corners of his mouth, and his hazel eyes were warm.

"I think it's my new favorite drink," she'd replied. Now, as she thought about him and their conversation, she couldn't help but smile. He wasn't thrilled with what she'd done, but he couldn't exactly argue with the outcome, and things could have been worse.

George's continued barrage of questions brought her back to the present. "What about everyone else involved? Allan Browne. Tammy. Lisa Linley. How do they fit in?"

"Allan Browne, as it turns out, while pompous as all-get-out, was an innocent bystander. He simply enjoys local lore and literature, in addition to theater. The money-making scheme that Josh alluded to was a pipe dream of Allan's. He wanted to purchase a parcel of land and create an outdoor theater with the money. That's why he was so anxious to have the murder mystery nights be a success. At first, they gave every indication that they would be a good source of revenue for both him and Lisa Linley. That is, until Holly was found murdered. Tammy being dosed with muscle relaxant didn't help matters."

Josh had informed everyone that Allan was writing a play based on the love story between Fitzgerald and "Genevieve." Maybe Allan would finally have the success he'd hoped for.

Callie continued, feelings of sympathy towards his folly outweighing any ill feelings she had for him. "Allan is a dreamer, but not a killer. As far as Tammy, she didn't know about the manuscript. Holly had hinted she was on the verge of something great, and I think Tammy was a little jealous, but not murderous. Tammy didn't like Allan, either. She wasn't sure if he had something to do with Holly's death, but she figured he was no friend of the actors. She suspected him of something, and was sure he was out to sabotage her performance because he wanted her to quit the troupe."

"Which brings us to Lisa Linley," George prompted, his ears all but pricked up. For all his admonitions, he loved to hear how his daughter had helped solve the crime.

"Yes. Lisa Linley was guilty of a crime, so to speak, but not the one we were thinking of. She's short on money after overspending on her purchase of The Harris House. April offered to cut corners. Instead of getting the necessary city permits, which, of course, requires inspections and possibly more renovations if they find violations in code, April simply went ahead with the work. I guess she figured she could make a quick buck and Lisa would be forced to work with her in the future. She falsified paperwork at Vintage Reno to cover her tracks."

George started to interrupt, but Callie held up a hand. "There's more. Apparently, Lisa wanted cosmetic changes only, and didn't want to know if there were other issues. She simply couldn't afford to know. Hugh claims April was the project manager, and he was in the dark. I guess I believe him. He was new to the company, after all."

"Why buy a hotel you can't afford to maintain? It doesn't make sense." George hadn't heard about Lisa's family and how they lost claim to the Linley mansion after a family spat, so Callie filled him in on the broad details. Lisa was only trying to recapture a dream along with some of the family honor, and Callie felt for her. When she was finished, he shook his head.

"I have to say, I'm happy Hugh and Raine didn't have anything to do with this. But that begs the question: Who put muscle relaxant in Tammy's drink the night she fainted at the performance?"

"That was April. I remembered, too late, that she had been complaining about muscle pain. She must have had a pretty strong prescription so it was easy for her. Plus, she'd been working at The Harris House earlier that day."

"But why Tammy?" George wanted to know.

"No real reason. It looks like she wanted to disrupt the murder mystery nights at The Harris House because they were getting in the way of her illegal activities regarding the renovation. I think she may also have been trying to cast suspicion onto Allan Browne and Lisa Linley, even Hugh and Raine, basically anyone but herself. That's what Sands thinks, too. April was also responsible for all of the Gilded Age Home break-ins. She knew her way around the security systems and with people out of town a lot, it probably wasn't that difficult for her. She was impulsive, greedy and vindictive, that's for sure."

"Fine. But what about... " George began.

Callie held up her hand to stop his flow of words. "Dad. Don't you always say 'All's well that ends well.' "

"I suppose." George's bushy eyebrows were drawn in a line across his nose in a gesture she knew all too well.

"I know it was risky, but all's well that ends well. I'm safe and a killer has been apprehended."

George rushed to Callie and enveloped her in one of his burly, warm bear hugs. "So it is. All's well that ends well. Isn't that the title of a Shakespeare play?"

"I can't handle any more talk of theater or plays right now," Callie said with a weary smile, eager to change the subject. "All I need now is a full-time cook."

"Yes," George said, distractedly so it seemed to Callie. "That *is* a problem. I love helping out here, but you know I can't for much longer. You'll need another person. Someone who knows the place inside and out. Someone who is passionate about food, and not crime solving." Callie smiled good-naturedly at his dig. "Someone who loves this place almost as much as you do."

Callie was growing more depressed with each word. She knew all of that already. Did George know that he was making her feel worse?

"You need someone like me," a familiar voice said from behind Callie. She whirled around, hardly able to believe her ears.

"Max!"

There he stood, spiky hair, eyebrow ring and all, sporting his farmer tan and sleeves rolled up to reveal his colorfully inked fore-arms. "I'd love to come back to work full-time, if you'll let me."

"Let you! Are you kidding? The job is yours as long as you want it. And you'd better want it a long time. It's been crazy around here without you." She smiled at George. "Dad, you've been great, but you've got your own business to run."

She turned back to Max. "This is wonderful news, but what about your father? I don't feel right about taking you away from him at this crucial time. How is he?"

"That's the thing. He's the one who wanted me to come back. In fact, George was really helpful in setting things up."

"George?" She turned to stare at her father, who was beaming at her.

"Can I tell it?" Max asked George, and he nodded vigorously. "Well, George came out to see me and my dad, a few days before you did, in fact."

"Is that what he meant by 'here's another one?' "

Max's laughter filled the room. "Yes, I was so mad at him when he said that! But George was persuasive." George shrugged in false modesty, and they all laughed.

Max continued his tale, his voice bright with enthusiasm. "George also told my dad that he might know someone who would love to apprentice as a farm worker. It's one of the waiters at The Olympia. My dad met him, and he's going to help out for the time being while dad heals and decides what to do with the farm."

Max turned to Callie. "At first he was angry at getting pressured by George and then by you, Callie. He didn't really show it when you were there. Later on, he told me that he realized I belonged here and that this is the life I should pursue. He sees the passion I have for working with food." He looked down, sheepishly. "I think my mom may have talked to him, too."

Callie looked from one to the other, incredulously. "This is almost too much. You guys saved my bacon, this time, and I mean literally. Thank you!" Before she knew it, the three of them were in a group hug. George kissed Callie on the cheek.

"One more thing," George said when they'd broken their embrace. "Your business is growing. You might want to give Josh another chance."

"Josh? I'm surprised to hear you say that."

"He was a good boy. He just didn't understand my style of teaching. But you? I think you can train him. He seemed to love food, and that's the important thing. Also, he wanted to learn."

"I'll definitely think on it, Dad."

"Good. Max, here you go." George removed his apron and handed it to Max. "Time to get to work."

"You bet, Mr. Costas!" Max put the apron over his head and tied it tightly.

Finally, Callie thought, smiling at the two of them, feeling like her heart would burst. Max was back where he belonged. Thank goodness for George and his interfering ways. She was lucky to have him in her life.

***

"So young Max is back in the kitchen?" Sands asked later that evening. Max had encouraged her to take an early leave from work, and Sands, happy at having the Holly Tennyson case solved, offered to take Callie out for a celebratory walk on the beach.

The "undiscovered" Fitzgerald manuscript was still being held as evidence, but Sands had told her that once it was truly authenticated by the author's estate, it was going to be held as part of the author's handwritten manuscript collection at Princeton. Callie was happy it would be in the right hands, but it was still devastating to think that a manuscript was the cause of Holly's tragic death.

The sun was setting as Sands and Callie walked, hand in hand, shoes off. Callie stood for a minute and listened to the peaceful sounds of the waves lapping at the water's edge. She also heard the beat of her heart, which always seemed to beat a little faster and more purposefully when Sands was around.

"He's back! This time, I hope it's for good. I don't know what I'd do without him."

"Hmm. If I were the jealous type, I'd be jealous, I think."

"Don't be silly. Max is wonderful, but he's way too young for me. Anyway, I'm taken."

"You certainly are," Sands said, squeezing her hand more tightly.

For a few minutes, they simply stood arm in arm, looking out at the peaceful expanse of Crystal Bay. The setting sun threw rays of orange and pink into the slate blue sky, now darkening to shades of purple as another day came to a close.

Across the water Callie could see the elegant homes dotting the shoreline. Each one had its secrets, heartbreaks, love, loss, death, hope, light and dark. She shuddered, and Sands held her closer.

"You know, we never did take that vacation," he said into her ear.

"No, we didn't. We just haven't had the time." *We have to make time*, Callie thought. *Nothing is guaranteed.* She realized with a start that Sands was becoming a seamless part of her life, and she couldn't picture a future that didn't include him. Just like with Max, she wouldn't know what to do without Sands.

"As I recall, your father said the trip would be better if it was a honeymoon."

Callie blushed furiously but relaxed when she saw the humor in Sands' eyes. He was teasing her, she could see that, but his loving expression spoke volumes. They would just have to take it a day at a time. For now, she would enjoy this peaceful moment.

Callie smiled. "That's George for you, but let's stop talking about him. At least for now. What do you say?"

"Agreed," Sands said, pulling her closer.

– THE END –

Author's Note

This is a work of fiction and the story is a product of my imagination. However, the inspiration for "Genevieve" comes from a real person. The names of all players have been changed, except for that of Fitzgerald himself.

As a fan of anything 1920s and in particular, the writings of F. Scott Fitzgerald, I have read many biographies of the author. One of them focused on his rocky romantic relationships with women. One of these young women was a Chicago debutante who travelled frequently to Lake Geneva and later married one of the Mitchells, a family with a grand estate in Lake Geneva, Wisconsin, the inspiration for "Crystal Bay". The young debutante, Ginevra King, and Fitzgerald exchanged several letters and he carried some of these with him for the rest of his life. She was also the supposed inspiration for characters in his short stories as well as Daisy Buchanan in *The Great Gatsby*.

I thought it would be fun to imagine that Fitzgerald had given Ginevra (renamed Genevieve for my book) a manuscript that she had then placed in a "hidden" compartment in the Lake Geneva home of her new husband. I have no evidence of this ever happening, of course. The romance and glamour of the "Gilded Age Homes" sometimes make you think things like this could be possible.

In addition, Fitzgerald's first novel, *This Side of Paradise*, includes Lake Geneva, Wisconsin, as the setting for the home of his protagonist's parents. It is easy to imagine a scenario where Fitzgerald could have visited one of the stately homes that still exist in Lake Geneva today.

First and foremost, despite some "real life" inspiration, the story-line is merely a product of my active imagination at work. Please don't go tearing up any walls.

Recipes from Callie's Kitchen

Greek Chicken and Lemon Soup (*Avgolemono*)

Ingredients:

8 cups chicken broth or stock (homemade is best, but Swanson's low-sodium is a good one, too.)
1 cup to 1-1/2 cups cooked white rice
1 cup cooked chicken, shredded or in bite-sized pieces
3 large eggs
1/3 cup fresh lemon juice (it has to be fresh, no bottled juice!)
1 tablespoon grated lemon zest
Salt and white pepper
2 tablespoons chopped fresh parsley

In a large saucepan, bring the stock to a boil over medium heat. Place the eggs in a mixing bowl and whisk until blended, then add lemon juice and zest. Whisk until well-combined. Reduce the heat of the chicken stock to very low.

While whisking the soup in the pan, slowly pour the egg-lemon mixture into the broth, whisking all the time to prevent curdling. The soup should thicken slightly.

Alternatively, use the following method, credited to my husband's *yiayia* (grandmother):

Add the eggs, lemon juice and zest to a blender and blitz until well combined. Take one cup of the hot stock and gradually add to the mixture in the blender. Cover the blender and zap it again. Then, slowly and carefully pour this mixture back into the broth and gently stir in, whisking all the while. This will help "temper" the broth so that it won't curdle.

Add cooked chicken and rice and gently cook for several more minutes at low heat until flavors blend. Don't set the heat too high, or you will curdle the soup (like Josh)! So have patience and you will have a delicious soup.

If there's any left over and you want to reheat it, put it in a saucepan on top of the stove over very low heat and stir frequently, to prevent curdling.

Sprinkle with parsley. Serves 6-8.

Squash Pie (*Kolokethopita*)

Ingredients:

½ lb phyllo sheets, thawed (Phyllo is found in the frozen section of the supermarket, frequently near the frozen fruit and desserts. Be sure to thaw thoroughly before using).

3 lbs zucchini squash, cleaned, shredded and drained or squeezed of excess moisture.

1 onion, chopped

8 eggs, beaten

1 tbsp butter

¼ cup olive oil

2 cups rice, cooked and slightly cooled

½ cup grated cheese (*Kefaloteri*, a hard Greek cheese is the traditional cheese. If you can't find it, use Parmesan or Romano.)

Preheat oven to 350 degrees F. Have ready a 10 x 15 baking pan.

Sauté onions in butter and olive oil. Add cleaned zucchini and cook a few minutes until softened. Allow to cool.

Combine eggs and cheese with squash mixture. Add cooked rice and combine gently until well blended.

Melt butter. Grease the baking pan, then place six phyllo sheets in the bottom of the pan, brushing each one with melted butter before adding another. Pour squash mixture in the pan and layer with eight more phyllo sheets, brushing each one with melted butter before adding the next. Brush the top sheet with butter and score into squares with a sharp knife.

Bake at 350 degrees for 15 minutes. Reduce heat to 325 F and bake for 30 minutes more or until golden brown.

12-14 generous squares, depending on how you cut them.

Greek Cheese Honey Pie (*Melopita*)

There are many recipes for *melopita*, a traditional Greek cheese honey pie. Unlike a creamy, dense cheesecake, this pie has a light, fluffy texture which makes it a nice ending to a heavier meal. It can be made with or without a pie crust; in fact many traditional recipes do not call for a crust. I include a crust because Callie definitely would and crust is good! Try it without sometime for a change of pace (and less calories). *Myzithra* cheese is the traditional ingredient, but if you can't find it (or it is too expensive as is often the case), then ricotta cheese is a good substitute.

Ingredients:

1 lb grated *myzithra* or 1 lb (1 regular-sized container) ricotta cheese
½ cup sugar
¼ cup honey plus more for topping
½ tsp salt
6 eggs
½ tsp lemon zest
1 tsp vanilla extract
Cinnamon
One half recipe "Callie's Perfect Pie Crust" (See next recipe.)

Preheat oven to 350 degrees F. Have ready a pie plate lined with pie crust (see next recipe).

Combine cheese, honey and sugar in a large mixing bowl. Beat eggs in a separate bowl and add to cheese mixture. Mix well to combine.

Pour into crust and sprinkle lightly with cinnamon. Bake for 30 minutes. Let cool, then serve sprinkled with more cinnamon and a drizzle of honey. Serves 8.

Callie's Perfect Pie Crust

A combination of butter and shortening is the secret to this flavorful pie crust.

Ingredients:

2 ¼ cups all-purpose flour
1 teaspoon salt
¼ tsp sugar
½ cup shortening (such as Crisco), very well-chilled
4 tablespoons unsalted butter, very well-chilled
6-8 tablespoons ice water

Mix flour, salt and sugar in a large mixing bowl or the work bowl of a food processor. With a pastry blender, or using a food processor, cut in shortening and butter until it resembles coarse crumbs.

Mix in the ice water, one tablespoon at a time, until dough forms a ball. If dough doesn't come together or looks crumbly, gradually add more ice water, a teaspoon at a time, until it does. Take the dough out of the food processor (if using) and knead gently with your hands a few times. It should feel pliable and smooth. If not, add a little more water and knead in. Don't overwork the dough.

Divide dough into two balls and flatten slightly into discs. Wrap well in plastic wrap and chill in the refrigerator for at least 30 minutes or even overnight before rolling. Before rolling out, take the dough out of the refrigerator to warm up slightly before continuing.

Using a well-floured surface and a rolling pin, roll each pastry disc from the center to the edges, forming a circle.

Roll each pastry into a circle that is several inches larger than a 9-inch pie plate. Place gently in pie plate and trim overhang.

Makes enough for a two-crust pie.

Pie crust tips:

Chilling and resting the dough makes the dough easier to work with. Let it chill for at least 30 minutes.

Once you've rolled out the bottom crust and placed it in the pie plate, chill it for an additional 30 minutes before adding filling and the top crust. This helps you avoid a "soggy" bottom crust after baking.

For extra browning, sweetness and sparkle, sprinkle one teaspoon white sugar over the top of the crust before placing it in the oven.

When a pie requires only a bottom crust (such as *Melopita*), make the entire pie crust recipe, divide into two discs and freeze one of the discs for future use. Well-wrapped, the pie crust will keep for several months in your freezer. Thaw thoroughly before rolling out.

Callie's Sour Cherry Pie

Ingredients:

3/4 cup – 1 cup sugar, or to taste (Note: this is a sweet-tart pie. If you want it even sweeter, you could add up to 1-1/4 cups sugar)
2 cans tart or "sour" red cherries (NOT cherry pie filling)
3-1/2 – 4 tbsp. cornstarch (depending on how much juice is in the can of cherries, you may need to add an extra tbsp.)
1 tsp vanilla extract
1 tablespoon butter or margarine
2 9-inch pie crusts (Callie's Perfect Pie Crust; see recipe.)

Preheat oven to 400 degrees F. Drain the cherries and reserve the juice from only one can.

In a saucepan, stir the cherry juice into the combined mixture of the cornstarch and sugar. Cook over medium heat, stirring constantly until thickened, but not gluey.

Remove from heat. Stir in vanilla extract, then gently stir in cherries.

Pour filling into pastry-lined pie pan. Dot with butter or margarine. Place second crust on top and gently seal by making a decorative edge with your fingers or the tines of a fork. Vent the pie by slashing the top crust several times. Or do as Max and Callie do, and use a shaped pie crust cutter to make decorative vents in the crust. (You can find inexpensive pie crust cutters at most kitchen specialty stores, online or at craft stores.) Place cut-outs on the crust and gently seal for additional decoration.

Bake 30-40 minutes or until crust browns and filling begins to bubble through the vents. Make sure it's bubbling or the filling will be too thin or "runny" once it cools.

If the edges of the pie are browning too quickly, cover with aluminum foil or "pie crust protectors" (found at kitchen stores) for the last 15 minutes of baking. Cool pie several hours to allow filling to thicken before slicing. Serve with vanilla ice cream.

Serves 8.

Beats on the Bay Blueberry Pie

Filling ingredients:

6 cups fresh blueberries, washed and drained
1-1/4 cup sugar
1 tbsp. lemon juice
¼ tsp. ground cinnamon
5-6 tbsp. quick-cooking (minute) tapioca (6 tbsp. of tapioca results in a firm pie filling; if you'd like it a little looser, use 5 tbsp.)
1 tbsp. butter, well-chilled and diced
Sugar for sprinkling the top crust

Make the crust first and chill. (See recipe for Callie's Perfect Pie Crust).

When ready to bake, preheat oven to 425 degrees F.

For the filling: mix berries, tapioca, sugar and lemon juice in a large mixing bowl. Let the mixture sit for 10-15 minutes so that the tapioca can begin to absorb some of the berry juices.

Pour the berry mixture into a pastry-lined pie plate. Dot with butter.

Place top crust over berries and gently seal, making a decorative edge with your fingers or the tines of a fork. Vent the pie by slashing the top in a decorative pattern several times or by making several cut-outs using small cookie cutters or decorative pie crust cutters.

If you like, place the cutouts decoratively on the top of the pie (not covering the vents you just created) and gently press to seal.

If desired, sprinkle the top of the pie crust with sugar.

Bake pie for 30 minutes, then cover edge with a pie shield or foil to prevent overbrowning. Reduce oven temperature to 375°F and continue to bake until crust is golden and filling is bubbling, 45 to 50 minutes more.

Allow to cool on a rack for at least an hour before slicing. Serve with vanilla ice cream.

Serves 8.

Pie filling tips:

To avoid "runny" fruit pie fillings:

Toss your fruit with the sugar, spices and quick-cooking tapioca and let it sit for several minutes to absorb some of the juices.

Vent your pie in several places and/or use decorative pie crust cutters to allow steam to escape and the liquid in the pie to reduce while baking.

Bake your pie at the higher heat setting before lowering oven temperature.

Be sure that the juices are thick and bubbling through the vents before removing from the oven. Browned pastry does not necessarily mean that the filling is finished.

For the blueberry pie: Use fresh blueberries if at all possible. They are generally available year-round in supermarkets and if they are not perfectly sweet, it's OK – you will be adding sugar and baking them in your pie, which make them delectable.

Frozen berries, while flavorful and readily available, give off much more liquid than fresh berries do. You will have to add additional tapioca to your pie filling if you use frozen. Make sure you bake the pie until bubbling hot.

Let your pie cool for several hours, preferably overnight. Fruit fillings set up as they cool, so the longer you can wait before slicing, the more firm your filling will be.

Greek Rice Pudding (*Rizogalo*)

Ingredients:

¾ cup long-grain white rice (NOT parboiled e.g. Uncle Ben's)
1-1/2 cups water
¼ tsp salt
4 cups whole milk (trust me on this one – you need the full fat milk)
2/3 cup sugar
1 tsp pure vanilla extract
Cinnamon, for sprinkling
Have ready 6 oz. custard cups or ramekins or a medium-sized heat-proof bowl.

Combine rice, water and salt in a heavy saucepan and bring to a simmer over medium-high heat. Reduce to low, cover and simmer until water is absorbed and rice is tender, about 15 minutes. Stir in the milk. Add sugar and stir until dissolved.

Cook uncovered over medium heat for about 30-40 minutes, stirring frequently. Watch carefully for boil-overs, especially near the end of cooking time. When the mixture looks thick and when large bubbles begin to appear on the surface, remove from heat. Do not overcook, or the pudding will be solid instead of creamy when cooled.

Off the heat, stir in the vanilla. Spoon pudding into custard cups (or one big bowl) and smooth the top. Place plastic wrap directly on the surface of the pudding to prevent a skin from forming.

Chill for several hours, then remove wrap and sprinkle with cinnamon before serving.

Serves 6.

Acknowledgements

I'm grateful to so many people. I'd especially like to thank:

Linda Reilly, for your support, encouragement, incisive commentary, enthusiasm and friendship. You always give me the boost I need.

Kathleen Costa, for your enthusiastic willingness to read my manuscript and for offering insightful feedback. You're the perfect beta reader!

Renee Barratt, for designing the beautiful cover that perfectly captures my book. Great job, as always! I'm so happy to be working with you.

Karen Owen, for setting up my Facebook launch party through your business, *Beyond the Bookmarks*. Your wonderful creativity is so appreciated.

Lori Caswell, for organizing my Great Escapes Book Tour. Your support of cozy mystery authors is just amazing.

Kim Davis, for being the best recipe tester and baking videographer, ever.

The wonderful book bloggers who've reached out to me and welcomed me into the world of cozy mysteries with open arms. Thank you for your support!

The readers! I couldn't do it without you. Thank you for buying my books, writing reviews, spreading the word about my books and most of all, for welcoming Callie Costas and crew to your Kindles and bookshelves.

My family and friends, for their love and support, as well as their efforts in helping me to spread the word about my books. A special shout-out to Patrick Gibson and Helen Kales for their input on the Greek Fest scene.

My two daughters, Alexandra and Zoe, for encouraging me in my writing efforts.

Last but not least, my wonderful husband, Jim, for his tireless tech support, editorial acumen and positive encouragement and love all along the way.

For anyone not mentioned here who helped me in some way with my writing journey – thank you!

And finally, a special note to readers: If you enjoyed this book, will you consider leaving a short review on Amazon? The more reviews that a book has, the more readers will see it. This helps writers keep writing books! Reviews need not be long and complicated – a simple "I liked it" means so much.

To those of you who have already taken the time to write a review, thank you! It is very much appreciated.

About the Author

Award-winning writer and blogger Jenny Kales worked for years as a freelancer, but fiction writing has always been a dream. Kales' marriage into a Greek-American Midwestern family inspired The Callie's Kitchen Mysteries, featuring Calliope Costas, food business owner and amateur sleuth. The setting of the story, "Crystal Bay", is inspired by Wisconsin's beautiful Geneva Lakes. Ms. Kales is an avid reader, cook and baker and she's addicted to mystery TV, especially anything on Masterpiece Mystery or BBC America. She lives just outside of Chicago with her husband, two daughters and a cute but demanding Yorkshire terrier, and is hard at work on her next book. Visit the author's web site at www.jennykales.wordpress.com. To keep up with author news, giveaways, recipes and other fun stuff, sign up for a FREE newsletter here: http://tinyurl.com/huv5pof.